# DEAD SILENT

# ALSO BY S.L. MENEAR

## The Jettine Jorgensen Mystery Series

Dead Silent

Dropped Dead

## The Samantha Starr Thriller Series

Flight to Redemption

Flight to Destiny

Triple Threat

Stranded

Vanished

Life, Love, & Laughter: 50 Short Stories

# DEAD SILENT

A JETTINE JORGENSEN MYSTERY, BOOK 1

S. L. MENEAR

ePublishingWorks!
love what you read.

Cover and eBook design by eBook Prep
www.ebookprep.com

September, 2021
ISBN: 978-1-64457-192-7

*ePublishing Works!*
644 Shrewsbury Commons Ave
Ste 249
Shrewsbury PA 17361 USA

866-846-5123
www.epublishingworks.com

*Dedicated to Niko and Meliodora Bujaj,*
*Owners of The Island Grill and Tiki Bar,*
*The finest restaurant in Palm Beach County.*

# ONE

*Rain pelts my castle.*
*Its mighty towers stand firm,*
*while the grey stones weep.*

A strange sense of foreboding prickled my skin as my journey home had almost reached an end. Luxury International Airlines Flight 1167 skirted the east coast of South Florida on its final approach to Palm Beach International Airport. A pang of mixed emotions jabbed my heart when I gazed out a passenger window and spotted my family's ancestral home on Banyan Isle, visible between rain clouds.

Shaped like a wide crescent moon, the quaint residential island extended a mere six miles north to south and a mile and a half east to west. Giant banyan trees with their multiple trunks looked like small forests and covered the island everywhere except the beach. My family's century-old castle stood on a six-acre lot fronting the ocean at the northeast end of the island.

Named Valhalla, its turrets jutted high above the broad branches that hid much of the island from an aerial view. The stone mansion had been built by my Danish ancestor as a tribute to his Viking heritage. The Norse theme had seemed out of place for my late mother, a Cherokee shaman, but she loved it. Tall and slender with golden skin, high cheekbones, long black hair, and golden eyes, Atsila could have passed for royalty in any culture. I was fortunate to resemble her, except I had my late father's electric-blue eyes.

My flight pulled into the gate at PBI, and I grabbed my wheeled carry-on the instant the seatbelt sign blinked off. After having worn a Navy officer's uniform for six years, I relished looking feminine again in a flowery sundress. A little unsteady in my new stiletto sandals, I exited the jetway and strolled to the arrivals area.

Gwen Stuart, my best friend since childhood, pulled up in her white Mercedes roadster, honked the horn, and waved. She rolled down the passenger window. "Hey, Jett!"

I tossed my bag in the trunk and slid onto the passenger seat. "Hi, Gwen. It's good to see you. Still driving the bait car, huh?"

"Yeah, but so far, no bites from the killer carjacker." She grinned. "It's been ages. How are you?"

"Jetlagged, but happy to be home." I leaned over and hugged her. "I have a month to chill out and make some big decisions."

"Good. We'll have loads of fun, and I'll help you figure out your future." She pulled into traffic and took the airport exit to I-95 North. "Any updates on your love life?"

"A total disaster. I needed this time off, and it took the better part of two days and several flights just to get here from Afghanistan."

"Wow, you must be knackered." Gwen changed lanes to avoid big trucks spraying road water from heavy afternoon showers.

I admired her thick red hair. "Your hair's a lot longer now. I like it."

"Thanks, I have to pull it back when I'm in uniform, but I'll be promoted to detective soon. Then I can wear civilian clothes."

"Congratulations, and I understand about your hair. I have to put mine in a bun whenever I'm in my Navy uniform. That'll change if I decide not to re-enlist."

We chatted like we'd never been apart as we zipped up the expressway and exited east through Palm Beach Gardens toward the Intracoastal Waterway. A few minutes later, we drove over the tall Banyan Isle bridge. I enjoyed looking out over upscale middle-class homes, condos, and shops, all in pastel colors, covering most of the island. They were four stories or less to preserve the small-town atmosphere.

Our brief drive to the east side of the island took us past the Banyan Harbor Inn on the southern curve. Inlets to the Atlantic Ocean separated the island from Singer Island to the south and from Juno Beach to the north. We made a left onto Ocean Drive and passed a beachfront hotel, a public beach, several pastel condo buildings, and the six southernmost mansions that had been converted to luxury condos.

Continuing north, we drove past several mansions built over a hundred years ago by industrialists from New York and Boston. At the northern end of the island, I clicked the remote gate control, and we turned in between tall stone pillars onto a tree-lined drive.

The gray stone castle, no longer warm and inviting, wept with cool, rainy tears. I bit my lower lip and reminded myself of all the wonderful family memories it held. Everything would be all right if I could just get through the first few days. Thank God I had Gwen to ease the loneliness.

"Let's leave your bag in the trunk until the rain stops." She held a large umbrella over us as we navigated through a typical afternoon downpour to the huge oak entrance door. "Too bad your ancestor failed to include a porte cochère when he built this Nordic stronghold."

Heavy raindrops hammered the puddles, splashing my open-toed shoes and lower legs with tepid water. "And stubborn Jorgensen descendants would rather get drenched than alter their patriarch's grand design."

"Typical Vikings," she joked. "Except you, of course."

We rushed up stone steps and ducked inside. I closed the heavy door behind us with a firm thud.

An only child like Gwen, I missed having my parents there to welcome me. I knew she was the one person who understood how I felt because she, too, had lost her parents.

I punched the code into the security panel and noted the normal indications. As I crossed the spacious foyer, I caught a whiff of perfume and froze. Had I imagined it? It wasn't Gwen's or mine. It reminded me of my mother's favorite fragrance. The weird thing was my mother had not been in the house since she perished in a plane crash with my father two years ago. The house had stood empty, yet the fragrance seemed real.

Gwen noticed my hesitation and stopped in front of one of the ten-foot winged Valkyries flanking twin marble staircases that ascended the two-story foyer.

A brief image of Valkyries escorting my parents to mythic Valhalla flashed through my mind. The fragrance I'd noticed seconds ago wafted past me again, jolting me back to reality.

"You okay, Jett? You haven't been home since the funerals. Would you like to spend a few nights next door at my place?"

My stomach churned. "Something's wrong."

She stared at me. "What is it?"

"I'm not sure." Goosebumps erupted on my arms as I glanced around the dark foyer. Lightning flashed, and something on the white marble floor glinted.

I gasped and dropped to one knee, tracing the moist marks with my fingertip.

Wet footprints, barely visible, glistened in the gray light cast by floor-to-ceiling windows and continued to the left staircase. Two sets, one from a man's shoes and the other from a woman's high heels.

Shoes like my parents had worn.

Thunder boomed, and I shivered as I pointed at the footprints. "My parents—"

Gwen's jaw dropped when she spotted the faint trail leading upstairs. "No, it can't be."

"But—"

She interrupted, "Listen, I know your mom was a shaman, but that doesn't mean your parents' spirits have returned. And ghosts don't leave footprints."

I pointed at the electronic panel. "The security system is on, and the only way to enter without triggering an alarm is with the key and the code, so who—" I inhaled through my nose. "Is that cigar smoke? It smells a lot like Dad's favorite brand." My mouth went dry.

She tilted her head, her long hair billowing in a light breeze that drifted down the staircase. "The odor seems to come from the second floor." She drew her police-issued Glock 40 from under her blazer. "Ghosts don't smoke."

I gazed up the left staircase and whispered, "It can't be relatives. They'd know Mom never allowed smoking inside the house."

The wet footprints were lost in the rich jewel tones of the Axminster carpet runner that ran the length of the staircase. Shiny brass stair rods held each section in place.

Gwen squeezed my shoulder. "Nobody you know would dare smoke here." She transformed into her cop persona as she started up the steps. "Stay behind me."

I passed a life-sized painting of my mother dressed in buckskin and flanked by timber wolves. Atsila held open flames in her outstretched hands, and her golden eyes seemed to follow me up the stairs.

We stopped at the second floor and followed the odor into the long, north hallway. Vivid portraits of Viking ancestors lined the fifteen-foot alabaster walls, their fierce gazes fueling my apprehension.

The oak floor creaked, and I froze.

Gwen hesitated. "Did you hear that? Sounded like a groan."

"Could be the storm." A humid breeze twirled my waist-length hair. "The cigar smoke is coming from that guest room." I pointed at an open door on the ocean side of the house.

We crept closer.

She grabbed my elbow. "Wait here."

"But—"

She gave me a stern cop's look.

I hung back a few moments, then followed her anyway. After all, I had survived three deadly terrorist attacks on the base in Afghanistan. My job normally involved gathering intelligence for SEAL missions, but I could handle myself in combat. How dare someone invade my family's home?

Gwen eased up to the door and peered inside. A brisk wind lifted her hair. She held her fingers to her lips and pointed.

I eased closer and peeked over her shoulder. Sheer blue curtains billowed in a fresh ocean breeze flowing through the open balcony door. A cigar smoldered in a crystal dish on the mahogany nightstand beside a whisky bottle and two glasses.

As I followed her inside, I caught another whiff of perfume. Goosebumps prickled my skin again. I peered at the king-size, four-poster bed with a royal-blue satin bedspread and a matching, satin-covered canopy. "Is that a man's shoe sticking out from under the bed skirt?"

"Yep, he must've undressed and kicked his shoes under the bed. I'll check the bathroom." She moved to the inner door and peeked inside. "Nobody there." She turned to me. "I'll search the closet while you check the shoe. Maybe it belongs to your uncle."

I eased up to the massive mahogany bed, leaned down, lifted the leather loafer, shrieked, and jerked my hand away like I'd touched a tarantula. "The shoe has a foot in it!"

Not the best reaction from a Navy Intelligence officer, but I was exhausted.

Gwen rushed over. She dropped to her knees and lifted the satin bed skirt.

"Not just a foot—there's a body under here." She paused. "Make that *two* bodies. A woman is lying beside him."

# TWO

"Two bodies! How could this happen here?" My gut churned.

Gwen holstered her weapon, crawled to the head of the bed, lifted the blue fabric, and reached underneath to check the man's neck for a pulse. "Still warm, but he's dead."

"Oh my God!" a squeaky voice shrieked.

Gwen glanced up at me. "Who was that, Jett?"

"Get me out of here!" A woman wriggled out from under the other side of the bed. Wide-eyed, she stood on wobbly legs. "Are you *sure* he's dead?"

My four-inch stilettos raised me above six feet. I towered over the short blonde and crossed my arms. "Who are you, and how'd you get into my house?"

The blonde stared at me and took a step back, bumping into a mahogany armchair with dark-leather cushioning. "She called you Jett. You must be Victor and Atsila Jorgensen's daughter. Sorry for your loss."

"Thanks, but why are you here?" I pointed at the bed. "And who's the dead guy?"

Gwen stood and looked over at the woman. "*Brenda*? What the heck?"

"Is he really dead?"

My cheeks burned as I clenched my fists. "Gwen, do you *know* this woman?"

A nod. "She's Brenda Carrigan—owns Treasure Chest Antiques on Main Street."

I sucked in a breath. "What were you doing, checking out my family's antiques?"

"Of course not, but if you ever wanted to sell—"

"Unbelievable." I shook my head. "Now, about the guy under the bed—"

Gwen kept her eyes on Brenda. "I checked his face with my cell phone light. It's Phil Peabody, Mayor of Banyan Isle, and he's definitely dead." She thrust her hands on her hips. "All right, Brenda, why were you hiding under the bed with the body?"

She gasped and slumped into one of the armchairs by the balcony door. "It's not what it looks like." Her voice panicky, she whimpered, "Phil and I were watching the rain while he smoked a cigar. He wanted some Scotch, so we circled the bed to the nightstand. He'd just taken his first drink when we heard you coming up the stairs. We thought the closet would be the first place you'd look, so we slid under the bed. Phil was alive when he scooted in beside me."

Gwen's tone darkened. "This looks like murder—probably cyanide poisoning. The mayor's lips are blue with foaming at his nose and mouth and a strong scent of almonds."

Brenda's taut, middle-aged face paled as she sputtered, "What? Poison? No. Must be a heart attack. Unless . . ." She stared at the whisky bottle. "Oh my—someone tried to kill me too. If I'd taken a drink of that Scotch . . . Did his wife find out about us? Or maybe my husband—he's got an Irish temper." She leaped up. "I have to get out of here!"

"Not so fast, Brenda." Gwen pulled out her cell. "I have to notify the police."

"No, don't do *that!*" she shrieked.

As Brenda, a member of the More-Botox-is-Better Club, sped through a wide range of emotions, I marveled that her face remained frozen in a neutral expression.

Gwen unlocked her cell phone.

"Wait! Please don't call the police," Brenda pleaded. "This'll be a huge scandal."

"And thanks to you, my family's good name will be right in the middle of it."

Gwen dialed 9-1-1 and spoke into her cell, "This is Palm Beach Police Officer Gwen Stuart reporting a possible murder at One Ocean Drive on Banyan Isle. Be advised I'm armed and inside the home with the homeowner. We found a body and a suspect. I'll brief the local police when they arrive."

I glared at Brenda. "It's obvious why you were here, but you still haven't explained how you got into my house."

She pointed at the bed. "It was Phil. He got a key and the security code from the maid." Her face flushed with bright-red blotches. "We weren't expecting anyone until later tonight."

"That's a lot of romance." Gwen smirked.

"He takes pills." She smiled sheepishly.

I nudged Gwen. "Make sure they arrest the maid too."

"I'm really sorry about this, Jett. And poor Phil. He just had his thirty-fourth birthday a few days ago." Brenda hung her head as her eyes filled with tears. She eased around the bed and glanced at Phil's well-polished left shoe, still on his foot. She sighed. "He always was a sharp dresser."

Gwen poked Brenda. "Let's get downstairs before the police arrive. Is there anyone else in the house?"

She choked back tears. "I hope not. This is going to ruin my life."

"I'll say. Now get going." I gave her a firm shove out the bedroom door.

"Wait a minute." Gwen grabbed Brenda's arm. "I didn't see any cars in the driveway. How did you and Phil get here?"

"We parked in the garage." She shrugged. "Don't look so shocked. There's plenty of room inside. Too bad we had to walk in the rain to get to the house."

Angry, my blood pressure shot up as the dejected suspect walked in front of Gwen, and we headed downstairs.

We stepped into the foyer just as the police rang the doorbell, booming the instrumental version of Wagner's "Ride of the Valkyries."

I opened the door to Mike Miller, my old boyfriend from summers in between college semesters, still handsome as ever. We'd lost touch when I joined the Navy. Actually, Mike had refused to answer my calls, texts, emails, and letters because he resented me joining up. I had no idea he'd become a detective for the Banyan Isle Police.

My heels raised me almost to his eye level as the wind whipped my hair. "Mike, it's been a long time."

Tall, dark, and brooding, he said, "Jett," in a curt tone and peered over my shoulder. "Gwen, I understand you found a possible murder victim, and you have a suspect?"

She shoved Brenda forward. "Here's your suspect, and Mayor Peabody is dead under a bed upstairs—looks like cyanide poisoning." She pointed. "Second floor, north wing, the first guest room on the ocean side."

"Don't listen to her, Mike. I'm innocent," Brenda pleaded. "What will my friends think?"

His eyebrows shot up as he snapped the cuffs on Brenda. "Gwen, did you just say the *mayor* was murdered?"

"Afraid so. It doesn't get any higher profile than this on Banyan

Isle. I'm guessing you'll call in the Sheriff's homicide detectives, their CSU, the works."

"That and I'll get somebody from the Medical Examiner's office over here pronto." He turned to a patrol officer behind him. "Read this suspect her rights and hold her in your car until officers from the Palm Beach Sheriff's Office get here. Keep the A/C on." Mike ignored me and said to Gwen, "I'm sorry about this, but I need you and Jett to wait outside the crime scene until the PBSO's team arrives." He pulled out his cell and made some calls.

Judging by his cold attitude toward me, Mike still resented my decision to join the Navy. Even though I had shared my plans with him, I guess he didn't understand I wanted to experience the world and serve my country before thinking about settling down. If only we could've talked it over and worked things out, but instead he shut me out. Not a word from him for six years.

Gwen and I walked outside. Lucky for us, the rain had stopped. Sunshine and a warm breeze scented with salt air caressed my skin.

Lost in our own thoughts, we sat on a sun-dried marble bench facing the enormous circular water sculpture that divided my driveway. A fifteen-foot bronze statue of Odin with his sword held high stood in the center of a white marble fountain surrounded by four snarling wolves spewing water from their fanged jaws. Each wolf faced one of the four cardinal directions.

The sound of steady splashes from the flowing fountain soothed me as the sun cast shadows over the sparkling water. I stared into its depths, my mind racing about the murder and the renewed pain of seeing Mike again.

A flaming wolf with gleaming golden eyes flashed into the water and seemed to rise up and hover in front of me.

I gasped and jumped up, my heart pounding.

The wolf vanished.

"You okay, Jett?" Gwen stared at me, worry clouding her face.

I'd never seen anything like *that* before, and I didn't feel like trying to explain it, so I came up with a more reasonable answer. "A reflection of one of the wolves startled me. Must've been the sun playing tricks with the light."

Or had it been a cryptic message from the spirit world?

# THREE

I slept late the next morning, snuggled under soft Egyptian cotton sheets in one of Gwen's guest beds. A gentle breeze drifted through the balcony's open French doors. The fresh sea air had deepened my sleep and pulled me into a vivid dream.

I stood on the tarmac at the Grand Bahama International Airport in Freeport, Bahamas, and watched my parents board their private Gulfstream G650 jet, taxi out, and take off. Their airplane climbed out over the water, and seconds later, a bright flash and a faint boom preceded the tail separating from the fuselage. The jet nosedived into the ocean, sending up a fountain of seawater.

"Noooo!" I shrieked and sprang up in bed. My heart hammered my chest as I gasped for breath, trying to recover from the shock and trauma of watching my parents die. It had all seemed so real, but I hadn't been in the Bahamas the day they crashed. I was halfway around the world in Afghanistan when it happened.

Gwen peeked into the room. "Are you okay? I heard you scream."

"Sorry, I had a really bad dream." I swung my legs over the side of the bed.

"Was it about the murdered mayor in your house?" She sat beside me and put her arm around my shoulder.

"No, I saw my parents' jet explode and crash into the ocean." I brushed away tears running down my cheeks.

"News reports never mentioned an explosion." Gwen grabbed a box of tissues from the nightstand and handed them to me. "Your subconscious is probably conjuring up catastrophes. Try not to think about it. The corpse in your house must've triggered the nightmare. Why don't you take a relaxing hot shower?"

I bit my lower lip, embarrassed Gwen had found me like this, and checked my watch. "Sorry I slept so late. It's almost time for lunch."

"No worries. Hugo and Leo are attending an art fair at Bayside Marketplace in Miami. Let me treat you to a late brunch at the new Banyan Isle Bistro. Their ham and Gruyère quiches are delicious."

I blew my nose and tried to shake off the traumatic image. "Sounds yummy. I'll be ready in twenty minutes." I stumbled out of bed and headed for the shower, eager to escape the lingering negative energy.

Forty minutes later, we sat at a table on an open deck overlooking the Intracoastal Waterway, which flowed past the island's west side. A wide sun umbrella shielded us from late-morning rays as salty air mixed with the savory scents of gourmet food in the light breeze. A water taxi filled with smiling tourists docked nearby, and gulls shrieked and dived into the water where a fisherman had tossed unwanted fish parts from a cleaning table.

I banished the nightmare's images from my mind, took in the scenic view, and felt better. "It all looks so normal. Hard to believe yesterday actually happened."

"The town's rumor mill is burning up Twitter." Gwen shook her head. "Half the people think the mayor's wealthy, much-older wife poisoned him, and the other half thinks Brenda's hot-tempered husband did it."

"I didn't know Mayor Peabody. He must've moved here after I shipped out. What can you tell me about him?" I took a sip of iced tea.

"Phil was only thirty-four and quite handsome—the town playboy. Three years ago, he married heiress Marjorie Wentworth—super-rich, razor-thin, and dripping with diamonds."

"But didn't you say she was a lot older?"

Gwen took a sip of her lemonade and lowered her voice. "Marjorie is sixty-five, but she's had a lot of work done and could pass for late forties. Everyone assumed the mayor married her for her money, but he behaved himself early on. Rumor has it the past two years he started drinking too much and having affairs with slightly older married women."

My jaw dropped. "Older than his *wife?*"

She laughed. "No, I meant older than Phil, like Brenda—early forties."

I stirred my tea. "Think he was messing around with more than one woman? The suspect pool could be bigger."

"I heard he had two or three on the hook." She rolled her eyes. "*Men.*"

"An equal opportunity guy—I guess married women can't be picky." I admired the sparkling waterway. "Is Chef Hugo still in love with your house manager?"

"They're seriously considering marriage. I want them to be happy, but Hugo and Leo are like family, and I'm afraid if they get married, they might move out. I can't bear to lose them."

I thought about them and chuckled. "They seem so mismatched— short and stocky Hugo with tall and elegant Leo."

"You left out their vast differences in style. Leo always looks like he stepped out of a page in GQ, and Hugo has zero fashion sense. Exact opposites."

"Yes, but they love each other. I don't think marriage would make them move out of a lovely oceanfront mansion where their rent is free in exchange for Hugo's cooking."

"And I pay Leo to run the household and handle all the paperwork," Gwen said.

I sipped my drink. "Do they still own the Gourmet Art Gallery on Main Street?"

"It's doing well. Leo keeps it stocked with beautiful paintings and sculptures, and Hugo prepares gourmet hors d'oeuvres for their popular Art Appreciation Hour."

"I've never heard of that. What's Art Appreciation Hour?"

"It's like a bar's happy hour, but with a free glass of wine and gourmet food. They told me it's been a big boost for their art business."

"Sounds fun. What about you, Gwen? Dating anyone special?"

She slid her glass in tiny circles on the table. "No, but I've got my eye on a hot homicide detective in the Palm Beach Police. What about you?"

"I dated a Navy officer who broke my heart when he married his childhood sweetheart while he was home on leave."

"The creep! I bet he never told you he had a girl back home."

"He said we were exclusive. I was shocked when he returned wearing a wedding band. I felt like such a fool, and everybody on the base knew we'd been dating."

Gwen touched my arm. "Just so you know, Mike Miller is still single."

"Yeah, but he crushed my heart when he ghosted me after I joined the Navy. It still hurts whenever I think about him cutting me out of his life. Besides, I'm not ready to date anyone."

"Hey, you know what they say about getting back on the horse." Gwen spotted someone behind me and sat a little straighter.

A whiff of aftershave reached my nose a second before a blond man in his mid-thirties, wearing an expensive suit, stopped at our table.

"I thought I recognized you, Gwen. It's been a few months." He smiled. "Your hair is longer. I'm at the end table and wanted to say hello."

She smiled at me. "Jett Jorgensen, meet Pierce Lockwood of the Lockwood Law Firm. We met last year at a charity auction."

"Seems like we cross paths every few months on this little island," he said.

I extended my hand. "Nice to meet you, Pierce." His deep-blue eyes sparkled as I gazed at his tanned face, his short sandy hair tousled by the breeze.

"We haven't ordered yet." Gwen pointed at an empty chair. "Would you like to join us? We'd hate for you to eat alone."

"Thanks, I'd love to if it's okay with Jett." His pearly whites showcased a warm smile in his chiseled masculine features.

"Of course, Pierce, have a seat. Gwen tells me the food here is superb."

He sat at our table just as the waitress arrived to take the orders. Gwen and I ordered the quiche, and he chose a brisket burger.

I admired his fit physique. "What type of law do you practice?"

He took a sip of ice water. "I handle corporate accounts, estates, and trust funds." He frowned. "Aw, forgive me, Jett. Your parents were Victor and Atsila Jorgensen, weren't they? I'm sorry for your loss."

"That's okay, Pierce. You don't know me, and I've been away in the Navy." I gave him a friendly smile.

He recovered quickly. "My dad handled the probate of your parents' will. They were good friends."

"I thought your last name sounded familiar. Your parents are Niles and Nancy, right?"

"They live about halfway down Ocean Drive from you." He

glanced at Gwen and back to me. "I heard you had quite a shock yesterday."

I laughed. "That's an understatement. Gwen was with me."

"The *Banyan Isle Bugle* reported Mayor Peabody paid off the maid to give him a key and your security code. Is that what happened?" he asked.

Gwen nodded. "That maid is in big trouble. Depending on who killed the mayor, she could be charged with accessory to murder."

"Are you staying at your parents' house, Jett?"

"I'm spending a day or two with Gwen until the police release the crime scene. She lives next door."

He smiled at Gwen. "You remained there after that carjacker killed your parents. When was that—ten years ago?"

"I was with them when it happened." Gwen touched her chest. "I spent two weeks in the hospital healing from a gunshot wound. My parents died in the street."

I patted her hand. "She wasn't quite eighteen."

"Sorry to bring up such a traumatic memory. I was away in law school when it happened. Did the police catch the killer?"

She shook her head. "He got away. Every now and then, a carjacking with the same MO comes across the police wire, usually down in Miami-Dade or Broward County."

"That's hard to take, but at least our cops caught the mayor's killer." He scanned the other tables. "I heard it was Brenda Carrigan."

I jumped in. "Gwen and I found her hiding under the bed, but she didn't seem to have a motive. The police might have other suspects."

"In any case, it's quite the scandal. They even mentioned it on the national news last night." He leaned back when his burger plate arrived.

"I still can't believe it happened in *my* house. I'd like to help the police catch the killer." The waitress served my meal, and the aroma of baked-on Gruyère cheese filled my nostrils.

"Why do you feel so strongly about this? You didn't know the victim, did you?" He squirted ketchup on his burger bun.

"No, but I hate that my ancestral home has been marred by murder. Did you know him?"

"We crossed paths occasionally because I'm a county commissioner. I heard he was playing around with local married women. Think one of them did it?"

Gwen lowered her voice. "It's not appropriate for me to speculate, but the local police are checking the security tapes to see who else may have met him there."

I patted my lips with a napkin. "Someone from the security company should've noticed the guest-room activity and checked with me or my uncle. I left our emergency contact numbers with them."

Gwen pulled out her phone. "I'll give Mike a quick call, cop to cop, and see what they found." She covered her food with a linen napkin to keep it warm and stepped away.

"I grew up here, but I don't remember you, Pierce. Have you been in Banyan Isle long?" I gazed at a passing yacht.

"All my life. I'm guessing you're about five or six years younger, so we weren't in school together or in the same circle of friends."

I swallowed a bite. "That makes sense. Are we still neighbors?"

"No, I moved into a hangar apartment out in Aerodrome Estates. I keep an airplane there."

"My uncle, Hunter Vann, lives in Aerodrome Estates. I think it's a fun pilot community."

"And it's near the international raceway. Your uncle and I had a blast taking our sportscars around the two-mile, ten-turn road course on a non-race day."

"I've done that with him too. He let me drive his McLaren 720S. That was the most fun I've ever had in a car. Uncle Hunter also taught me how to fly. I love his antique cabin biplane."

"Right, his red Staggerwing Beech is a beauty. My airplane is more about speed," Pierce said. "After the USSR disbanded, I got a great deal on an older generation L-39 Czech fighter/trainer jet. You should fly it with me sometime."

"Every pilot has dreams of flying a fighter. I'll definitely hold you to your offer once I'm settled. I'm glad we finally met, Pierce."

"Me too." He smiled warmly. "What brings you home?"

"I'm near the end of a six-year tour in the Navy, and I have to use up my accumulated leave before I decide whether to re-enlist."

Gwen rejoined us looking concerned. "Mike told me the security videos for your home showed an empty house and grounds yesterday while we were there. Turns out someone rigged the system with a recorded loop every afternoon between two and five. This could've been going on for almost two years while the house stood empty. The Sheriff's team is looking into whether someone at the Elite Security Company was paid off."

"Wow, I can't even trust the firm I pay to protect my home." I took a moment to control my anger. "Does this mean they have no way of knowing who else the mayor was playing around with in my guest room?"

"They don't have video evidence, but they found some personal items in that guest room that didn't belong to Brenda or Mayor Peabody." Gwen uncovered her meal.

"Whose were they?" Pierce asked after swallowing a bite of his burger.

"They're verifying the suspects now." She shrugged. "A small community like this—we'll probably hear all about it on the evening news." She stabbed a fork into her lunch.

I waited while Gwen savored a few bites of her meal. "Think I should change security companies?"

Pierce shook his head. "I'd keep their service and make them post guards on the grounds free of charge for a few months to compensate for their mess up."

Gwen patted her lips with a napkin. "He's right. A scandal like this could sink their company. They'll bend over backwards to win you back and restore their reputation."

He checked his watch. "I've got to dash. I have a court case in West Palm Beach." He signaled for the check. "Lunch is my treat. Thanks for the company, ladies." He stood as the server ran his card through her electronic tablet.

"Thanks for lunch." I waved goodbye to him.

I grinned at Gwen. "He was nice. Did you two ever date?"

"No, we tried a few times, but never managed to sync our schedules." She checked the time on her phone. "I have the whole day off. Let's go to Elite Security, and maybe we can find out who tampered with your video feed."

"I would like to feel safe in my home. Armed guards for a while would be nice."

Gwen finished her meal. "I'll flash my badge when we meet the CEO. It might help with the negotiations on your security upgrade."

# FOUR

I slid into the passenger seat of Gwen's roadster and pulled my hair in front of my shoulder. I held it so it wouldn't blow around with the top down.

The drive to Elite Security in West Palm Beach took fifteen minutes. I gave my hair a quick brush as she pulled into a parking spot.

We strolled up to the receptionist, and Gwen said, "Officer Gwen Stuart and Jettine Jorgensen to see your CEO." She flashed her badge. "He'll know what this is about."

The receptionist, a blonde in her mid-twenties, stiffened when she heard my name.

Bad news traveled fast.

"Do you have an appointment?" She tapped her computer keyboard.

I leaned forward. "After what happened yesterday, we shouldn't need one."

"No, and I'm sorry you went through that." She made a call, gave our names, and listened to the response. "Our CEO, Mr. Spencer, will see you now in his office." She pointed at an elevator bank. "He's on the top floor."

I smiled. "Thank you."

We entered the elevator, and a few seconds later, the doors opened. A tall brunette rose from behind her desk and ushered us into the CEO's office. Tall windows on the east side showcased the nearby Intracoastal Waterway.

A middle-aged man of medium height with graying temples walked around his L-shaped cherry desk, introduced himself, and offered his hand. "Miss Jorgensen, Officer Stuart, thank you for coming. Please, be seated." Spencer waved at cushy leather chairs.

As we settled in, he sat behind his desk. "Miss Jorgensen, I heard about what happened at your home yesterday. Is that why you're here?"

I crossed my arms. "Please tell us who tampered with my home security system and what you're doing about it."

"We haven't discovered the guilty party yet—could be an outside hacker. But don't worry, we've added several additional layers of security oversight to your system."

Gwen joined in. "One of your employees might be an accomplice to murder, putting Miss Jorgensen at risk."

"I'd like to talk to your head of security." I arched an eyebrow. "Now, please."

He picked up the phone and punched in a number. "Send Wilfred Sims to my office right away." Replacing the receiver, Spencer smiled. "He's coming."

Moments later, a skinny man wearing wire-rimmed glasses entered the office and closed the door. His weasel eyes focused on me, and he froze.

Something about him made my skin crawl. I shot a glance at Gwen. Her eyes telegraphed the same reaction.

"Have a seat, Sims," the CEO said. "Miss Jorgensen and Officer Stuart would like a word with you."

The weaselly guy stared at me. "Sorry about the trouble at your house."

"You mean the murder." Gwen zeroed in on Sims. "Why haven't you identified the employee who tampered with the Jorgensen's video feed?"

"Whoever did it covered his tracks." He swallowed hard, still staring at me, and licked his lips, like a lizard about to eat a fly. "Could've been an expert hacker."

Sims behaved like he was guilty of something. I said nothing and gave him the Aniwaya evil-eye glare my mother had taught me. It seemed to be working. The longer I stared back, the paler his face became and the more he squirmed.

"How do you intend to catch the culprit?" Gwen asked.

"I have all the employees who had access under surveillance," Sims replied.

"That's it?" Gwen raised her eyebrows. "You're not doing anything else?"

Spencer said, "The police are running checks on all my employees' financial records. They'll find whoever received a big payoff or steady payments over the past two years."

The little head of security shifted in his seat, chewed his thin lips, and eyed the door like he was about to make an escape.

"Not if the guilty party was paid in cash," I pointed out, still focused on the creepy head of security.

Gwen leaned forward. "Well, Spencer, how are you going to make things right for Miss Jorgensen?"

"There's no evidence we were at fault." His eyes darted from her to me.

"In that case, I'll tell all my neighbors how you treat customers when there's a security issue." I stood. "Cancel my contract. I'll find a company with better customer service."

"Wait, how about free round-the-clock security guards and the Tier-One Package for the next three months?" Spencer continued, "After that, a fifty-percent discount on whatever services you choose to continue."

"Make it six months and I won't sue, provided a guard begins walking the grounds today."

Spencer bit his lower lip. "Agreed. I'll have a guard there in two hours."

"Good, and don't forget to notify the Banyan Isle Police about the guard," Gwen said. "The home's interior is still taped off as a crime scene."

We kept our expressions neutral as we exited the building.

As we drove back to Banyan Isle, Gwen turned to me. "Wow, Jett, you really gave Wilfred Sims the evil eye."

"He's guilty of *something*. Mom taught me that guilty people will squirm if I focus my eyes on them like blue laser beams." I chuckled. "Hey, I took a shot. I wouldn't be surprised if the cops find evidence Sims rigged the video."

"Do you think you inherited any of your mom's psychic abilities?"

"Maybe a few fragments here and there, but it has never helped me pick the right boyfriend." I paused, remembering her. "She was guided by wisdom and kindness and had a strong connection to the spirit world. I really miss her."

Gwen drove over the bridge to our island community. "I wonder if you'll get a call from the Banyan Isle cops soon, telling you who's responsible for your altered security tapes."

"I hope so." I leaned back. "And maybe I'll get a call from Pierce Lockwood."

# FIVE

That evening, Gwen and I enjoyed a quiet dinner on her screened-in, oceanfront terrace. We ordered a thin-crust pizza delivered from Luigi's Italian Ristorante on Main Street. A chilled bottle of chardonnay complemented the meal.

I took in a deep breath of fresh ocean air as small rollers broke on the sandy beach fifty yards from the elevated terrace. Palm trees swayed in the warm breeze as twilight set in, the sun slowly setting behind us in the west.

"It must've felt good to get free armed guards for your home security today." Gwen handed me a plate with two slices of pizza on it.

"It's only fair." I breathed in the enticing aroma. "It was their job to keep me safe at home. Armed guards were the least they could do after what happened yesterday."

"And what about Pierce? Do you like him?"

"He's smart, handsome, and charming, and we seem to have a lot in common." I smiled. "Yeah, I like him."

"Good. You should date him. Best cure for a broken heart, and you'll be less likely to stay in the Navy."

"Just because I like him doesn't mean I'm ready to start dating again." I changed the subject. "Why don't you call Mike and see if he has any news on murder suspects?"

Gwen made the call, listened to Mike's answer, and rolled her eyes. She pocketed her phone. "He said they have too many suspects now."

"Too many? Did he give you any names?"

"Well, there's the mayor's vengeful wife, Marjorie, of course. And Brenda's jealous husband, Andy, who owns Carrigan's Irish Pub."

"Brenda already mentioned them." I sipped my wine. "Who else?"

"Technically, I'm not supposed to say, so this is just between us. Could be Dolores Delgado, owner of Fit and Fabulous, a new health club here on the island. The CSU techs found a hairbrush with her hair, fingerprints, and her company's name on it behind the nightstand."

"Hell hath no fury." I chuckled. "She must've found out about the other women."

"Or it could've been her husband, Manny. He owns Paradise Construction Company, rumored to have Mafia connections, and he's known for his hot Latin temper."

"Oh boy, I wouldn't want to be in Dolores's shoes if Manny finds out about all this."

"Yeah, but then there's Victoria Master, owner of Master Realty, whose gold Montblanc pen was found under the bed. It had her initials engraved on it, and it was covered with her fingerprints. And Victoria's husband, John, is a real estate lawyer in the same company. If he knew about the cheating, he'd have a motive too."

"Those are a lot of suspects. Who do you think did it?"

"Who knows? Here's the kicker: none of them have alibis for that afternoon."

"I suppose anybody could've poisoned the Scotch, but Brenda's husband is the most likely culprit. He owns a bar that specializes in top-shelf Irish and Scotch whisky." I took a bite. "The mayor's wife is the other major suspect. Were her fingerprints on the bottle?"

"No, just the mayor's prints."

"So maybe Andy Carrigan sold the mayor the poisoned Scotch and was careful not to leave prints."

"Ah, but that's where the plot thickens. Carrigan's Irish Pub doesn't sell Glenglassaugh whisky, the brand of Scotch found in your guest room. Nobody on this island carries it."

"That complicates things, but I'm sure there are plenty of places on the mainland that sell that expensive whisky." I reached for my other slice. "And anyone in the mix could've been vengeful enough to take action. Mike must be getting gray hairs over this one."

"They all had motives if they knew about the cheating. That's seven people."

I chewed on a bite of pizza and thought about the suspects. "The thing is, the Scotch could've been poisoned any time after the mayor bought it, like the day before the murder. Maybe he was the only target."

"I bet his wife gave him the poisoned whisky and didn't care which tart drank it with him. Revenge is a strong motive. So is jealousy. She must've felt betrayed by her husband." Gwen leaned forward. "I forgot to tell you one of her stick-on nails was found on his right sleeve."

"That could've happened at home." I admired a full moon rising over the ocean. "I don't envy Mike trying to solve this."

"You're right. This is a tough one. PBSO is doing everything they can to help."

"Has your perspective on solving crimes changed now that you're a cop?"

"When my parents were murdered, I couldn't bear the injustice of the killer getting away, and I poured out my anger on the police officers assigned to the case." She turned to me. "Now I understand how difficult their job can be. I've since apologized to all the cops involved."

"But you're still trying to catch the guy who did it, right?"

"That's why I drive my fancy bait car. I research all unsolved carjacking cases with the same MO, most of which are in other counties. If that monster ever comes back to Palm Beach County—"

I interrupted, "You'll catch him and lock him in a cage for the rest of his miserable life."

Gwen touched the center of her chest where the bullet wound had left a scar from the surgery. "No danger of me forgetting him—not with this souvenir front and center. I still have nightmares about him—those evil eyes are forever burned into my soul."

"Sounds like your memory of the carjacking is still crystal clear."

"Just before he drove away, he shot us and laughed. He *laughed*. Only a monster would behave like that." She took a big sip of wine. "He's the reason I became a police officer. I *will* catch him."

Gwen's French chef, Hugo Fournier, and her Spanish house manager, Leonardo Pérez, returned from Miami and joined us on the terrace.

"Jett, darling, sorry about that nasty business with the mayor and his floozy, but you look marvelous. The Navy must agree with you." Leo nudged me. "How's your love life?"

"Not so good. My boyfriend dumped me and married his childhood sweetheart."

Hugo joined in with his heavy French accent, "Sorry, Jett, but you know what they say. Best way to get over a man is to get under another."

Gwen laughed. "That's kind of what I've been telling her."

I smiled at the men, Leo dressed in a pale-blue linen suit, and Hugo in khaki shorts and a floral Hawaiian shirt. "Did you find anything at the art fair?"

"A few paintings and a fabulous bronze mermaid sculpture." Leo covered a yawn with his manicured hand. "It's been a long day. We're turning in early. See you girls at breakfast."

# SIX

Later that night, I went to bed in the same third-floor guest room at Gwen's house and left the doors to the balcony open to let in the fresh sea air and moonlight.

I experienced a vivid dream that my mother visited me. She led me downstairs, out the terrace screened-door, across the back lawn, through the beach gate, and across the sand to our back gate. Mom walked right through the gate, but I had to climb over it. I trailed her to our house, where she walked through the glass terrace doors. I tried to follow her, but my head banged against the glass, waking me. Confused, I stared into the great hall. No one was inside. It had all seemed so real.

Gwen yelled, "Jett! Wake up!" She ran onto the Italian-tiled terrace, barefoot in her nightgown, and grabbed my arm.

I faced her. "Are you in my dream, or is this real?"

"You were sleepwalking. I followed you over here." She touched my forehead. "That's going to leave a bruise. Does it hurt?"

"It's not bad, but more important, I've never sleepwalked in my life."

"How would you know you sleepwalked if you ended up back in your bed?"

"I've been in the Navy for six years. *Somebody* would've noticed."

"Were you dreaming?"

"I thought I was. Mom led me here. I woke when I slammed into the glass door." I rubbed my forehead. "I've never experienced anything like this before."

Gwen patted my back. "The mayor's murder must've triggered the dreams and sleepwalking."

"If that's true, why was last night's dream about my parents' jet crash and tonight about Mom leading me home?"

Gwen and I were barefoot and wearing nothing but knee-length satin nightgowns.

"Freeze! Hands up!" An armed security guard pointed his weapon at us.

I turned around. "It's okay. I'm the homeowner."

"No, you're not. This home is unoccupied." He pulled out his cell phone and called the police. "Wait right there until the cops arrive."

Frustrated and embarrassed, we sat on white woven chairs and waited for a police officer.

"We must look foolish out here in the middle of the night," I said to Gwen.

"We look like idiots. No wonder the guard called the cops."

"Well, I hope whoever comes will be someone we know."

She straightened her nightgown. "I'm hoping it'll be someone I don't know."

"Good thing we aren't wearing see-through nighties." I smoothed the fabric.

We sat in silence, staring out at the dark ocean as whitecaps breaking on shore glistened under a bright moon. A steady breeze made me shiver and rub my arms.

Ten minutes later, a deep voice said, "Jett? Gwen? What are you doing out here so late?"

It was Detective Mike Miller. Why couldn't it have been a patrol officer?

*Great, my old boyfriend will either think I'm drunk or stupid.*

Gwen and I exchanged glances, not sure what to say. Would he believe I had sleepwalked here?

She stood. "There's a perfectly reasonable explanation for why we're here. Go ahead, Jett, tell him."

That was fair. After all, my dream had led us to my house, so why should Gwen have to come up with a plausible explanation?

I began, "Dealing with the murder has been stressful—"

She interrupted, "Yes, very stressful."

I continued, "I might've had too much wine, and I couldn't sleep, so I stood on the guest room balcony, looking at the beach. Thought I saw someone climb over the beach gate and run into my backyard. Not really thinking, I yelled and rushed downstairs and out the back door."

Gwen broke in, "I followed her, thinking she was sleepwalking or something."

"I forgot to bring my key, and the guard found us here on the terrace. No intruder. End of story." My face flushed. "Sorry."

Mike stared at me. The judgmental look on his face told me he didn't believe my story. "Lack of sleep can make people do strange things. Come with me. I'll drive you two back to Gwen's house."

I peered into his tired brown eyes. "Why are you here in the middle of the night? This isn't a detective's call."

"I was at the office late, working on the murder case, when the intruder report came in. I thought maybe it would lead to a break in the case, so I took the call."

Gwen patted his back. "Thanks for coming, Mike."

We circled the house, following the tiled terrace that wrapped around the north wing, bordering the ballroom and swimming pool. "Has the crime scene been released yet?" I glanced at my front door on the way to his car.

"Yes, the tape has been removed, and the guestroom floor was professionally cleaned. You're free to go home whenever you want. Don't forget to alert the security company."

Before I climbed into the unmarked police car, I waved at the security guard who had followed us. "Good job. And just so you know, I'll be living here starting tomorrow. Good night."

When Mike dropped us off, we were too wired to sleep, so we settled on comfy chairs in Gwen's living room and sipped wine.

"Mike didn't believe my story, and I wish he didn't act so cold toward me."

"*Act* is the key word," Gwen said, her tone guarded.

"What do you mean?"

"I guess I should've told you sooner, but the time never seemed right, and I didn't want to reopen the wound after you'd healed." She took a sip of wine. "Four months after you went in the Navy, Mike took me out for a drink to celebrate my new job with the Palm Beach Police. He'd been hired two months earlier with the Banyan Isle Police. We ended up having a lot of wine and a long, serious chat."

"What did you talk about?" I worried it had been about me.

"We discovered we were both drawn to law enforcement careers because we had lost family members to unsolved murders and wanted justice for ourselves and others."

"Right, I remember his younger brother Matt was our age when he was found murdered at our prep school. He was only sixteen, and the killer was never caught."

Gwen frowned. "That was twelve years ago, but it seems like yesterday."

"Are you saying your long conversation was strictly work-related?"

"It started that way, but then he told me how he'd blown it with you. He admitted you'd told him all along you intended to join the Navy and serve your country." She bit her lower lip.

"I don't understand. Did he say why he shut me out?"

"He was big-time in love with you, and your relationship was going well, so he assumed you'd changed your mind. He even bought an engagement ring, but before he had a chance to propose, you left for the Navy and crushed him."

I gulped the wine. "Why didn't he tell me any of this?"

"He felt hurt, betrayed, and abandoned. A typical alpha male, he didn't want to show any weakness. By the time he admitted to himself his bad reaction wasn't your fault, you'd stopped trying to contact him. He assumed it was too late and you had moved on. He asked me not to tell you. Sorry."

I felt sick. "Well then, why did he miss my parents' funerals two years ago?"

"He was in D.C. attending a criminal investigations class taught by the FBI. He didn't find out about them until it was too late to get there. He felt really bad about missing the services and appearing not to care. He probably assumed that was the final nail in your relationship's coffin."

I emptied my wine glass. "I'm here now, so why is he still so cold toward me?"

"I'm guessing it's because you're only here for a month, and he doesn't want to get hurt again when you return to the Navy." She drained her glass. "Why did you join, anyway? You could've been an executive at Jorgensen Industries."

"I've never had Father's passion for business, and I don't have Mother's spiritual and healing abilities. I wanted to do something that would make a difference, protect people. You and I were never cut out to live like spoiled socialites."

"You got that right. Have you decided to re-enlist?"

"I've been so distracted by the mayor's murder and my disturbing dreams I haven't thought about the Navy at all." I sighed. "And now I'm not sure what to think about Mike."

"A more important question is how do you *feel* about Mike?"

"Crap, I don't know. I thought he hated me." I stood. "I can't think about this right now. Let's go back to bed."

# SEVEN

After finishing breakfast, I re-packed my bag, and Gwen dropped me off on her way to work. That might've seemed like an unnecessary gesture, but the estates didn't have side access to each other for security reasons. Each driveway was the length of a football field, and the entry gates were separated by more than twice that distance. That would've been a long trek pulling a wheeled suitcase.

I used my key, opened the heavy door, punched in the code, and walked past the twin stairways and winged-Valkyrie statues. The house seemed eerily quiet.

I hit the number-four button and took the elevator to the top floor. Turning right, I pulled my bag down the long hallway in the south wing, which was on the opposite side of the house from the murder. The twelve-foot walls paneled in golden teak held paintings of Nordic landscapes and Viking battle scenes.

My bedroom suite occupied the south end. Narrow spiral stairs in both corners led up to turret rooms guarding the castle. My south balcony faced the lower north balcony in Gwen's third-floor bedroom next door, but it was too far away to see her without binoculars.

When we were children, we played spies and sent each other messages in Morse code using light signals. We had fun and learned a skill seldom used in the modern age. Ironically, I ended up putting that knowledge to good use on four occasions during my service in Navy Intelligence. Good thing I was blessed with an eidetic memory like my father.

I took a moment and sprawled across my king-size, four-poster bed. The rose satin bedspread felt cool against my skin, and the thought of sleeping in a familiar bed again comforted me. After unpacking, I drew open the heavy rose draperies and stood on my east balcony, staring out at the Atlantic Ocean sparkling under the bright morning sun.

My first order of business would be getting the door locks and codes changed and then hiring a new cleaning service after I ran them through the same intense scrutiny I'd employ for a suspected enemy operative. No more betrayals by dishonest maids.

Until I figured out what was causing my dreams and sleepwalking, I didn't want to hire any live-in staff who might react badly to my nocturnal antics. Was my mother's spirit trying to help me solve Mayor Peabody's murder?

After completing my to-do list, I needed to restock the refrigerator and pantry. I grabbed the keys to Mom's SUV and drove to Giorgio's Gourmet Market near the north end of Main Street on the island. The extra-wide street accommodated huge Banyan trees that lined broad sidewalks and provided a thick canopy shading the thoroughfare from the blazing sun. I pulled into Giorgio's small parking lot.

I grabbed a big cart and filled it with my favorite foods. After I finished shopping, I loaded the bags into the SUV and drove down the street to the Upper Crust Bakery. A few comfort snacks would be good to have on hand to ease the trauma from disturbing dreams. That was my excuse anyway. I bought chocolate brownies, chocolate chip cookies, and chocolate biscotti sticks. I assumed Gwen would eat half of everything, and I'd burn off the calories swimming laps in my pool.

As I exited the bakery, I bumped into Pierce. "Hey, thanks again for lunch yesterday. I'm back at my house now."

He smiled. "Good. I hope the security company provided an armed guard."

"They did. Are you here for a caffeine and sugar fix?"

"Just caffeine. They have the best cappuccino in town. Join me for a cup?"

"Sure, and I have goodies if you change your mind about something sweet." I held up the bags. "I'll grab an outside table."

We sat at a tree-shaded sidewalk table and sipped our beverages.

I opened the bags. "Would you like a chocolate chip cookie, fudge brownie, or a chocolate biscotti stick?"

"Knowing my luck, I won't get time for lunch, so how about a brownie?"

"My pleasure." I set it on his napkin and stuck a biscotti stick into my cappuccino.

Pierce savored a bite of the brownie. "How's the Navy treating you?"

"Navy Intelligence has been interesting work, but after six years I might be ready for a change." I gazed into his sexy eyes. "How do you like being a lawyer?"

"I enjoy my job, but I have political aspirations."

"What office are you shooting for?"

"I'm already a county commissioner." He lifted his glass in a mock toast. "Next step is the State House, then governor of Florida, U.S. senator, and maybe president one day."

"Wow, Pierce, I'm impressed." I bit off the end of the biscotti stick. "I like an ambitious man with a solid plan. With your family's connections, you're bound to go far."

His cell pinged with a text message, and he frowned. "I'm needed at the courthouse, but I was hoping to get an update from you on what's happening with the mayor's murder. Any chance we can continue this conversation over dinner tonight at the Banyan Harbor Inn?"

"Thanks, but I just went through a rough breakup. I'm not ready to date."

"No pressure, just a friendly dinner." He held up his hand. "Scout's honor. Pick you up at seven?"

"Okay, as long as we're just friends." *Is this a good idea?*

He stood. "Good, I'll see you tonight." He dropped his paper cup in the trash bin and whistled the tune for "You Give Love a Bad Name" as he strolled down the street to his red vintage Corvette.

I deposited the baked goods in my car and then entered the LBD Boutique next door. I needed a little black dress for dinner at the elegant restaurant. The store had a wide selection of cocktail dresses, and it had been several years since I had bought any new clothes. Three dresses fit me perfectly, enhancing my modest curves. I found matching stilettos and handbags for each dress: one black, one red, and a light-blue one. Retail therapy.

––––––

The Banyan Harbor Inn sprawled across the southern end of the island midway from east to west and included a yacht harbor with boats and jet-ski rentals, a long, four-story hotel with two swimming pools, tennis courts, and an elegant waterfront restaurant and bar. We sat at a table overlooking the ocean inlet between Banyan Isle and Singer Island.

Pierce admired my sleeveless black cocktail dress. "You look beautiful in that outfit, Jett."

I smiled. "Thank you. It's nice to wear a pretty dress after wearing a uniform for so long."

He perused the wine list. "How about a bottle of Pessimist from the Paso Robles Vineyard? It's my favorite blended red."

"Yes, please. I'm craving red meat. I could never get a good steak in Afghanistan." I surveyed the menu. "Ooh, I love Béarnaise sauce."

He signaled the waiter and ordered a bottle of wine and Châteaubriand Béarnaise for two. "Afghanistan sounds like a miserable place."

"It is, but the Taliban keeps us busy. It's a never-ending struggle."

"It's like the story of Sisyphus forever rolling that boulder up the hill." He shook his head. "A no-win situation."

"That constant frustration is one reason I'm thinking of leaving the Navy." After the waiter poured wine into my glass, I swirled it and took a sip.

Pierce tasted his wine. "Are you planning to live here again?"

"The trust my great grandfather created to maintain Valhalla requires a Jorgensen family member to live there." I swirled my wine. "After my parents died, I used some of my inheritance to fund a local shelter for battered women. I'd like to expand the charity to include college scholarships with free room and board for the women to attend nearby colleges."

"Good idea, Jett. You'd help a lot of women get a fresh start and improve their lives."

"I'd like to hold a charity ball at Valhalla to raise funds for the scholarships. It's just that there's something I need to resolve at home first."

He arched an eyebrow. "The mayor's murder?"

"I'll help the police if I can, but I have a personal matter to deal with."

He reached out and patted my hand. "I'm here for you if you need me."

The server arrived with our dinners.

"This looks delicious." I took a deep drink of the red elixir and sliced into a piece of meat as tender as butter.

He lifted a silver sauce boat. "Béarnaise?"

"Yes, please, pour a little on everything."

"Any new gossip on the murder case?" He finished serving the sauce.

"They have seven possible suspects now." I left out their names, but the local paper had printed everything in a front-page story in the evening edition. Secrets didn't last long on Banyan Isle.

# EIGHT

W e were down to the last few bites of steak when I scanned the people occupying the many tables on either side of us and on the levels that covered two graduated tiers above us.

I recognized Manny and Dolores Delgado from pictures on the front page of the *Banyan Isle Bugle*. Pictures of the mayor's wife, Marjorie, Andy and Brenda Carrigan, and John and Victoria Master also had been included in the story circulated early this evening.

A broad guy with no neck at a table behind the couple seemed a little too interested in Manny and Dolores as they appeared to be having a heated discussion. A skinny guy in a Tommy Bahama shirt and tan slacks two tables away from us seemed to be watching them too.

As I dawdled over my wine, I scanned the other tables. Brenda and Andy Carrigan were seated one tier above the Delgados at the opposite end. A guy in a cheap sport coat sitting alone watched them. Had Mike put the couples under surveillance? I whispered, "Pierce, look who's here." I nodded in the direction of the Delgados and then the Carrigans.

"Interesting, and did you notice the men watching them?"

"The observers don't look like cops, especially the guy with no neck. He looks like a mobster." I grinned. "Let's see what happens."

We had just started our second glasses of wine when Dolores got up and headed for the bathrooms in the front of the restaurant near the entrance.

"Look, No Neck and Tommy Bahama followed her." Pierce pointed.

I peered left and spotted Andy heading for the restrooms followed by the sport-coat guy. "This just became even more interesting. I'll go to the ladies' room while you keep an eye on Manny and Brenda."

When I entered the restroom, Dolores wasn't there. I refreshed my lipstick and turned in the opposite direction when I exited. No Neck and Tommy Bahama waited outside on a bench between two indoor palm trees while the sport-coat guy paced nearby.

An intimate alcove decorated with tropical plants bordered the hallway twenty feet past the restrooms. I peeked inside as I strolled by and spotted Andy in a steamy lip-lock with Dolores. I pulled out my cell and snapped a picture.

The hulk with no neck sat staring at his cell phone. The other two observers ignored each other and pretended to make calls. None of them noticed me taking their pictures.

I returned to our table, and Pierce pointed at Brenda and Manny sharing an intimate chat down near the docks where they smoked cigarettes in the designated area. I snapped their pictures too. Marital intrigue galore.

Brenda checked her watch and scurried back to her table. I wondered what would happen next when someone eased close behind me.

"Hello, Pierce, mind if I have a word with Miss Jorgensen?"

"I'm not leaving, but you're welcome to join us." Pierce pulled out a chair and introduced Andy Carrigan.

Andy smiled and sat beside me. "Jett, would you be willing to testify at my divorce hearing? I just want you to tell the truth about finding Brenda with the mayor."

Pierce answered for me. "Jett doesn't need to testify because the police report states she found your wife with Mayor Peabody's dead body. That fact is not in question."

"Well, okay then. Have a good evening." Andy returned to his table.

"Thanks, Pierce. Let's finish the wine and enjoy the spy-versus-spy cheating spouses show." I took a sip.

He grinned. "I'd bet a case of Pessimist wine two of the spies are private investigators. Not sure what to think about the big guy. Probably works for one of Manny's silent partners."

"I guess the women are trying to get dirt on their husbands before the divorces." I laughed. "Looks like the cheating wives have cheating husbands who are cross-pollinating their marital beds."

"This is way more complicated than I originally thought. Think Victoria Master's husband is involved with one of the other wives too?"

"And maybe Victoria is playing around with Manny or Andy or another married guy we don't even know about." I chuckled. "This is juicy stuff. Navy Intelligence isn't nearly this fun."

"You could leave the Navy and become a P.I.," he joked. "Later, you'll have plenty of material to become a best-selling author. Just change the names to avoid lawsuits."

"Who knew Banyan Isle could provide so many alternatives to the Navy?"

"Too bad you aren't ready to date. With your Cherokee heritage, you and I would make the ideal political power couple."

"I guess my ethnic diversity would look good to the voting public." I grinned. "I could end up in the White House as your first lady, but if I had to put up with the media nightmare that goes with it, I'd rather be the one in the oval office."

"No harm in thinking about it." He sipped his wine. "Hey, I'm going out to your uncle's place tomorrow to fly my L-39 fighter jet. I keep it in his hangar. Want to come?"

"I've got some interviews scheduled in the morning—I'm looking for a new maid service, but my afternoon is free."

"Pick you up at noon?"

"Sounds perfect. I'll bring the Nomex flight suit my uncle gave me. Do the ejection seats still work in your old-generation fighter?"

"It's not *that* old, and I keep everything in tip-top shape. But just in case, you're qualified in parachutes, right?"

"Yeah, but how long has it been since you've flown it? A lot can go wrong with that older technology."

"Don't worry, I flew it last week, and your uncle's maintenance shop keeps it airworthy." He drained his wine glass. "Looks like the players are leaving."

I turned as the couples and their spies weaved their way through the tables to the valet stand.

He checked his watch. "It's a little after ten. Want to go somewhere for a nightcap?"

"No, thanks. I want to swim early-morning laps in my pool before the interviews start tomorrow." I stood.

"Of course. Let's go." He placed his hand at the small of my back and guided me to the valet stand.

Five minutes later, he pulled in front of Valhalla, hopped out, and opened my car door. He walked me to the front door, waited until I unlocked it, then kissed my hand. "See you tomorrow."

The hand kiss made me tingle all over. Maybe Gwen was right about me dating again. Especially since the enormous empty castle magnified my loneliness. I double-checked the security system and then headed up four flights of stairs to the top floor, listening to every sound along the way. I changed into my nightgown and slipped under the covers. The wine I had enjoyed with dinner made me drowsy. It wasn't long before I dropped into a deep sleep.

My mother visited me in a dream. Her radiant golden eyes focused on me as her long black hair cascaded over a billowy powder-blue dress. Beckoning me to follow, she led me downstairs and into the study, located on the first floor in the southwest corner. Floor-to-ceiling oak bookcases lined the walls, and a Persian rug in vibrant hues accented the oak floor. She pointed at a book on a shelf full of mystery and thriller novels. Books I'd read.

I reached for the book. As I pulled it off the shelf, the phone on the desk rang, shattering my dream. Waking with a sudden jolt made me drop the book. Confused, I turned and stared at the ringing phone, illuminated by moonlight shining through tall, corner windows. *Is this still a dream?*

Lifting the receiver, I answered, "Hello?"

"Jett, it's Gwen. Sorry to call so late, but I tried your cell earlier, and you didn't answer. I was worried."

I concentrated on keeping my voice steady as I recovered from the shock of another sleepwalking episode—one I wasn't ready to discuss. "Don't worry, you didn't wake me. I forgot to turn my cell phone's ringer back on after dinner."

"Good. Did you have a nice time with Pierce?"

"Yes, and there are several new developments related to the murder case. I took pictures. I'll be busy during the day, but we can meet here tomorrow night for dinner. Do you think Mike will want to see the evidence I gathered?"

"I'll ask him to stop by your house around seven with a big sausage pizza, and you can tell us all about it."

"See you then." Disconnecting, I surveyed the dimly-lit room. Wine-colored cordovan armchairs and a matching sofa stood in a semi-circle in front of a stone fireplace built into the south wall.

Bookcases flanked the hearth, and I spotted an action thriller nearby on the rug.

My breath caught when I picked up *Stranded* by S.L. Menear and remembered the jet airliner depicted on the cover had crashed because of sabotage. Goosebumps erupted on my arms as my shaking hand returned the book to the shelf.

*What's happening? Is Mother trying to tell me she and Dad were murdered?*

I collapsed into the wine-colored cordovan desk chair and stared at a framed picture of my parents perched on the desktop. Moonlight illuminated my blond father's handsome face. His brilliant blue eyes stared back at me as my beautiful mother stood beside him, smiling.

*Are they trying to tell me something about their plane crash? Why wait until now? Am I reading too much into my dreams?*

# NINE

The next morning, I popped out of bed and pulled on a bathing suit, a terry robe, and flip-flops. I breezed down the stairs and cut through the great hall, which had a magnificent thirty-foot vaulted ceiling and oak-paneled walls. On the ocean side, tall windows showcased the ocean view, and wide glass doors opened to the broad oceanfront terrace. A long, outdoor infinity pool, level with the terrace, bordered the ballroom.

I swam laps for thirty minutes, trying to burn off anxiety about my dream's possible message. The warm water and early morning breeze caressed my skin.

After a hearty breakfast, I dressed for the maid service interviews. All the companies had excellent reputations, so I chose the one that gave me the most positive feeling. Sterling Maid Service emailed the contract, and I completed the transaction online. Problem solved.

I grabbed my cell as I trotted upstairs to change for the flight. The phone vibrated. It was Pierce.

"Hey, Jett, hold off on eating lunch and I'll bring a picnic basket of goodies for us to enjoy after our flight. It's best to eat after the G-load."

That sounded ominous. "Alrighty, then, I'll wait. See you soon."

I rushed to change into shorts, a fancy T-shirt, and sneakers. I folded the Nomex flight suit that would fit over my clothes. I'd pull it on right before the flight so I wouldn't overheat.

As I waited downstairs for Pierce to arrive, I relaxed in a comfortable leather armchair and called Uncle Hunter. I decided not to tell him about my dreams until I was sure what to say. He was my mother's younger brother—tall and muscular with thick black hair, golden skin, and golden eyes. A former Navy fighter pilot and current airline pilot, he owned a flight school and a maintenance facility that also restored antique airplanes and built experimental aircraft. At forty, Hunter Vann was a confirmed bachelor and my closest relative. I loved him dearly.

He answered on the third ring. "Hi, Jett, I was planning to visit you later today."

"I'm coming to Aerodrome Estates. Pierce Lockwood is picking me up in a few minutes, and he's taking me for a ride in his fighter jet. After that, we're having a picnic lunch, and I'd like you to join us."

"That's even better. I can't wait to see you, sweetheart. Sorry I was working a three-day trip when your flight arrived. Otherwise, I would've picked you up. I heard about the murder. Are you okay?"

"I'm fine, but it was quite a shock. Where should I meet you?"

"I'll be in my workshop. Stop by before you go up in the jet."

"You think it's safe for me to fly in the L-39 with Pierce?" I decided it didn't hurt to ask, even though my gut said it was okay.

"We keep that fighter in pristine condition, and Pierce is a good pilot. You'll be fine."

"Good. I'll see you soon." The instant I disconnected Pierce rang my Viking doorbell.

We climbed into his vintage Corvette and cruised over the Banyan

Isle bridge with the top down and the sun overhead. It was a perfect day for flying with clear skies and light wind.

"Do you mind if we stop by Hunter's workshop and say hello before we launch?"

"I planned to do that anyway," he said with a smile. "I want to put the picnic basket inside his giant refrigerator while we're up flying."

"You'd better give me some stick time. That fighter must be a thrill to fly."

"You'll love it. The controls are instantly responsive, and it really rips through the sky. Just limit the G-load so you don't black out."

"Oh, right, I don't have a G-suit, just the fire-retardant flight suit."

"That'll be fine, and I'll go easy on you." He grinned, brimming with confidence.

We arrived thirty minutes later, and I gave my uncle a big hug.

"Jett, you look as beautiful as ever." He lifted me up and spun me around.

Pierce laughed. "Looks like you're preparing her for aerobatics in the L-39."

"She'll be fine. Jett has a cast-iron stomach. If aerobatic lessons with me didn't make her sick, nothing will." He set me down and grinned.

"Uncle Hunter, you're way too good-looking. Flight attendants must have a tough time concentrating on their jobs when they work with you."

"Is that why they act so silly around me?" He laughed. "Mystery solved."

I playfully punched his bulging biceps. "You're so bad."

"Can't help it, sugar. It's the wild Cherokee in me." He took the picnic basket from Pierce. "Want me to put this in the fridge?"

"Thanks, and please join us for lunch when we get back. We have plenty."

After a detailed thirty-minute briefing about the L-39, its ejection system, and our planned flight, we were suited up and strapped into the sleek fighter-trainer jet. The takeoff pinned me to the seat, and the brief, vertical climb was exhilarating. I loved it.

"Woohoo! This is so fun, Pierce!" I was in pilot heaven.

Minutes later, he said, "We're in the practice area over the Everglades now. I like to stay near the southwest corner of Lake Okeechobee. Don't forget, the hard deck is at ten thousand, so we don't have to worry about the speed limit at the lower altitudes. Keep it between twelve and sixteen thousand feet." He wiggled the control stick slightly. "You have the airplane."

I took hold of the control stick with my right hand and put my feet on the rudder pedals. "Here come some aileron rolls." We spun horizontally for several rotations before I stopped it back in the upright position. I couldn't believe the lightning-fast roll rate.

"Do a wide loop to limit the G-load. Expect to use about three thousand feet vertically."

I gave it a try. What a rush! The speed was addictive, and the dives were thrilling.

We played around, zooming up, diving down, and banking in steep turns as we rocketed around the Everglades. Time went by too fast. Soon Pierce took the controls, and we headed back to Aerodrome Estates. He made a whisper-soft landing and taxied to the jet-fuel pumps.

My veins hummed with adrenaline when I climbed out. "What a thrill! No wonder you enjoy flying this so much." I hugged Pierce and then pulled off my Nomex suit. "It must be fun and fast for traveling."

"No traveling. The FAA has it in the Experimental category, which restricts me to local flying only, except waivers for airshows." He wriggled out of his flight suit. "You flew it like a pro. We'll have to do this again soon." Concerned, he asked, "Are you ready for lunch or does your stomach need to recover first?"

"I'm good. Let's put your baby in the hangar and then dive into that picnic basket."

We strolled to my uncle's workshop and found him changing a spark plug on the radial engine of his beautiful red Beechcraft D17S Staggerwing. His antique cabin biplane was one of my favorites. When it was running, the big Pratt & Whitney R-985 engine made a deep rumbling that vibrated the cabin and made the airplane seem to come alive. I felt an almost spiritual connection to the venerable aircraft.

"Hey, do you still have your old Panhead Harley?" I scanned the maintenance hangar.

Hunter pointed at a shiny Harley Davidson motorcycle parked in a back corner. "Yep, it's powder-coated, fully chromed, and ready to roll."

Pierce stood, hands on hips, looking at me. "I had no idea you were such a motorhead."

I blushed as Hunter said, "She's only like this when she's hanging out with me. I taught her to appreciate fine machinery." He wiped his hands on a rag. "I'm starved. Let's eat."

Pierce grabbed the basket from the fridge, and Hunter took cold bottles of water. We found a picnic table under a big shade tree and settled in.

Pierce handed out gourmet ham and cheese sandwiches from Giorgio's and opened a big bag of baked potato chips with sea salt. No one spoke until we'd inhaled half the sandwiches.

Hunter put his arm around me. "I have a nice surprise for you. I hope Pierce won't mind taking it back to your house in his Vette."

"A greasy old motorcycle won't fit anyway." Pierce took a swig of water.

"Nothing like that. I assure you they're clean." He finished his sandwich. "Wait here while I go get them."

"Them?" I arched an eyebrow.

He grinned. "You'll see."

A few minutes later, he returned with two balls of fur in his arms. He set them down beside me. A honey-colored male puppy and a black and tan female puppy.

Pierce studied them. "Are they German shepherds?"

"Nope, they're Timber-shepherds—half timber wolf and half German shepherd from different parents so they can be mates," Hunter explained. "They're ten weeks old."

I sat on the grass and let them climb over me and lick my face. "They're sooo cute! They remind me of the Timber-shepherds my family bought when I was twelve. They were so smart, they never barked at intruders. Instead, they snuck up and positioned themselves in front and behind, ready for an attack if necessary."

"They're yours if you want them." Hunter ruffled their fur.

"I love them, but I won't be able to keep them if I go back to the Navy."

"No problem. This early stage is critical in their training, and you're so good with animals. If you return to the Navy, I'll see to it they're taken care of here."

Pierce nudged me. "Are you a dog trainer?"

"No, but I have a way with animals." I caressed their butter-soft fur.

He reached down and stroked them. "Wolf puppies look a lot like regular dogs."

"What are their names?" I asked as I cuddled them.

"That's up to you." Hunter smiled. "What names would you like?"

I noticed the sleek Staggerwing Beech sitting in the open hangar in the background, and an idea popped into my head.

"I'll name the male Pratt and the female Whitney."

Hunter laughed. "Pratt and Whitney, like your favorite aircraft engine manufacturer. Perfect."

I suspected the puppies were part of a calculated plan to ensure I stayed in Florida, but they were so darling, I didn't care.

Pierce pulled Pratt onto his lap, and the puppy sniffed his shorts like a vacuum cleaner. "I bet he smells Mom's cats on me." He set him down and brushed cat hairs off his shorts. "I visited my parents this morning and petted Mom's Persians. She has two big ones."

Hunter ruffled the dogs' fur. "They haven't met any cats yet. The yellow tabby who patrols the hangar has steered clear of them."

"Your mom's Persians must smell strange to him." I pulled Pratt to me.

"If you'd rather not have the dogs in your car, I can drive Jett home," Hunter offered.

"No, I'm sure they'll be fine." Pierce packed up the picnic basket. "Ready to go, Jett?"

"Oh yes, I can't wait to shop for puppy stuff. They'll need collars, leashes, dog beds, toys, food, the works."

Hunter laughed. "Dog beds? I know you. They'll be snuggled in your bed tonight and every night."

"I wouldn't want them to feel frightened in an unfamiliar place. They'll need time to get used to that huge house, and they might be too little to climb the stairs. Good thing there's an elevator." I scooped them up. "Let's go." I kissed my uncle's cheek. "Thanks for the fur babies. I love them."

He grinned. "I'll walk you to the car." He took one wiggling puppy out of my arms so it would be easier for me to carry the other one.

When we arrived at his Corvette, Pierce popped open the trunk. He dropped in the picnic basket and pulled out a blanket for the dogs.

I sat in the passenger seat, and he spread the blanket over my lap.

Hunter deposited Pratt beside Whitney and then leaned down and kissed the top of my head. "Call me if you need anything."

"No wonder you've always been my favorite uncle." I waved goodbye.

As we drove away, he yelled, "I'm your only uncle."

————

I convinced Pierce to stop at The Pampered Pet on Banyan Isle. "Keep an eye on them while I grab some essentials. I'll only be a few minutes." I dashed out of the car.

Inside the store, I grabbed a shopping cart and dropped in the best organic puppy food I could find, collars, harnesses, leashes, a few small toys, and water and food bowls.

I wheeled the cart outside. "I think this stuff will fit."

Covered in wiggling puppies, Pierce struggled to unlock the trunk.

I loaded the purchases and parked the cart in a return stall. When I slipped into the passenger seat and lifted the dogs, they greeted me with enthusiastic kisses. I turned to Pierce. "Thanks for stopping here. I hope they weren't too much trouble."

"Not at all. They kept busy playing with each other." He pulled away from the curb and headed for my house.

He parked in front, and I unlocked my front door and held the puppies while he unloaded the car.

"Thanks for a fun day, Pierce."

"My pleasure. We should do this again soon, and when you're ready to date, I hope you'll give me a shot."

He carried the bags into the foyer. Before he hopped back in his car, he leaned down and gave me a quick, feather-light kiss on the lips.

My heart raced as I watched him drive away. Was it because Pierce kissed me or because I hadn't been kissed in two months?

# TEN

I deposited my furry friends on the front lawn so they could take care of business before entering the house. They romped around a few minutes, wrestling each other and chasing lizards before finally emptying their bladders.

When I opened the front door, Pratt and Whitney raced around the foyer, their little nails clattering as they slid on the smooth marble floor. They plowed into me a few times, almost knocking me down when they tried to dart between my legs as I carried bags into the spacious kitchen and pantry.

Good thing my uncle had given me two puppies. They could wear each other out while I organized everything.

I carried the food and pet dishes into the kitchen. After removing the stickers and washing the stainless-steel dishes, I poured filtered water into their drinking bowls and then filled their food dishes.

Following my scent trail, the puppies rocketed into the kitchen and misjudged their stopping distance. They slid across the tiled floor into the cabinets and rolled up into a ball of tangled limbs.

In seconds, they were back on their feet. I led them to the water bowls. "Thirsty?"

They lapped up the water, then sniffed the kibble and dived right in. The food was gone in record time.

I stroked their silky fur and scratched behind their ears. "I'm glad you have healthy appetites. Let's have a look at the backyard now. And don't bite the guard." I led them through the great hall, out the terrace door, and onto the grassy back lawn.

They romped around, pooped, and then took a defensive stance in front of me when they spotted the guard rounding the corner of the house. They raised their hackles and snarled at him.

How adorable. They were protecting me.

I waved at him. "Just so you know, I have two dogs now."

He tipped his cap. "I'll watch where I step."

Pratt and Whitney held their stance until the guard walked away. Such good doggies.

I herded them inside and called Gwen. "Come and see what Uncle Hunter gave me."

"Just got back from Giorgio's with salads to go with dinner. I'm pulling up in front now."

I rushed to the front door with the puppies close on my heels and checked that Gwen's car was parked before I opened the door.

Gwen took one look at the pups and shoved the bag of food into my arms. "Oh, my goodness, they're sooo cute! Come to Auntie Gwen." She kneeled on the foyer floor and opened her arms.

The puppies rushed forward and licked her face as she ruffled their fur and cooed to them like they were baby humans.

"I'll take the food out to the terrace. Mike will be here soon with the pizza." As I headed outside, Gwen rolled on the floor, giggling, with the puppies climbing over her.

When I returned to the kitchen to grab plates, flatware, and wine glasses, Gwen rushed to help and almost tripped over the dogs.

"I'll get the chardonnay out of the fridge. Have the puppies eaten?" She opened the door to the big refrigerator.

"They've been fed, watered, and walked. They should be good for a while." They tugged on my shoelaces as I carried everything to the round terrace table.

Gwen uncorked the wine and poured two glasses. "What are their names?"

"The male is Pratt, and the female is Whitney." Both dogs looked up at me upon hearing their names.

"Pratt and Whitney? Isn't that the name of an aircraft engine manufacturer?"

"Yes, they make my favorite airplane engines."

"You named your dogs after an aviation company? Seriously?" She shook her head.

"I happen to love their engines, especially the old radials. They make such a wonderful sound." I took a sip of chardonnay.

Gwen rolled her eyes. "Pratt and Whitney aren't dog names."

"They're actually half timber wolf and half German shepherd. That means they'll be bigger and smarter than regular shepherds." I patted their cute little heads. "Won't you, my darlings?"

They wagged their tails and licked my legs. The doorbell rang, sending a booming instrumental rendition of Wagner's "Ride of the Valkyries" through the house. I laughed. "The puppies will learn Viking classical music every time the doorbell rings."

Gwen jumped up. "That must be Mike. I gave him your new gate code. I'll let him in." She trotted through the terrace doors, and the dogs stayed with me.

A few minutes later, she returned with Mike carrying a big pizza box and a six-pack of cold beer.

Gwen gushed, "See? Aren't they cute? You'll never guess what she named them."

He set the beer and pizza on the round, glass-top table and ruffled the pups' fur. "Knowing how Jett loves old aircraft, she probably went with antique airplane names, like Stearman and Waco, or WWII fighters, like Spitfire and Bearcat."

"Nope, I named them Pratt and Whitney." The puppies looked at me when I said their names. Such smart ones.

He laughed, despite his attempt at maintaining a cool attitude toward me. "Well, I hope you named the female Whitney." When he said her name, the puppy licked his hand.

I grinned. "See? She already knows her name."

Mike cleared his throat and put on his serious face. "Gwen told me you have some new evidence regarding the mayor's murder."

"Got it last night at the Banyan Harbor Inn. Hang on while I get the pictures I printed." I headed for the study, and the puppies bounded after me.

When I entered the room, the dogs rocketed past me, misjudging their speed, and slammed into a brass etagere. The collision rocked the shelves and caused the plastic model of my parents' Gulfstream jet to fall to the oak floor and break where the tail attached to the fuselage.

The dogs froze, sensing they'd done something wrong.

I picked up the two pieces of the broken jet and felt a chill shoot down my spine. My breath caught as I stared at the model. *This can't be another coincidence.*

My dogs cowered, not realizing my distress had nothing to do with their innocent accident.

"It's all right. I'm not angry." I patted their cute little heads and gave myself a moment to recover from the shock of seeing the tail come off my parents' airplane again. I set the pieces on the desk. "Pratt and Whitney, come."

When we returned, I heard Mike say, "Look at them. They stick with Jett like glue. I thought you said she just got them a couple hours ago."

"Her Uncle Hunter gave them to her this afternoon after she went for a ride with Pierce Lockwood in his fighter jet."

I dropped a handful of pictures in front of him. "This first one is Dolores Delgado smooching with Andy Carrigan in a secluded spot at the restaurant."

The puppies rubbed against my legs. I snatched up Pratt and held him on my lap, and then I handed Whitney to Gwen. Content, the dogs curled up and immediately fell asleep.

Mike sat straighter as he studied the picture. "This certainly complicates things."

"You have no idea." I explained the pictures of the three guys who'd been watching either Dolores or Andy.

"I know who they are," he said. "The guy with no neck is a low-level mobster who works for Manny's silent partner, Vito Giordano. The other two are private investigators."

I tapped another photo. "And here's one of Brenda Carrigan with Manny Delgado near the docks."

Gwen joined in, "Looks like a lot of inter-marital fooling around."

"Andy stopped by our table and asked me if I'd testify in court for his divorce."

"Who were you with?" Mike popped open a beer.

"Pierce Lockwood. He told Andy I didn't need to testify because my statement is in the police report."

He frowned. "You should steer clear of Lockwood. The guy's a player."

"We're just friends. I'm not up for dating right now."

"Seems like you're spending a lot of time together for just friends." He arched an eyebrow.

I crossed my arms. "Why would you care? This is the first time we've had a real conversation in six years."

"All right, you two," Gwen said. "We're getting off track." She lifted the box. "Pizza anyone?"

"In a minute." Mike sounded curt. "Was there anything else, Jett?"

"Yes, something big, and I'd appreciate it if you'd take me seriously, both of you, because this is important to me." I took a deep breath and fidgeted with my wine glass. "Last night, I had another sleepwalking dream. Mom led me to the study and may have showed me that my parents' plane crash wasn't an accident." I bit my lip. "They were murdered."

His jaw dropped. "Your mother? Murder?"

Gwen nudged him. "Actually, that was the real reason we were on her terrace the other night. Her mom led her there in a dream, and Jett didn't have her key. Then the guard showed up."

"You've seen your mother twice in dreams?"

"I've had three dreams about my parents." I described seeing their plane crash in the Bahamas and everything that happened in the study last night and a few minutes ago. "I think my mother is showing me they were murdered."

"She could be right, Mike. Why else would Jett dream these things?"

He focused on me. "I don't know. I can't help wondering why you didn't have the dreams two years ago."

"I was too distraught to be open to dream messages right after their deaths."

"Okay, but why wait two years?" Mike sat back and crossed his arms.

I blew out a sigh. "Maybe their deaths are somehow connected to the mayor's murder."

Gwen took a sip of wine. "Did the authorities send divers to the crash site?"

"No, the Bahamian government doesn't investigate private aircraft accidents. They did autopsies on the pilots, but that was because Hunter paid divers to retrieve their bodies along with my parents. My uncle identified the bodies and warned me not to see my parents like that. And forget about the FAA and NTSB. They only investigate foreign crashes if a U.S. airline is involved."

Mike sipped his beer. "No one investigated why the plane crashed?"

"No, but if the jet had gone down in shallow water, the locals would've picked it clean. The ocean floor at the crash site is at a hundred and seventy feet."

"I recall you saying you've gathered intel for a lot of SEAL missions. Any chance you could get a few of them to dive on the wreck and check it over for you?" Gwen asked.

"Good idea. My SEAL friends are expert divers. They'll know how to spot evidence of an explosion. And I know a lot about airplanes, thanks to my uncle. As far as the authorities are concerned, it's just another wreck on the bottom. They won't care if we dive there."

"How much dive experience do you have?" Mike asked. "That's way too deep for a sport dive."

"I've been diving with my uncle since I was twelve. I'll be fine with a SEAL for a dive buddy." I sipped chardonnay and gazed down at Pratt, who was sound asleep on my lap.

Gwen nudged me. "You should ask Hunter to go with you."

Mike said, "Better yet, have Hunter dive with the SEAL while you watch the boat."

I smiled at him. "If I didn't know better, I'd think you were worried about me."

His face flushed, and he checked his watch. "I should go. Lots to investigate. Enjoy the pizza." He grabbed the pictures and left before I had a chance to respond.

Gwen grinned. "Mike still loves you."

"Right. That's why he left without eating dinner or finishing his beer." I opened the pizza box. "More for us. I'm starved."

Gwen petted Whitney, who was sound asleep on her lap. "You're going to need someone to look after the dogs while you're away. A kennel might be too traumatic, and I have to work."

"I need a live-in dog nanny. I don't suppose you know any?"

"No, but I can run your final applicants through the police database. Better check the Internet for dog sitters and get cracking on setting up interviews for tomorrow."

"What if the nanny sees me sleepwalking? I don't want Valhalla labeled a weirdo's house."

"Ask the applicants how they feel about paranormal stuff. Say you're just trying to get a feel for their personality. See what they say." She bit into a slice of pizza.

I laughed. "Yeah, that won't sound strange or anything. I think I'll reserve that conversation for the person I like the most."

"When you have the list narrowed down to a few, call me. Hopefully, they'll have clean records."

I took another slice of pizza. "Hey, I forgot to ask. Any news on your promotion?"

"Yep, my detective shield will be awarded on Sunday, and that just happens to be when Aunt Liz and Uncle Clive are arriving from England. I'm supposed to meet them for cocktails and dinner at The Breakers Hotel in Palm Beach, and they asked me to bring you."

"An evening with the Duke and Duchess of Colchester? Count me in." I raised my glass. "Cheers!"

# ELEVEN

I posted the dog nanny job on several Internet sites after dinner. The responses were quick. A good salary and free room and board in an oceanfront castle turned out to be a big draw. I had five interviews with the best prospects set up starting after lunch the next day.

I decided to hire the pet nanny before calling my uncle about the possible murders. As he'd predicted, the puppies spent the first night in my bed. They only needed two nocturnal trips outdoors. Despite the sleep interruptions, I slept more soundly with two warm, furry bodies snuggled against me. They filled a deep need I hadn't realized had been missing. And the big house didn't seem empty anymore.

After Pratt and Whitney had their morning meal, I took them out back for a run, then played with them inside and familiarized them with the first and second floors. The huge ground-floor ballroom, similar in size to a basketball court, would be an ideal place for the dogs to play fetch and catch frisbees on rainy days. Tall windows on three sides let in plenty of light, and the smooth oak floor gleamed through a heavy coat of clear varnish. I ran the dogs through some obedience drills and decided I'd save the third and fourth floors for another day.

Pratt and Whitney snuggled next to me on a cordovan sofa in the study and fell asleep while I made phone calls. I wanted them rested so they'd be back to full energy when the interviews started.

My first call was to a SEAL I'd worked with many times in Afghanistan. Snake Sanchez was a tall Texan with short brown hair, hazel eyes, and hard muscles. Like every SEAL I'd ever met, he was good-looking, sexy, and brimming with male bravado.

"Snake? Hi, it's Jett. I'm calling from sunny Florida."

"Jett, how the heck are you?" he answered, his voice deep with a Texas twang.

"Fine, but I need your help." I explained I had uncovered evidence my parents may have been murdered. "I want to dive on the crash site and see if the jet was sabotaged."

"They crashed two years ago. Tropical storms and hurricanes go through there every year, so the bottom could have changed since then."

"I know, but I still have to look. This is important to me."

"How deep is the crash site, and how strong is the current?"

"It's at a hundred and seventy feet in calm, crystal-clear water. It's not far from Freeport, but it's well east of the Gulf Stream."

"We'll use trimix in our scuba tanks so we can stay down long enough to do a thorough search without having to worry about narcosis, but it won't be easy. The wreckage could be buried in sand, or a hurricane could've moved it." He hesitated. "Look, I know you're a licensed pilot, but if you really want to know what happened, you'd better bring an expert airplane mechanic."

"My uncle is a former Navy fighter pilot who operates his own aircraft restoration and maintenance facility. He knows airplanes inside and out, and he's an experienced scuba diver."

"Perfect, then find a good equipment source. Money isn't an issue for you, so I'd rather use a local dive shop you trust and include one of their best people to make sure the dive operator in the Bahamas does the trimix correctly when they fill our tanks."

"Pura Vida Divers on Singer Island has an excellent reputation and top-notch people. My uncle and I have taken many of their dive charters. I'll set everything up through them. We'll have reliable equipment and a tec diver with us who's done plenty of dives on trimix."

"My team is on call right now, but I have a few days off next week. Make all the arrangements, I'll fly down from Virginia Beach, and we'll shoot over to the Bahamas."

"Thanks, Snake. I'll send the company jet, and I'll owe you for this."

"Grill me a big ol' juicy ribeye, supply me with plenty of cold beer, and I'll be happy. See y'all next week."

Elated, I did a fist pump before I called Pura Vida Divers and explained what we needed. I waited while Andrea checked with the manager.

"No problem, Jett, as long as everyone is trimix certified. We have everything you'll need, and Justin Newton is Advanced Trimix and Full Cave certified, a PADI Master Scuba Diver Trainer and a PADI Tec Deep Instructor. He'll see to it you get the right trimix in the Bahamas and the proper air tanks for decompression on the ascent."

"We're all trimix certified, and we want full face masks with comms so we can talk to each other during the dive. And be sure to include your best dive computers."

"Since you're planning to go deep, we recommend two dive computers for each diver."

"Okay. Count on four divers, including Justin. Ask him to bring everything to Vann's Flight School and Maintenance Facility in Aerodrome Estates at nine o'clock Wednesday morning. We'll fly to Freeport in a private aircraft and then take a chartered live-aboard dive boat to the crash site south of the airport. We might stay a day or two."

Next, I booked a dive boat in Freeport that had everything we'd need, including four private cabins. I hoped I'd find a dog nanny during the afternoon interviews so I could call my uncle and convince him to dive with me in the Bahamas. I remotely opened the gate and left it open for the interviewees.

The doorbell played, and both puppies sprang awake.

"It's okay, my darlings. No barking. I'm expecting someone. Come along and be nice."

I strode to the entrance, and the dogs trotted beside me. They sat and waited when I opened the door.

A young woman, barely twenty-one, with long stringy hair and wearing torn jeans and a Taylor Swift T-shirt, stood outside holding her cell phone. She was thirty minutes late.

"Hi, I'm Krissy Simmons, here for the dog nanny interview."

"Hi, please come in."

She stepped in and glanced around the foyer, then stared at the winged Valkyries. Her clothes reeked of marijuana. "This place is really something."

"Thanks. I'm Jett Jorgensen, and these are my puppies, Pratt and Whitney."

Krissy smirked. "Their names are Pratt and Whitney? Kinda dumb names for dogs, but whatever. How often am I supposed to walk them? Will I get nights off?"

"This is a live-in position, so you'd be on duty five days a week with two days off." I peeked at the dogs, who were still waiting for Krissy to interact with them. "Your duties will include feeding, grooming, walking, and playing with the puppies."

She stared at text messages on her phone. "Huh? Five days? But I can have my boyfriend here while I'm on duty, right?"

The girl seemed far more interested in what was on her phone.

She hadn't even petted the dogs, who sat waiting for some indication she'd noticed them. The strange scent on her clothes made them hold back.

"What floor is my room on, and when do I get a tour of the castle?"

"No tour. We're done." I escorted her the few feet back out the door. "I'll call if you get the job. Have a nice day." I closed the door before Krissy had a chance to object.

I fussed over my doggies. "You were so well behaved. I'm very proud of you." I checked the time. "Let's go in the backyard before the next interviewee arrives."

Thirty minutes later, a slender woman around my age arrived wearing a navy skirt suit and matching stilettos. She carried an electronic tablet and wore her blond hair pulled back in a bun like a legal secretary. Her perfectly manicured nails were painted a pale pink.

She paused beside a Valkyrie statue and held out her hand. "Hi, I'm Jennifer Maxwell." She perused her tablet. "Right on time for my interview. You must be Miss Jorgensen."

I shook her hand. "Call me Jett, and these are Pratt and Whitney, the pups needing a nanny."

Jennifer reached down and gave each furry head a light pat. She held her stylus perched against her tablet. "I'm sorry, what did you say their names were?"

"The male is Pratt, and the female is Whitney." I pointed at each dog.

The stylus slipped out of her hand and bounced across the marble floor. Pratt remained beside me while Whitney rushed to retrieve the plastic pen-like object. She grabbed it with her tiny needle teeth, trotted back with it in her mouth, and dropped it at the woman's feet.

Jennifer picked it up. "Eeew, dog slobber." She wiped it off with a tissue from her purse and then doused her hands with liquid sanitizer. Stylus poised, she asked, "How do you spell their names?"

"Never mind. This isn't the right job for you." I eased her out the door. "Thank you for coming." I closed the door. "Two down, three to go. Mommy needs a glass of chardonnay."

The puppies wrestled and played as they followed me into the kitchen. I pulled a bottle from the refrigerator and poured a glass. After taking a sip, I said to the dogs, "I didn't think it would be this difficult to find you a good nanny." I took another drink.

Candidate number three, Iris Jenkins, was a no-show. I finished the glass of wine.

An hour later, Becky Sue Simmons arrived with a lit cigarette hanging out of her mouth. When I opened the door, the woman exhaled smoke into my face and moved to enter.

I blocked her. "Sorry, no smokers. I made that clear in the ad." I closed the door in her face and sucked in a deep breath to calm myself. "What a rude person! Let's hope number five turns out to be just right." I petted my dogs and took them out through the terrace doors to romp on the back lawn.

Sophia DeLuca arrived promptly at four o'clock carrying a large handbag. Under five feet tall, she wore tennis shoes and a tan pantsuit in a cotton-poly blend. Sixty years old, she had short curly hair dyed dark brown with a reddish sheen. Slender with a kind face, her nails were short, clean, and free of polish.

The instant she stepped inside, she dropped to her knees and fussed over the puppies. She looked up at me. "Sophia DeLuca here for my interview. You must be Jett. Your fur babies are adorable." She leaned down so they could lick her face. "Such cuties! Grandma Sophia loves you."

I offered her a hand. "Welcome, Sophia. Come with me into the great hall so we can sit and chat." I helped her up and led her to a sitting area where dark-brown leather sofas and chairs formed a rectangle.

Sophia perched on a sofa and reached into her purse. She pulled out two Ziploc bags, one filled with tubular pastries and another with small dog biscuits. "I figured you'd be hungry after conducting so many interviews. Cannoli with chocolate bits for you and my home-baked dog biscuits for the puppies, if that's okay." She offered me cannoli on a paper napkin.

"Thank you. It smells wonderful, and I'm sure my dogs would love some of your dog biscuits." I took a bite. "Delicious! Did you make this?"

She smiled. "I love to cook. Glad you like it. Have another. There's plenty."

The puppies made short work of the dog biscuits and licked her hand.

"You're welcome, my little dears." She caressed their fur. "I should get them some water. They look thirsty."

"They know where their water dishes are. Can I get you something to drink? Iced tea? Something stronger?"

"Iced tea would be great. Need any help?" Sophia glanced around as she petted the dogs, her gaze pausing on a large painting of Viking longships under sail, a nearby statue of Thor, and then a broadsword mounted on the east wall between windows.

"Relax, I'll be right back." I headed for the kitchen, and the puppies followed. They lapped up water from their bowls while I prepared a tray with a pitcher of iced tea and two glasses.

I served Sophia and then settled across from her. "Do I detect a New York accent?"

"Brooklyn. I come from a big Italian family." She lifted the dogs and placed them on either side of her. "My father, Francesco Calabrese, was an immigrant from Sicily."

My jaw dropped. "Not Don Calabrese?"

"Yes, dear, you're looking at the Mafia Don's daughter, may he rest in peace." She crossed herself. "Don't worry. I don't participate in Mob business. After my sons were raised, I moved to Florida to get away from those over-protective goombahs." She twisted her napkin. "I had a nice nest egg from my late husband's life insurance, but I lost a big chunk of it in the recent stock market crash. I'm afraid if I ask my sons for help, they'll insist I move back to Brooklyn."

"How long ago did your husband pass?" I smiled at the way Sophia automatically petted the puppies while she talked.

"Twenty years ago, that worthless *imbroglione* was caught in bed with the wife of a lieutenant from a rival family. I was humiliated, and my father was furious. Nobody ever saw my Vincent again. He's probably wearing cement overshoes on the bottom of Long Island Sound." She made a gesture with her arm and a balled fist. "Good riddance! I'm done with men. The only thing they want with a woman my age is a free cook, housekeeper, and nursemaid. Who needs them?"

"I can see you love dogs. Do you have any experience with big ones?"

"I used to breed Italian *Cane Lupino del Gigante* dogs. They're big and look a lot like German shepherds. My dear Bello passed away four months ago. I feel lost without him."

I took a sip of iced tea. "Sophia, you seem ideal for this job. If my cop friend does a background check on you, will it come back clean?"

She crossed herself again. "May God strike me dead if it doesn't."

"How are you at keeping secrets?"

"What kind of secrets are we talking about? I don't put up with sexual shenanigans. And if you're sneaking around with married men, fuhgeddaboudit. I'm outta here."

"No, no, nothing like that. It has to do with me and this house, which was built in 1908."

"Well, if your house is that old, it's probably haunted. Are you afraid of ghosts, dear?"

"No, are you?" I studied her face to judge her reaction.

"When I was growing up in Brooklyn, the body count was pretty high, and back then they laid out the corpses in open coffins in our living room. I've seen plenty of ghosts." She noted all the Norse statues. "You got some Viking ghosts here?"

"No ghosts, but my mother was a Cherokee shaman—"

Sophia broke in, "A shaman? Is that a medicine woman?"

"She was a spiritual leader and a natural healer." I bit my lip. "I've seen her in my dreams three times this week, and two of the times involved me sleepwalking."

"That's no big deal as long as you don't fall off a balcony." She bit into a cannoli. "Won't bother me. I've seen real ghosts."

"No kidding? What have you seen?"

"The worst one was my Uncle Benny, walking around with blood oozing from bullet holes in his chest and forehead. He was grotesque." She grinned at me. "Of course, he wasn't much better looking alive."

"Let me make a quick call. While I'm gone, think about when you can move in." I strode out onto the terrace, closed the glass door, and called Gwen. "I think I found the perfect dog nanny. How fast can you run a check on Sophia Calabrese DeLuca, sixty, from Brooklyn, currently living in Silver Lakes in West Palm Beach?"

"Hang on, I'll run it now," Gwen said as she typed in the info. A few seconds later, she said, "Whoa, Jett, she's Francesco Calabrese's daughter. He was Don of the biggest Mob family in New York until he died eight years ago and passed the torch to his two grandsons, Domenico and Marco."

"She already told me all that. Is her record clean?"

"Yes, but Mafia women usually steer clear of the wet work. That doesn't mean she's an angel."

"My dogs love her, and so do I. She's a real peach. Says exactly what she thinks, and she loves to cook. She brought me the best cannoli I've ever tasted. I can't wait for you to meet her. Thanks for the background check."

I walked back in. "You're hired. When can you move in?"

"Is tomorrow too soon?"

"Tomorrow is perfect." I smiled. "Come any time after ten in the morning."

# TWELVE

I called Hunter after Sophia left. "Hey, I love the puppies, and they're super smart. So easy to train. I think it's the wolf in them."

"Glad you like them. Any news on the mayor's murder?"

"I have something you need to see, but you have to come here to see it, and you might want to stay overnight. Any chance you can come tonight? It's important."

"Is this something you want to keep private or can I bring my date?"

"We definitely wouldn't want your date involved."

"Is it okay if I arrive around ten? I'll take her to an early dinner and drop her off before driving out to Valhalla."

"Ten will be fine. I'll look forward to seeing you tonight. Bye."

---

The dogs and I greeted Hunter when he arrived in his black McLaren at 10:15 p.m.

I hugged him. "Thanks for passing up the rest of your date so you could come here."

He leaned down and petted the puppies. "I swear they look bigger already. Now, what's so important?"

I bit my lower lip. "Brace yourself. Your sister … my mother … has returned in my dreams to show me that she and Dad were murdered."

He raised an eyebrow. "After two years? Are you sure about this? What did Atsila tell you?"

"Come in, have a drink, and we'll talk about it." I led him to the great hall. "What would you like?"

"Beer is good." He sat on a sofa and surveyed the room like he was expecting to see his sister step out of the life-size portrait of her and my dad over the fireplace.

"Is Coors okay?" He nodded as I headed for the kitchen.

I handed him a cold bottle and settled beside him with a glass of merlot. "The first time I saw something weird was out front at Odin's fountain right after the mayor's murder. Just a glimpse, but I'm certain it was Mom's wolf spirit."

"How can you be so sure?" He took a swig of beer.

"It was a flaming wolf with golden eyes. Mom had golden eyes, Atsila means fire in the Cherokee language, and she was shaman of the Aniwaya Clan. You know Aniwaya means wolf. Hence, a flaming wolf with Mom's golden eyes."

"Okay, that makes sense, but you only had one brief glimpse of it, right?"

"Yes." Then I described every dream and sleepwalking episode in detail. "The day after she showed me the book, the model of their jet broke at the tail."

He rubbed his chin. "So, this has nothing to do with the mayor? It's just about Atsila and Victor?"

"She wants me to know their jet was sabotaged, but I don't know if it has any connection to the mayor's murder or why two years passed before I had the dreams."

"Okay." He crossed his arms. "What do you want me to do?"

"Dive on the crash site with my SEAL friend, Snake, a tec deep diver named Justin, and me to look for evidence. I booked a dive boat for next Wednesday in Freeport."

He took another swig of beer. "Show me the broken airplane in the study."

"Good idea." I stood and headed down a hallway to the southwest corner of the house. The pitter-patter of eight tiny feet trailed behind us.

We settled on a cordovan sofa and examined the broken tail and fuselage.

"Small charges set on the attach bolts and timed to explode during the climb out would separate the tail from the airplane. It would only require small explosions to shear the bolts. It's possible someone did that."

"I won't rest until I know for sure. Will you dive with me?"

"Yes, of course, I'll come." He handed me the plastic T-tail. "Any developments on the mayor's murder?"

I filled him in. "They still don't know who rigged my security feed to look like no one was here every afternoon. They suspect it was an outside hacker."

"Why be satisfied with one hacking fee from the mayor? If it had been me, I would've gone a step further and installed a tiny video camera the size of a pencil eraser to use for blackmailing all the players. Did the cops find a hidden camera?"

"Not that I've heard. Do you know what one looks like?"

"I may or may not have put one in my bedroom," he said with a wink. "Show me the room where the mayor died."

The dogs weren't big enough to climb the stairs easily, so we picked them up and carried them to the second floor. When we entered the guest room, we set the dogs down, and they sniffed under the four-poster bed where the mayor had died.

A large oil painting hung over a low dresser on the wall opposite the bed. The picture depicted a rocky shoreline in Denmark. Lots of shiny black rocks with waves washing over them fronted a stone fortress looming in the background.

Hunter searched the painting for several minutes. "Aha! You'd never see it if you weren't looking for it, and crime scene techs would've been reluctant to mess with this valuable painting." He pointed at a quarter-inch diameter camera hidden among the rocks. Lifting the painting, he found a tiny antenna taped behind the camera. "See this? I bet it transmits the images to a video recorder in a closet directly above us on the third or fourth floor."

"I can't believe you found this." Amazed, I gawked at the miniature spy apparatus.

"Let's go find the recorder." He bounded out of the room.

I rushed to catch up. "Wait. I need you to carry one of the dogs."

He scooped up Pratt, and we trotted upstairs past a huge portrait of my great-great grandfather, whose steely-blue eyes seemed to follow me.

"We'll look on the third floor first." He turned left into a wide hallway with a twelve-foot ceiling. Tall, Nordic statues spaced every ten feet lined both walls in between vibrant-hued oil paintings.

We turned into the bedroom directly above the murder room, and I switched on the light. Twin brass beds flanked a nautical-themed brass and teak dresser. A round mirror over the dresser looked like a large, brass-framed porthole.

When he opened the closet door, the dogs pounced on an overturned cardboard shoebox on the floor. I pulled them back, and Hunter used his house key to lift the edge of the box. A video recorder was hidden underneath, and it was still on.

"I'd love to know what's on it, but Mike Miller will have our hides if we mess with this. He's the lead detective on the case."

Hunter arched an eyebrow. "Mike, huh? Are you two back together?"

"Seriously? After six years of him ignoring me?"

"Whoa!" He held up his hands. "I didn't mean to hit a nerve."

"We're on speaking terms again because of the murder." I pulled out my cell and called him. "Mike, it's Jett. Better come to the house right away. Hunter found a video camera hidden in the murder room and a recorder in the room above it." I rolled my eyes. "No, we didn't touch them. Are you coming?" I hung up.

Hunter smiled. "I take it he's coming."

"He'll be here by the time I get downstairs to let him in." I picked up Whitney.

"Alrighty, let's go." He scooped up Pratt and headed for the stairway.

The doorbell rang as we reached the foyer. I set Whitney on the floor and opened the door.

Mike's facial expression was all business when he walked in. He shook my uncle's hand. "Good to see you, Hunter. I hear you found a hidden camera upstairs."

"And a video recorder in the room above it. Looks like it's still turned on."

Mike turned to me and arched his eyebrow. "Am I going to find your fingerprints on it?"

"No, but you might find some from the killer or maybe little paw prints." I nodded at the dogs. "The puppies pounced on the cover."

Mike shook his head. "I can't believe the CSU missed this."

"Come on, Mike. You'll understand why when I show you." Hunter headed upstairs.

I called up after them, "I'll wait down here with the dogs." I took Pratt and Whitney out on the terrace so they could take a run on the back lawn. When they finished, I led them into the great hall and lifted them onto a sofa with me. "Are Mommy's little soldiers all tuckered out? Take a nap. I have a feeling this is going to be a long night."

———

Hunter, the puppies, and I waited on a sofa in the great hall while Mike observed CSU techs recover the video camera and recorder. Embarrassed about missing the spy equipment, the team was very thorough and didn't leave my home until well after midnight.

Mike strode into the great hall to give us an update. "Thanks for calling this in. The memory card in the recorder was from the day of the murder until now. A tech played it for me on a portable screen. It recorded everything that happened that afternoon and since."

I had to ask, "Did it show who poisoned the Scotch?"

"No, but everyone told the truth about what they did in that room, including Brenda Carrigan. No prints on the camera, recorder, or memory card. Whoever installed the system was a pro. I'm hoping he's the same person who hacked your video feed, but I still don't have a clue that'll help catch him."

I speculated, "I think it's safe to assume he had regular access to this house so he could retrieve the video cards and install new ones. Ask the women how long they'd been meeting the mayor here and if they were being blackmailed."

Hunter added, "I'd lean real hard on that maid who supplied the key and code to the mayor. She might've given copies to the blackmailer."

"She'll end up with a public defender, and they're always eager to make a deal. I'll stop by her house in the morning and tell her we found the camera. She might be partnered with the pro. This'll be her chance to roll over on him to avoid being charged with blackmail and accessory to murder."

"I hope you catch him, Mike." I moved to stand, and the puppies woke.

Mike held up his hand. "Stay put. I can let myself out. Good to see you again, Hunter." He strode to the front door.

Hunter nudged me. "There's noticeable tension between you two. I get the impression he's trying to remain aloof, but he's struggling with it."

"He's slowly warming to me." I petted the dogs. "I'll take them outside before bed."

He picked up my wine glass and his beer bottle. "I'll clean up."

He hugged me when the dogs and I walked back inside. "We're in this together, sweetheart. I'll rearrange my schedule and do whatever it takes to help you investigate the crash. Give me Snake's and Justin's cell numbers so I can coordinate with them."

He handed me his phone, and I entered the info. My photographic memory came in handy. I didn't need to look up the numbers.

He petted the puppies, who were watching us. "That reminds me, who's going to take care of them while we're in the Bahamas?"

"My dog nanny is moving in tomorrow." I grinned. "The dogs love her, and so do I."

"You thoroughly vetted her, right?"

"Oh, yes, I know everything about her. She's quite a character, and she doesn't care if she sees me sleepwalking. She's seen real ghosts."

He smiled and checked the time. "One-thirty already. Better hit the sack. Breakfast at eight?"

"Count on waking to the aroma of fresh-brewed coffee and bacon." I kissed his cheek. "Sleep in whichever room you like. All the beds are made up and ready."

# THIRTEEN

I got up at seven, showered, dressed, and took the dogs out for their morning run. Before starting the bacon, eggs, and toast for breakfast with my uncle, I fed the puppies and brewed coffee.

Hunter sauntered in. "Smells great." He poured himself a cup of coffee. "Let's eat on the terrace. It's nice and cool on these January mornings."

We loaded two trays with our food and beverages and settled at the round, glass-top table overlooking the ocean. Italian tile flooring in multiple shades of blue glistened in the morning sun as a mild sea breeze ruffled the leaves on nearby banyan trees.

"I've been thinking about the crash site." He took a sip. "Even if we locate it and find evidence of sabotage, it might be difficult to prove who did it. Don't be disappointed if this turns out to be a long, frustrating investigation."

"I agree this won't be easy, but I'm determined to do whatever it takes to find that wreck." I took a bite of bacon. "And if we discover evidence of sabotage, we'll look for someone with a motive and maybe catch the killer."

"Your Navy Intelligence experience should come in handy." He reached down and gave each puppy a small piece of bacon.

"Hey, don't teach them bad habits, like begging at the table." I crossed my arms.

He grinned. "Don't get your panties in a bunch. Everybody knows dogs haven't lived until they've tasted bacon. They'll be fine." He patted their little heads.

My cell rang. I noted the caller ID. "Good morning, Mike."

"Is Hunter with you?"

"We just finished breakfast. What's up?"

"Put the phone on SPEAKER. Do you still have an armed guard patrolling your grounds?"

I hit the SPEAKER button. "Elite Security is providing guards for six months. Why?" I gave Hunter a nervous glance.

"I went to the maid's house an hour ago." His voice sounded strained. "I found her body. Looked like cyanide poisoning, same as the mayor." He waited a moment to let that sink in. "Then I called Elite Security. Wilfred Sims hasn't been seen or heard from in two days, so I checked his house and found his body. Cyanide poisoning. Someone is eliminating loose ends. If he thinks you know too much—"

"The locks and code have been changed," Hunter explained. "Jett's trained for combat, we'll get weapons from her dad's vault, and I'll make sure she's safe. Thanks for the warning, Mike."

"Okay, good. Be careful, Jett. I'll be in touch." He hung up.

I frowned. "This is getting complicated. The blackmailer who installed the camera is probably also the guy who hacked my security system, like you suspected. And Sims gave off guilty vibes when I met him at Elite Security. He probably hired the hacker after the mayor asked him to have someone rig my tapes. Then when the mayor was murdered, the hacker decided to cut his losses. I bet he copied the murder method to throw the police off track."

"Sounds plausible, but how did he know about the cyanide?" He poured another cup of coffee.

"Everybody knows. Brenda Carrigan blabbed it to the press." I picked up Pratt and cuddled him on my lap. He sniffed at the table. "See? Now he's looking for more bacon."

Whitney pawed to get up on Hunter's lap. He picked her up, and she sniffed the table too.

He laughed. "The dogs are fine, and we have bigger worries."

My cell rang. It was Sophia.

"Good morning, Jett. Is it okay if I move in now, or should I wait until ten?"

"Now is perfect."

"Good. I'll be there in five minutes. Should I use a servant's entrance?"

"Never. Come to the front door, and we'll help you carry in your stuff." I hung up and poked my uncle. "My dog nanny is moving in any minute. You'll get to meet her."

Right after we cleared the terrace table and carried everything into the kitchen, the doorbell rang, booming out the familiar beginning of Act III of Wagner's *Die Walküre* opera.

I opened the door to Sophia, who stood beside four large wheeled suitcases. "Come in, Sophia. We'll help you with the bags."

Her eyes lit up when she spotted Hunter. "Please introduce me to this magnificent man."

He grinned. "Hunter Vann at your service." He took her hand and kissed it. "Let me get these for you."

He picked up two suitcases. "I'll come back for the rest. Which room?"

"Second floor, north wing, the large suite next to the room the mayor was in." I turned to Sophia. "He's my uncle on my mother's side."

Smiling, she whispered, "Is he single?"

"Oh yes, and he loves women, but he doesn't want to be tied down. He says it's the wild Cherokee in him."

"I hope he visits often. I could get used to looking at that kind of handsome. Does he like cannoli?" Her eyes focused on his well-shaped posterior as he climbed the stairs.

"He'll love anything you make. Would you like a cup of coffee?"

"Thanks, but at my age, I have to limit the caffeine." She leaned down and petted the puppies. "How are my little darlings doing? Have they been fed?"

"They're fine for now. We had breakfast out on the terrace, and they took care of business on the lawn."

He trotted down the stairs and grabbed the last two bags. "Be right back, Sophia. We need to talk."

"We'll wait for him on the terrace." I led her and the dogs outside.

He joined us and smiled at Sophia. "I don't want to alarm you, but there might be a killer lurking nearby. We have excellent security here with an armed guard and video surveillance, but I want you to be on the alert for anyone sneaking around."

She reached into her enormous handbag and pulled out a Glock 26 handgun with a laser sight. "No worries. If he threatens us, I'll blow him away."

Hunter and I stared at the weapon, our mouths hanging open.

He pointed at the handgun. "Do you know how to use that?"

"Darn straight. I was raised in a Mafia family. I know guns, and I'm not afraid to pull the trigger." She slipped the pistol back into her purse. "And I have a license to carry."

I touched my uncle's arm. "Sophia is Don Francesco Calabrese's daughter."

His jaw dropped again. "*The* Don Calabrese from New York?"

"Brooklyn. He ran the family for forty years. May he rest in peace." Sophia crossed herself.

He smiled at the short woman with the red sheen on her dyed brown hair. "You're quite the little spitfire, aren't you?"

"Sweetheart, if I were twenty years younger, I'd give you a run for your money."

"I have no doubts, Sophia. My niece is in good hands. You ladies will be just fine." He kissed her hand again.

He stood. "I have to go. Lots to do before our dive trip." He kissed my cheek, petted the dogs, and sauntered out.

She watched him go. "What a man!"

# FOURTEEN

GWEN

While Jett spent the day with Sophia, familiarizing her with the house and getting her settled, Gwen started her first day as a detective in the Palm Beach Police. Chief Rod Malone assigned her to a robbery investigation and explained it was to help her gain experience.

Gwen spent hours interviewing neighbors and sifting through evidence on a Maserati SUV break-in, looking for something that might lead to the thief, but the burglar must've worn gloves. No prints. She wished she was working Homicide with the handsome lead detective, Clint Reynolds. He'd been called to an apparent murder/suicide at the northern end of the island. The bodies of a wealthy elderly couple had been discovered by their maid.

Time dragged by, and her shift finally ended. She checked her watch. It was almost time to meet her aunt, uncle, and Jett for cocktails and dinner at the Seafood Bar in The Breakers Hotel, one of her favorite restaurants in Palm Beach. She was excited to see her closest relatives, especially since she hadn't seen them since her quick visit to England last summer. Her aunt was her late mother's older sister. She and Gwen's uncle tried to fill the role of parents after her parents were killed.

She grabbed her clothes bag and changed in the ladies' room. A floor-length mirror showcased her black stilettos and sleeveless black cocktail dress. She released her hair, gave it a quick brush, and strolled to her car. It was a short drive from the police station to the hotel.

Her cell chirped as the valet jumped into her car under the portico at The Breakers. It was Chief Malone calling. She strolled around the car and stood to one side.

"Gwen, we're short-handed. Go to the charity polo match on the golf course at The Breakers pronto. We've got a DB in a Rolls near the party tent. I'll meet you there."

Her boss was a gruff man of few words, but he had the respect of her coworkers.

"On my way," she said as a valet drove away with her car. Good thing her weapon and shield were in her purse. She approached another valet and flashed her badge. "I need a ride to the polo match. Police emergency." *My first dead body as a detective.*

A valet took her in a golf cart to the tailgating area across the street from the hotel's long entrance drive. She spotted a pale-blue Rolls Royce Corniche with the top down parked under a shade tree. Yellow crime-scene tape separated the Rolls from the elaborate party tent that anchored the site. Aromas of grilled steaks and galloping horses wafted through the warm air as elite patrons dressed in casual designer silks and linens sipped champagne and watched the polo match.

An approaching siren overpowered thundering hooves, noisy revelers, and loudspeakers booming play-by-play calls.

A patrol officer guarding the scene checked out her cocktail dress and five-inch stilettos. "Hot date, huh, Gwen?"

She rolled her eyes and ducked under the tape. The handsome man sitting in the driver's seat of the Rolls appeared to be sleeping. Around forty, he had a chiseled jaw, blond crew cut, and fit physique. He wore mirrored aviator sunglasses.

She asked the patrol officer, "Are you sure he's dead? Maybe he drank too much."

"One of his friends said he didn't have a pulse and called it in."

She thought about how embarrassing it would be if it turned out the man wasn't dead. Better to verify it herself. She pulled on latex gloves she kept in her purse and pressed her fingers a little too firmly against his neck. His body fell like a rag doll over the center console, and his sunglasses slipped off, revealing dull blue eyes.

The police chief walked up, shaking his balding head. "Real smooth, Gwen. The M.E. is going to have your butt. Didn't your fancy finishing school teach you not to touch dead bodies?"

Blushing, she pulled back her long red hair and focused on the body and the convertible's interior. No signs of a struggle. No visible marks on the body. No obvious cause of death. *Probably not murder, so no handsome Detective Clint Reynolds joining me later.*

Rod thrust his hands on his hips. "I should've known this case is too high profile for a newbie. Denton Donley is a Palm Beacher with deep pockets. The press will be all over this."

"Dent Donley? Isn't he the creep who allegedly raped those young women?" She Googled him on her cell. Yep, he was that guy.

"Expensive lawyer got him off." He stared at the body. "Guess too much high living did him in." He appraised her outfit. "Nice dress."

When the medical examiner arrived, Rod stepped aside.

The M.E. pulled on his gloves and opened the car door. He arched an eyebrow and asked the chief, "Is this how you found him?"

"Our new detective knocked him over." Rod glared at Gwen.

"According to the guy who called it in, Donley was found behind the wheel with his body slumped back against the seat. He assumed Donley was taking a nap. Eventually, he needed to pop the trunk to get to the champagne cooler. When he couldn't wake him or feel a pulse, he called 9-1-1."

The short, gray-haired man frowned at Gwen. "What were you thinking?" He turned back to the body. "Never mind. Probably natural causes anyway." He pierced the body's liver area with a device that resembled a meat thermometer. "Yep, died about two hours ago. Is he high profile?"

Rod said, "Big money. We'll need an expedited autopsy."

Several news vans raced up, vying to be first on the scene. An overeager young female reporter must've recognized the body in the Rolls. She reached over the yellow tape and aimed her microphone at Gwen's face. "Isn't that Denton Donley? What happened? Did one of his alleged victims get revenge?"

Rod gave Gwen a let's-see-you-handle-this look, so she stepped forward. "Mr. Donley passed away in his car. An autopsy will determine the cause of death. Please step back so the medical examiner can remove the body. Thank you."

Cameras flashed behind her as the M.E. zipped the body bag over Donley's face. After he was wheeled away, she turned to the police chief. "Where's the crime-scene truck? The Rolls should be swept for evidence."

"Our team is working a murder/suicide on the north end. A county CSU will be here in a few minutes. Work the crowd. See what you can learn."

She stepped away, called her aunt, and explained she'd be a little late.

After circulating through the crowd and asking questions for an hour, she hadn't learned anything new. Her spike heels were covered with dirt and had made more divots than the horses.

She was about to leave when she turned and bumped into Pierce.

"Hi, Gwen. You look great in that dress. Here for the polo match?"

"Actually, I was about to meet my relatives for drinks and dinner when I got called over here." She smiled up at Pierce, who wore a cream linen suit. "Do you know Denton Donley?"

"I see him at all the charity events, but we're not friends. Why?"

She turned and pointed. "He was found over there in his Rolls, dead."

"Really? What happened?"

She shrugged. "Don't know. That's the M.E.'s problem. I have to run. See you around."

Five minutes later, a golf cart took her down the stately drive lined with royal palms. The entry lane divided around a massive fountain near the front of the hotel. On the way, she reached down with a tissue and cleaned the dry dirt off her shoes. Under the portico, she straightened her dress and gave her hair a quick brush before breezing into the magnificent lobby.

The Breakers was a picture of Old-World elegance with thirty-foot coffered ceilings adorned in unique artistic designs. Her heels clacked on the polished marble corridor as she walked south through the lobby and turned east into the hall leading to The Seafood Bar.

Her aunt and uncle sat with Jett at a table overlooking the Atlantic Ocean. The tall windows were so close to the water that the view was similar to dining on a cruise ship.

"Auntie Liz and Uncle Clive, it's good to see you. Hey, Jett. Love your blue dress." Gwen leaned over and kissed her aunt on the cheek. "Sorry I'm late." When her uncle rose to pull out her chair, she hugged him. "How long will you two be in Palm Beach?"

Liz smoothed her elegantly coiffed white hair. "Just January for the high season, my dear Gwen. I do hope we'll see you often. Is your new job keeping you busy?"

"It was a slow day until a wealthy Palm Beacher died at the polo match. Did you know Denton Donley?"

The waiter poured Gwen a glass of Opus One, her favorite blended red wine, and presented the menu. She smiled, always enjoying visits with the Duke and Duchess of Colchester.

"We had drinks in his tent earlier this afternoon." Clive glanced at Liz. "We left the match early so we would have plenty of time to relax and dress for dinner. He seemed fine when we left."

Clive's answer surprised Gwen. "Did you know him well?"

"Not really. We heard he was quite the womanizer," Liz said. "You know the type. I wasn't fond of him, but we fulfilled our social obligation to the charity organizers. I heard he was accused of raping several women and escaped prosecution."

Jett said, "Whoa, Gwen, did you get a murder case on your first day as a detective?"

"I doubt it. He probably had an undiagnosed heart defect. Divine justice." She sipped the wine, savoring the delicious blend from the Rothschild and Mondavi vineyards. "According to Google, the women who accused him last year were merely the tip of the iceberg in his alleged rape history. He should've spent the rest of his life behind bars. Our legal system failed. At least he can't hurt anyone else now."

Her uncle swirled Glenglassaugh whisky in his glass. "Could someone seeking justice have caused his demise?"

"I suppose it's possible." Gwen pursed her lips. "There was no obvious cause of death."

"Considering his alleged crimes, you shouldn't rule out the possibility someone killed him." He downed his Scotch. "We want you to do well in your new position."

"Thanks, Uncle Clive." She nudged Jett. "I ran into Pierce at the polo match. He looked dapper in a linen suit."

Liz asked Gwen, "Pierce who? Are you dating him?"

"Pierce Lockwood, and Jett's dating him."

Jett shook her head. "Not true. We're just friends."

"Jett, darling, men are never *just friends* with beautiful young women." Liz patted Gwen's hand. "And what about you, dear? You look fit and fabulous in your little black dress. Anyone on your dance card?"

"Thanks, Aunt Liz, but no. I have my eye on a handsome coworker, but he hasn't shown any interest." She couldn't help thinking she'd never look good in a bikini again with her ugly scar front and center, courtesy of her parents' killer.

Liz studied her face. "You're thinking about *him*, aren't you?"

"Sorry, I was thinking about my scar." Gwen took a soothing sip of wine and changed the subject. "I'm looking forward to our opera night at the Kravis Center on Tuesday. *Carmen*, isn't it?"

Liz smiled warmly. "Yes, dear, we have fifth-row orchestra seats." She patted Jett's hand. "Jett's been telling us about the murder you two discovered at her home. How dreadful. Any leads?"

"Not yet, but stay tuned." Gwen lifted her glass.

"I think you two need some fun," Liz said. "Plan to meet us thirty minutes before the curtain for cocktails."

Jett said, "Thanks, and if you visit Gwen in Banyan Isle, please stop by Valhalla and meet my fur babies and their new nanny. The puppies are half-wolf, and their nanny is the daughter of a famous Mafia Don."

Clive arched an eyebrow. "Are you sure it's safe to have a Mafia woman in your home?"

"I'm positive. Sophia has a heart of gold, but there have been some recent developments I haven't had a chance to share with

Gwen." She glanced sideways at her best friend. "Is it okay if I tell them *everything*?"

"You mean about your sleepwalking?" She laughed. "Have you forgotten they live in an eight-hundred-year-old castle? Nothing shocks them. Go ahead and spill."

Jett brought Liz and Clive up to date, including all the new happenings when Hunter came to visit. She ended with, "It's a good thing the opera is Tuesday night because I'm leaving with Hunter and two divers on Wednesday. We're going to dive on the crash site near Freeport."

"My goodness, you do lead an exciting life. I hope you find the answers you're looking for." Clive patted Jett's hand.

"And you girls stay safe with possible murderers sneaking around Banyan Isle," Liz said.

Gwen and Jett bid goodbye to Liz and Clive and returned to their homes.

Gwen checked her messages. Donley's family physician reported he'd been in perfect health.

She went to bed in her queen-size canopy bed and slipped into her recurring nightmare of the deadly carjacking.

# FIFTEEN

JETT

At 3:14 Monday morning, the puppies woke me. At first, I assumed they needed a trip outside, but instead, they stared at the closed bedroom door and growled softly, warning me. Typical of wolves, they didn't bark, intending to hunt and corner the intruder. I slipped on a robe and grabbed my handgun and a mini flashlight. My eyes were accustomed to the dark, so I put the little flashlight in my robe pocket. I didn't want to alert an intruder to my presence.

When I eased the bedroom door open, the dogs crept into the hallway all the way past the elevator. They slowly descended the stairs to the second floor, turned into the hallway, and stopped short of the north hall with their heads cocked, listening and sniffing.

The threat of imminent danger heightened my senses as muffled sounds drifted down the dark hallway. I hid behind a sturdy statue of a Viking chieftain, standing midway between the twin staircases, and strained to identify the source of the soft noises.

Peeking around the statue, I didn't see anyone. The door to the murder room had been kept closed, but now it was open. I crept closer, and the dogs took a protective stance in front of me.

Sophia yelled, "Freeze, dirtbag!" followed almost instantly by a loud gunshot.

I racked the slide on my pistol and ran forward, yelling, "Sophia? Where are you?"

"Don't shoot!" She stepped into the hall, wearing night-vision goggles and her PJs. She pointed. "He's in there. Dead."

"Grab the puppies and keep them away." I switched on the bedroom light.

Dressed in a guard uniform from Elite Security, a man lay on the floor, a pool of blood haloing his head. A bullet had pierced his forehead, and a black bandanna covered his face under his eyes. A handgun with a silencer attached lay close to his gloved right hand. The oil painting above the dresser had been placed face-down on the bed.

I turned back to Sophia. "What happened?"

She had removed her goggles and was crouched, clutching the dogs' collars. "I'm a light sleeper. I heard noises in the room next door, so I pulled on my night-vision gear and grabbed my Glock. He was putting the painting on the bed when I peeked in. I yelled, he drew on me, and I blew him away." She held out her pistol with the red laser. "I never miss with this laser sight. Is he the killer Hunter warned me about?"

"Probably." I backed out and closed the door. "Night-vision goggles?"

"What? I can't sleep with a light on. I keep the goggles on the nightstand so I can find my way to the toilet in the middle of the night." She held them up. "Army surplus."

Despite the grave situation, I smiled at the tiny woman wearing flannel PJs. "I'll go call the police. I have a bad feeling there's a dead guard somewhere on my property."

Sophia reached in her pajama pocket and pulled out her cell phone. "Use mine."

"Thanks." Instead of dialing the emergency number, I called Mike's cell.

He answered on the fourth ring. "Who is this?"

"Mike, it's Jett. I'm calling on my dog nanny's phone. I need you to come right away and call in a CSU and the medical examiner. There's a dead body in the room where the mayor was murdered, and I'm afraid you may find another body on the grounds. Please hurry."

"Grab a weapon, get somewhere safe with the nanny and your dogs, and I'll be there in five minutes." He hung up.

I handed her the phone. "Lock yourself in your room with the dogs. I need to let the cops in." I ran up to my room, grabbed my cell, and rushed downstairs. I arrived just in time to open the door for Mike.

He pulled me against him, hugged me, and asked, "Are you hurt?"

I felt a surge of warmth, reminding me of what we had shared long ago. "I'm all right, and the nanny is locked inside her room with the puppies. The DB is in the room where the mayor was killed. It's next door to hers. I think the intruder stole the guard's uniform. I noticed the pants are too short and the uniform is tight."

He sucked in his breath and searched my eyes. "Did you shoot him?"

"No, the nanny shot him when he drew on her." I noted his frown. "Sophia has a license to carry, and the dead guy had a SIG with a silencer attached."

He released me and opened the door to the sound of approaching sirens. Soon there were cops searching my home and grounds.

My cell rang.

It was Gwen. "What's going on over there?"

I explained what happened. "Don't worry. Mike and a bunch of cops are here. Get some sleep and I'll call you at work later with some answers."

The medical examiner arrived several minutes before the CSU van, and Mike led him upstairs to the body.

I waited in Sophia's suite with her and the puppies and squeezed her hand. "Are you feeling okay after that traumatic event?"

"I'm good. The guy I shot, not so much. Have the police identified him?"

"I don't know. I guess Mike will tell us once he has everything handled out there."

"And who is Mike to you?" She studied my face. "I sensed you share a bond with him."

"He was my boyfriend until I joined the Navy. Since then, he hasn't spoken to me until a few days ago when we needed to discuss the mayor's murder."

"How do you feel about him?" She patted my hand.

"I'm not sure. I feel a strong attraction to him, but the tension between us twists my stomach into a knot." I chewed my lip. "I'm afraid he'll hurt me again."

"I saw him when he escorted you in here. Very handsome." She tilted her head. "Not quite on the same level as your uncle, but then few are."

I grinned. "Women do tend to swoon over Hunter."

"I sure did. He's quite the manly man." She sighed. "Ah, if only I were younger."

An hour went by before Mike knocked on the door. I opened it, and he walked in. "Are you two okay?"

"Yes, but we're eager to know what's going on. Any news?" I asked.

"We found marks in the sand where a body had been dragged into an inflatable boat. Probably dumped him in the ocean. The boat is pulled up on the beach now, and a man's jeans and shirt are in it."

"Have you identified the guy Sophia shot?" I asked.

"I sent the intruder's picture to Elite Security. His name's Mark Morgan. He doesn't work for them anymore, but he was the one who originally set up their video surveillance system."

"Do you know who the missing guard is?" Sophia asked.

"We're waiting until his kids leave for school to notify his wife." He pulled out a large plastic evidence bag and reached for Sophia's weapon. "I'll need your full name for my records, and we'll have to run this weapon through a ballistics check. Standard procedure."

"And leave me unprotected? I don't think so." She held the pistol close to her.

I leaned in and whispered, "I'll give you another one as soon as he leaves."

She held out the weapon, barrel down. "All right, but I want this back. My name is Sophia DeLuca, maiden name Calabrese, originally from Brooklyn, and yes, *that* Calabrese family, so get over it already."

Mike's jaw dropped, and he stared at the tiny woman, not even five feet. "Do you have a police record?"

"I'm clean, the gun is registered to me, and I have a license to carry. Did you think Jett would hire a criminal to take care of her precious fur babies? You should know better."

"Sorry, Mrs. DeLuca, but I had to ask. I'm just following procedure." He glanced at me. "I wish I could say for certain Mark Morgan is responsible for all the murders, as well as tampering with your video feed and installing the spy camera."

"Looks to me like he was covering his tracks to avoid charges for blackmail and accessory-to-murder for the mayor. He must not have known the police already had the hidden camera and recorder." I shook my head. "Now, we'll never know for sure if he killed the maid and Sims."

Mike sealed the bag holding Sophia's gun. "Chances are he's our guy for the breach in security and the possible blackmail. The mayor probably hired Sims to rig the security feed, but he might not have known Morgan's identity. The guy was a pro. Probably never met with the mayor in person. He might not be the maid's killer, but he had a motive for taking her out if she's the one who gave him the key and the code. And he was probably working with Sims, blackmailing clients."

"I'm guessing Morgan hacked my system under orders from Sims," I said. "But I don't think either of them killed the mayor, because then their opportunity to collect more blackmail money would've ended. Morgan killed Sims and the maid to hide his identity."

"It's possible he intended to kill you too, Jett." Mike gave me a worried look.

"Good thing he didn't know about me." Sophia grinned. "Poison is a woman's weapon of choice. My guess is the mayor was killed by a jealous lover, and Morgan staged the other murders to look like the same killer did them all."

Mike frowned. "We have four suspects in the lover category but no definitive evidence."

I checked my watch. "It's almost five. I'd like to get to sleep before the sun comes up. Sorry about another late night, Mike. I'll let you out and lock up after you."

"Good night, Mrs. DeLuca." He petted the puppies and followed me to the front door.

# SIXTEEN

GWEN

While Jett tried to catch up on some sleep, Gwen spent Monday morning researching Denton Donley. That afternoon, she interviewed six rape victims and their parents. They all had alibis.

Gwen stopped by the M.E.'s office. The scent of disinfectant permeated the air.

"Donley's death seemed natural until the autopsy changed everything." The M.E. checked his report. "Enough sedative was found in his body to drop him into a deep sleep, and a tiny puncture wound was discovered over the right carotid artery. No poison. No toxic residue at the puncture site."

Another mystery, Gwen thought. "Thank you, Doc. Call me if you discover the COD."

When she arrived home, she called Jett. "I'm dying to know what happened last night at your house."

Jett yawned into the phone. "Sorry, I didn't get enough sleep." She gave a recap of the early morning events.

"Your sixty-year-old dog nanny shot the intruder? I've got to meet her."

"Better come now. We just had an early dinner, and I don't think we'll last much longer before we dive into our beds."

"I'll be right there." Gwen hung up and drove next door.

Jett answered the door and handed her a glass of chardonnay. "How's it going?"

She surveyed the foyer. "Where are your puppies?"

"They're on the terrace with Sophia. How's your murder investigation?"

"It's a little like the mayor's murder. More questions than answers." She gave her a quick recap as they strolled out to the terrace. "I'm supposed to interview Donley's friends tomorrow."

They walked around a chaise lounge where Sophia and the puppies were snuggled together, sound asleep.

"Aw, look at them—so cute together. Don't wake her. I'll meet her tomorrow evening when I pick you up for the opera. I'll swing by at five, so we'll have time to chat a little."

———

Gwen spent Tuesday interviewing Donley's close buddies. First up was William Branson of the Boston Bransons. He led her into the study on his family's oceanfront estate in Palm Beach.

She had deliberately worn a fitted skirt suit, conservative but sexy, and four-inch stilettos to see how her interviewees would behave. Branson fit the privileged playboy stereotype.

He poured himself a Scotch. "May I offer you a drink?"

"Ice water, please. I'm on duty." She chose a cordovan wingback chair so she wouldn't have to sit beside him in the secluded room. "Thank you for seeing me."

"My pleasure." He handed her a crystal glass filled with iced water. "Lady cops have come a long way since the dowdy meter maids of yesteryear." He sat across from her and leered at her legs. "There's something sexy about an armed and beautiful woman."

She pulled out her electronic tablet. "How long had you known Denton Donley?"

He furrowed his brow, doing math in his head. "Twenty-four years, off and on. We were roommates the last two years of prep school, went to different colleges, then attended Harvard Law together. After graduation, we ran in the same social circles here and in Boston."

"And you remained friends throughout the rape charges and trials?" She studied his eyes.

He stared out the narrow floor-to-ceiling windows in the corner. "Those charges were bogus. Greedy tarts hoping for a big payday turned vindictive when he refused to pay them off. It was their word against his. He was never convicted of anything."

She checked her notes. "Over the years, twenty-eight women accused him of rape. You didn't find that number excessive for an innocent man?"

He frowned. "I'm surprised there weren't more. Gold diggers are a dime a dozen."

She sucked in her breath to maintain her composure. "Can you think of anyone who might have wanted him dead?"

He choked on his Scotch. "No, why do you ask? Was he murdered?"

"Cause of death has not been determined, so we're looking into every possibility."

He peeked at his watch. "I just remembered I have a client coming in." He stood. "If there's nothing else?"

She stood. "Thank you for your time." She handed him her police business card. "If you remember something helpful, give me a call."

"It would be helpful if you'd have dinner with me tonight. Sevenish?" He grinned.

"I have plans, but thank you, and have a nice day." She bolted for the main door.

Her other interviewees turned out to be worse than Branson, the sessions resulting in multiple passes, lewd suggestions, and no clues to help her catch a possible killer.

After a long, frustrating day, she relaxed in a hot shower, dressed to the nines, and drove next door to Jett's house.

Sophia answered the door with the puppies flanking her and wagging their tails. "You must be Gwen. Jett will be down in a minute. I'm Sophia DeLuca, the dog nanny."

She leaned down and petted the dogs. "Careful, Auntie Gwen has to stay clean for the opera." She straightened and offered her hand to Sophia. "So nice to meet you."

"I suggest you take a chair opposite one of the sofas, and I'll keep the little ones next to me." Sophia led her into the spacious great hall beyond the foyer. "Can I get you a drink?"

"No thanks." She regarded the diminutive woman. "I heard you blew away a bad guy your first night here. Well done."

She held her hands palms up. "The way I see it, anybody who draws on a Calabrese must want to die."

"I'm glad Jett has you to look after things. It's obvious the puppies adore you." She smiled at the dogs, snuggled against Sophia on the couch.

"Jett told me about her mother communicating with her in dreams. What do you think about that?" Sophia asked.

"Her family moved next door when I was twelve, so I knew her parents most of my life. Atsila was an extraordinary woman. If she and Victor were murdered, I want to help catch the person responsible." She lowered her voice. "I haven't said anything to Jett yet, but it occurred to me that her mother might be trying to protect her from the killer."

Sophia's jaw dropped. "You mean their killer might want to murder Jett too?"

"It's possible. Why else would her mother invade her dreams after two years?"

Jett walked in. "What's possible?"

Gwen stood. "I was just telling Sophia about my new theory." She explained it.

Sophia lifted her skirt and revealed a handgun in a thigh holster. She patted the weapon. "No worries. I've got things covered."

It was Gwen's turn for a jaw drop. "You're not concerned about living in potential danger?"

"Are you kidding? My life in Silver Lakes was a snooze, surrounded by geezers complaining about their medical problems and pressuring me to join all their senior-living clubs. Life here is almost like being back in Brooklyn. I like the danger. It makes me feel alive."

"Well, Jett, you really lucked out finding her. She's exactly what you need." She checked the time. "We have to go. See you later, Sophia."

They drove to the Kravis Center in downtown West Palm Beach and valet parked. The two-story lobby covered in glass on three sides had a lovely outdoor terrace and fountain on the main level.

Gwen headed for the Will-Call booth. "I'll pick up our tickets. Liz said to meet them inside by the bar."

Jett waited for Gwen and then pointed at the nearest end of the bar. "There they are."

Clive handed them glasses of red wine. "Welcome, ladies. You look lovely."

Liz introduced them to several of the old-guard Palm Beachers. Soon, they were immersed in conversations.

Opera night with the duke and duchess was turning out to be fun and festive. They enjoyed glasses of Robert Mondavi's 50 Harvests Cabernet Sauvignon in the lobby bar before the show. Liz and Clive knew how to work the room and have a good time. Gwen and Jett relished the celebrity treatment with everyone crowding around the icons of British nobility.

Gwen nudged Jett. "Is that Pierce Lockwood standing over there?"

Jett turned just as he spotted them. He sauntered across the lobby and joined them.

"Hello, ladies. You look stunning this evening. I see you're here with the Duke and Duchess of Colchester."

"What about you? You're not flying solo tonight, are you?" Jett asked.

"No, my parents roped me into escorting Prissy Parker." He rolled his eyes. "We're here with her parents and mine."

"They mean well." Gwen smiled. "I meant to ask if you know anyone who might want to kill Denton Donley. I'm working every angle."

Pierce paused in mid-sip of his Scotch. "The news didn't say anything about murder."

"We don't have a cause of death yet. Murder is just one possibility we're checking."

Pierce shook his head. "Sorry, I didn't know him well enough to speculate."

Chimes signaled it was time to be seated for the performance.

"See you later, Pierce." Gwen set her glass on a high-top table and followed Jett and her aunt and uncle into the orchestra seating section, where they sat five rows from the stage.

During the intermission, their party gathered at the bar for second glasses of wine and more socializing. Gwen stood at a high-top table with Jett while her aunt and uncle made the rounds.

"What time are you leaving for the Bahamas?" Gwen surveyed the room.

"I'm meeting the men tomorrow morning at nine o'clock. My uncle is borrowing a friend's propjet that has plenty of room for all our dive stuff."

"I know you'll be careful. Let me know what you find down there."

The chimes sounded. Intermission was over.

Gwen surveyed the bar. "I don't see my aunt and uncle."

"They're probably inside the theater." She set her glass down. "Let's go."

They slipped into their seats beside Liz and Clive moments before the lights dimmed.

Later, she hugged her aunt and uncle after the performance. "Thanks for a fun evening. Jett and I have to run. We both have busy days tomorrow."

The valet pulled up in Gwen's Mercedes, and she and Jett hopped in. After dropping her off, Gwen returned home feeling relaxed. She slept soundly. No nightmares about the carjacker.

# SEVENTEEN

JETT

I rose early and played with Pratt and Whitney before breakfast, teaching them to catch a canvas-covered foam frisbee. Half the time, they played tug-of-war with it, trying to make each other let go. I didn't bother doing laps in the pool because I would get plenty of swimming later in the Bahamas.

My cell rang. It was Gwen. I said, "Hey, I'm just about to leave. Wish me luck."

"Oh, Jett, I'm so embarrassed. I don't know how I'll face Detective Hottie and the chief."

"What's wrong?"

"A man died last night at the Kravis Center while we were there."

"What happened? Was he murdered?"

"Not sure yet, but the circumstances are similar to the Donley case. It was another rich guy from Palm Beach, Bradford "Binky" Worthington. He's had four wealthy wives who died under suspicious circumstances, but prosecutors couldn't prove he killed them."

"But we didn't see an ambulance or any cops there."

"After most people had left, he was found dead on the outdoor terrace sitting on a bench with a cigar and a glass of Scotch."

"The mayor had a cigar and a Scotch. Was Worthington's whisky poisoned?"

"I don't know. West Palm Beach Police have jurisdiction over this one. I'm on my way in to face the teasing. Wish I hadn't told my coworkers about the opera."

"I know what you'll be doing while I'm gone. I hope you crack the case. I'll call when I get back."

"Be careful, and try not to have too much fun with three handsome men."

"How do you know they're all handsome?"

"Because you're lucky that way. I'd bet my Mercedes the SEAL and the guy from the dive shop are almost as handsome as your uncle."

"The SEAL is. I haven't met the other guy yet."

"Take pictures and text me. I need something to make me smile today. Bye."

I tossed my bags into the trunk of my dad's sedan and left the SUV for Sophia in case she needed it for the puppies. Pierce drove up as I exited the front gate. I pulled over.

He jumped out of his car. "Hey, Jett, I was hoping to catch you for an impromptu breakfast at the Banyan Isle Bistro. I'd like to catch up after the strange goings-on at the polo match and the opera. I'm getting worried. Seems like somebody has it out for wealthy younger men like me."

I peeked at my watch. "Sorry, I have a plane to catch. I'm going scuba diving with Hunter and some friends. Would you like to join us?"

"Wish I could, but I have clients in court today. When will you be back?"

"In a day or two. Why don't you call Gwen? She's handling the Donley case, and she'll look into the other case to see if there are similarities."

"Good idea." He leaned over and gave me a soft kiss. "Have fun and call me when you get back."

His sweet kiss flooded me with warmth. I smiled as he drove away.

———

I parked next to my uncle's hangar and lugged my duffle bag to the King Air 350iER. The men had almost everything loaded in the roomy turboprop aircraft.

Snake turned around, gave me the once-over, and grinned. "Dang, woman, I've never seen you out of uniform. You look hot in shorts."

Hunter crossed his arms. "Cool it, big guy. You're not here for romance."

"Speak for yourself." Snake hugged me.

I kissed his cheek. "Thanks for coming. Kidding aside, you know what happened in Afghanistan with Commander Jones. I'm taking a break from so-called romance."

"Sorry, Jett. Everybody at the base knows what he did to you. We gave him such a hard time he asked for a transfer."

"Too bad *everyone* didn't know about his fiancée." I switched gears. "My focus now is on finding out if my parents were murdered. And just so you know, my mother was Hunter's older sister."

A tall man finished loading equipment into the baggage compartment and joined us. "Hi, I'm Justin Newton from Pura Vida Divers. You must be Miss Jorgensen."

I smiled at the six-four man in his early thirties with blue eyes, chiseled features, and a fit physique. *Gwen was right. Three handsome men.*

"Please, call me Jett, and thanks for joining our dive excursion. We're counting on you to help us with the correct trimix and decompression fills in the Bahamas." I offered my hand.

"No problem. I enjoy a challenge, like diving on a deep crash site." He gently squeezed my hand. "I hope we find what you're looking for."

Hunter herded us to the entry steps. "Time to launch. Climb aboard while I button up the cargo hatch."

I went forward to the cockpit. Buckling into the copilot seat, I scanned the instrument panel.

Hunter joined me. "I'll give you some stick time once I get us on course. You'll love flying this propjet. She's smooth and fast."

"And it has Pratt & Whitney turboprop engines." I grinned. "Which reminds me, I sure do love my puppies. Thank you."

"I knew they'd be perfect for you. How's their training working out?" He handed me a printed card with the aircraft's checklists.

"Training the puppies is easy. I don't know if it's the wolf in them, but they seem to instinctively know what to do. They've never had an accident in the house, and they alerted me to the intruder without making noise to draw his attention. Of course, it didn't matter because Sophia shot him."

He froze with his hand on a switch. "Sophia shot an intruder?"

"Oh geez, I forgot to tell you. So much has happened since you left Sunday morning after Mike told us the maid and Sims had been poisoned." I filled him in on the intruder murdering the guard, Sophia shooting the intruder, and the mystery involving two rich dead guys from Palm Beach.

"I don't like this. The body count's getting high, and you're in the middle of most of it." He shook his head. "Your life could be in danger."

"Gwen thinks Mom is trying to protect me from the killer by helping us expose him."

"Then let's get cracking. Read me the Before Start checklist."

# EIGHTEEN

I checked my handheld GPS and signaled the Bahamian captain of the live-aboard dive boat to stop. He dropped anchor over the crash site while Justin helped Hunter, Snake, and me organize our dive tanks. The boat rocked in three-foot swells covered with white caps in the brisk east wind.

"We'll dive with the trimix doubles and clip the other tanks together beside the anchor," Justin said. "We marked our tanks for the decompression stops, so we shouldn't have any confusion on the ascent. And we have two tanks marked LIFT for inflating all the lift bags if you decide to raise something big to the surface. Check your dive computers and ensure your gas blocks are selected to your trimix tanks."

I checked both my dive computers and my mask. "Will the integrated comm units in these full facemasks work when we're on the bottom?"

Justin said, "They have a range of six hundred feet, so you'll be able to talk to the boat captain too."

"And I brought some tactical lift bags from the SEAL's equipment locker." Snake held one up. "Snap the cuff closed around something under two hundred and fifty pounds, and a $CO_2$ cartridge will instantly inflate the bag and yank the item to the surface."

Justin smiled. "These will be great for lifting small pieces of wreckage."

Snake handed a tactical lift bag to each of us. "Just clip it to your vest." He thumbed at the weapons. "And don't forget the spearguns and dive knives, just in case."

I nudged Snake. "Are you expecting a shark attack?"

"Naw, but SEALs like to be prepared for anything." He sat on the side rail. "Let's go. I'm gettin' hot in this wetsuit."

After donning our dive gear and double-checking everything, we rolled backward into the ocean and waited for the captain to hand over all the extra tanks we would take down with us. We descended ten feet, checked our dive computers again, and did a comm check before continuing down.

The warm water helped calm my anxiety. I wasn't sure how I'd react to visiting the place where my parents died. *Suck it up. They aren't there now, and I want to find out what happened to them.*

We descended slowly in the crystal-clear ocean, clearing our ears. Penetrating sunlight transformed our air bubbles into sparkling diamonds as bright-colored fish darted around us, and a huge school of small Atlantic silversides zipped past. A loggerhead turtle the size of a tractor tire glided past me and turned in front of the men.

As we descended deeper, the light in this tranquil world dimmed into shadows as huge schools of crevalle jacks swam by. Some fish were close to four feet long. But the jacks were small compared to the Goliath grouper we encountered. The size of a MINI Cooper sedan, the huge grouper meandered by unconcerned with four scuba divers.

As the depth increased, so did my sense of foreboding. How would I feel when I faced my parents' watery crash site? After several minutes, we reached the anchor resting on the sandy ocean floor a hundred and seventy feet from the surface.

Although the water was cooler at this depth, my full wetsuit kept me comfortable.

A five-foot barracuda flashed past, chasing a school of spadefish that resembled large angelfish except they had silver bodies with irregular black vertical bands.

Justin said, "Clip all the tanks together, and then I'll tie them to the anchor."

Once the spare tanks were secured, I checked my compass and pointed. "Locate the wreck and find the tail section. It should be right over there on a 330-degree heading."

We swam in calm water to a dark, raised area covered with soft corals, sponges, and barnacles. As our spotlights passed over the wreck, gray colors turned into bright oranges and yellows. Red lionfish hovered over the site, their bold zebra-like stripes and elongated dorsal-fin spines making them look beautiful while hiding their painful venom.

My stomach churned when I shined my powerful dive light on the airplane's cabin. *Don't get upset. Nobody's in there now. Focus on the mission.*

Disturbed by my light, a Spotted Eagle Ray sprang up from the bottom silt and swam past me. Its back was covered with white dots on a black background.

Finding the tail section turned out to be harder than we'd expected because it wasn't with the rest of the wreckage. The fuselage was in one piece, but the wings had been ripped off, and the cockpit windshield had buckled. The entire wreck was covered with bright orange, yellow, and red sponges, truncates, anemones, sea worms, and corals that only revealed their colors in the spotlights and camera flashes.

"Look at this." Hunter pointed and took pictures of charred areas marking the attach points where the tail should have been. His flash illuminated large orange and yellow sponges.

"Good thing Hunter paid to have divers retrieve the bodies, or my parents and the pilots would still be belted into their seats." I stared at the cracked fuselage.

"No tail plus these burn marks make this look like sabotage," Snake said.

Hunter speculated, "The jet took off to the southwest. If the tail came off during the initial climb with the wings generating maximum lift, the airplane's forward motion would've carried it away from where the tail fell into the ocean. The jet would've dropped to a vertical nose-down attitude, and the wings would've ripped off on impact with the water, slowing the descent."

Justin scanned the area. "If storms haven't moved the tail, we should search northeast of the airplane's trajectory. I suggest we spread out, keeping the diver next to you in sight."

"Good idea. I want Hunter and Snake on my left and Justin on my right. Let's go."

We had covered a hundred yards when Justin warned, "We'd better find it soon, or we'll run out of bottom time."

I spotted a raised area twenty yards diagonally to our right and led the team there. We converged on an object protruding out of the sand. Lionfish hovered over the tail section. We used our spearguns like sticks to push the venomous fish out of the way.

Barnacles, sponges, delicate anemones, sea fans, and small corals covered the empennage. I scraped away some barnacles and recognized my family's company logo on the vertical stabilizer, a Viking ship encircled by a wreath with wolf heads in the top and bottom of the wreath.

"This is it. We found it." I pointed at the logo.

The severed T-shaped tail had landed upside down in the sand with the vertical part sticking up. It had separated from the airplane where it had been attached to the fuselage between the tail-mounted engines.

I watched as Hunter used his knife to scrape away some barnacles. "See the burn marks where bolts attached the tail to the fuselage?" He took pictures, the flash illuminating brilliant corals and sponges nearby. "You were right, Jett."

"These match the burn marks on the fuselage where the tail was blown off." I clenched my jaw, trying to control the anger welling up. "Mom and Dad were murdered."

"Looks like small explosives were used. It would help if we could find parts of the detonators. Feel around carefully and try not to create a silt cloud." Snake gently slipped his hand into the sand.

Justin checked his dive computers. "Better hurry. Fourteen minutes of bottom time left."

Snake shined a light inside the tail cone. "I don't believe it." He reached inside amidst the growing tube worms and sea fans and pulled out a small piece of debris with wires attached. "Part of a detonator got trapped inside. I think we have what we need to prove sabotage." He held it in front of us while Hunter took a picture.

Justin tapped his dive watch to indicate we should go. We were fifty yards from the anchor and spare tanks when a loud explosion at the surface sent shock waves to the bottom, hammering us into the seafloor.

I noted pieces of debris drifting downward. "Somebody just blew up our dive boat. I hear another boat driving away."

"We have bigger problems." Justin pointed up. "Hurry and grab our spare tanks before it's too late!"

As I swam hard with the men, the dive boat's heavy inboard engine descended toward our spare tanks clipped to the anchor. Before we could reach them, the engine block landed on most of the tanks, pinning them under it.

As my heart pounded my chest, I reminded myself not to gulp air.

We managed to pull out the two tanks that had been intended for inflating lift bags and one decompression tank, but most of our air tanks were trapped. We started digging out the sand underneath using our hands.

"Diggin' won't work fast enough," Snake said as a silt cloud formed around us. "Attach all our lift bags to this side of the engine." He threaded a line through one end of the engine while he could still see it. "Clamp your tactical bags to this line, and then we'll attach our large lift bags and fill them."

The tactical bags inflated, which did little to lift an engine weighing at least a ton. I tied my large lift bag to the line and filled it with air.

"These lift bags should be enough to raise one end of the engine so we can pull out our tanks." Snake tied another bag to the engine and inflated it.

"If this doesn't work, we're in big trouble." Hunter attached his lift bag and filled it.

"And if we don't start up in the next four minutes, we won't have enough air for a safe decompression." Justin filled his bag, using the last of the air in the two fill tanks.

I kept digging with the men after all the lift bags had been filled. I tried not to think about the boat captain. *He's probably dead. Maybe in pieces. How awful.*

"It's moving." I felt one end of the engine rise above the tanks in the heavy silt cloud.

We worked by feel to pull out the air tanks. One tank had a bent air valve, and air steadily escaped in a stream of bubbles, which only added to the murky water. We were in zero visibility.

Justin said, "I pulled down the severed end of the anchor line, wedged the anchor under the engine, clipped myself to the engine, and tied the anchor line to several inflated lift bags so the bags will be available to us when we reach the surface. Then I untied the lift bags from the engine and let them pull up the anchor line. We'll use it to stage the decompression stops."

"Good thinking, but we're one tank short." I discarded the leaking tank.

"We'll ascend close together and remind each other when to stop and switch to a deco tank. Conserve your air," Justin advised. "We might need to buddy-breathe in pairs before we reach the surface."

"Everybody, take your tanks and start up." Snake rose above the silt cloud.

We began a slow ascent, careful to follow the decompression schedule to avoid having nitrogen trapped in our joints, a painful and deadly condition known as The Bends. It would be well over an hour before we safely reached the surface. By then, any rescue boats might have come and gone, thinking no one had survived. And the surface was rough with white caps, making it difficult for boats to spot our bubbles.

I faced my dive partners in clear water at the first decompression stop. "I guess the boat captain is toast. Any chance this could've been an accident?"

"Not likely," Snake said. "Who knew where we'd be diving?"

"Sophia, Gwen, her aunt and uncle, and Mike knew we were going, but not exactly where, and I told Pierce I was taking a short dive trip."

"Did he ask where?" Hunter asked.

"No, he just said to call when I returned. What about you, Justin? Did you tell anyone?"

"Just the people who run the dive shop. They needed to know."

"Maybe the killer has had someone keeping an eye on this spot to see if anyone mounts a dive mission," I said.

"For two years? Unlikely," Hunter countered. "Someone has been watching you and keeping track of what you do and where you go."

"Then I guess it's good we have to stay down so long. He'll think I'm dead."

"I'm glad we brought spearguns," Snake said. "We might need them."

I scanned the distant surface. No boats, but plenty of shark activity.

Hunter peered up. "Must be blood in the water from whatever's left of the boat captain."

Several Caribbean reef sharks searched the debris field. I didn't want to think about what they might be eating up there.

# NINETEEN

GWEN

Gwen walked into the Palm Beach Police Station, and the first person she saw said, "Hey, Gwen, heard you had a great time at the opera last night. Too bad you missed the final act."

She decided to face the music in Rod's office first thing and knocked on the police chief's open door.

"Come in, Gwen." He waved to a chair. "Have a seat. Don't be embarrassed about last night. There's no way you could've known about the dead guy on the terrace. Let the bozos have their fun teasing you and move on. Any thoughts on your case?"

"There might be similarities between the Donley case and the death at the Kravis Center. With your permission, I'd like to meet with the detective on that case and compare notes."

"Good idea. Maybe the deaths are connected," Rod agreed. "I hope you find something."

She returned to her desk and called the lead detective on the Binky Worthington case at the West Palm Beach Police Department.

"Detective Palmer here, how may I help you?" a deep voice said.

"I'm Detective Gwen Stuart from the Palm Beach PD. I believe your rich dead guy has a lot in common with my rich dead guy. I'd like to compare notes over lunch today somewhere on your turf. How about E.R Bradley's?"

"Sounds good. I'll meet you there at noon."

Three hours later, Gwen walked into E.R. Bradley's fifteen minutes early and snagged a water-view table. The wide part of the Intracoastal Waterway known as Lake Worth sparkled in the noon sunlight. A balmy saltwater breeze out of the east mixed with the pleasing aroma of food in the open-air restaurant. She ordered an iced tea and gambled on a coffee for Detective Palmer.

Confident she could spot a detective among the lunch crowd, she noticed a man who surveyed the restaurant like a lion hunting prey. The attractive man in his early forties wore gray polyester pants and a sport coat. She waved.

"Detective Palmer?"

He smiled and flashed his badge. "Call me John. I assume you're Detective Stuart."

"Gwen, and thanks for coming, John." She gave him her best smile and flashed her shiny new badge. "I ordered coffee for you. Hope that's okay."

His alert eyes noted the coffee and focused on her face. "Thanks, Gwen. Been on the force long?" He settled across from her.

She smoothed her red hair. "Six years. I moved up to detective a few days ago. Denton Donley is my first murder case."

"The alleged rapist?" He scanned the menu. "I heard he was found dead in his Rolls."

A waitress appeared with her pad and pencil ready. Gwen ordered the grilled chicken salad, and John got a burger with fries.

He smiled at the waitress and flashed his badge. "We'd appreciate it if you'd expedite our food order."

Gwen waited until the waitress walked away. "Donley's like your rich dead guy—a relatively young Palm Beacher in good health with no obvious cause of death. He was charged with several rapes but never convicted. The M.E. found a pinprick in his neck and enough sedative to put him to sleep. We don't know what killed him, but it looks like murder."

John drained his coffee and waved for more. "Worthington also avoided prosecution. Four rich wives died under suspicious circumstances, but the D.A. couldn't make anything stick. Binky died a very wealthy man."

"Has the M.E. finished his autopsy?" She took a sip of iced tea.

"He worked all night and finished early this morning. Found a pinprick in Worthington's neck and a strong sedative in his system. No poison. No cause of death."

Gwen's eyes widened. "Sounds like the same MO. I'd like to know if it was the same sedative used on Donley. Was it injected into his neck?" She leaned back as the server placed her meal in front of her.

John waited until the waitress served him and walked away. "The M.E. found traces of the sedative in his cocktail glass. I checked out the bartender. He's clean." He bit into his burger.

She swallowed a bite of grilled chicken. "Any chance Worthington and Donley were partners in a shady Mob deal?"

He reached for the ketchup. "Worthington hung out with spoiled rich guys. I didn't find any Mob connections or any reason he would be involved with them."

"The Mafia angle was a long shot. The deaths are clearly connected. If we can figure out the connection, we'll catch the killer."

"Both men did terrible things and got away with it. That's the connection." He dipped a fry in a small pool of ketchup. "Maybe some of their victims got together and hired a pro."

She paused with her fork halfway to her mouth. "A hitman?"

"Gwen, I've worked plenty of murder cases. Both of these have the earmarks of professional hits—deaths that appear natural with no evidence of the killer. I'll ask around if a heavy hitter is in town." He focused on finishing his burger.

"I know I'm new and a little naïve, but I'm confident if we keep digging and go by the book, the killer will end up behind bars along with the people who hired him."

He sounded skeptical as he summoned the check. "I hate to burst your bubble, but I've seen lots of bad guys walk, even though the cops did everything by the book. We have no cause of death, no murder weapon, and no suspects. See if you can turn up evidence proving their victims communicated with each other. If we can find a link there, we can squeeze them and see who caves." He dropped money on the table and stood.

She rose to shake his hand. "Thanks for your help. I'll let you know what I find on the victim angle. Call me if you hear anything about a hitman."

# TWENTY

JETT

We buddy-breathed in pairs from our last tanks before we finished the final decompression stop and surfaced amidst chunks of flotsam from the explosion. There were no boats in sight, but a few sharks still circled.

"Ignore the men in gray suits, and they'll lose interest," Snake advised. "Whatever blood was in the water is gone."

I nudged him as we swayed back and forth, clutching the lift bags. "You said SEALs are prepared for anything. What's your backup plan?"

"Yeah, Snake. Any ideas?" Hunter asked. "It's a long way to shore."

Justin reached inside his BC vest. "I have a Nautilus Marine Rescue GPS. It's a locator beacon."

Snake pulled a sealed bag out of his vest. "I can do you one better." He held up a waterproof satellite phone and two flares. "We don't know who we can trust in the Bahamas, so I'll call my SEAL buddy in Virginia and let him handle this."

When he finished the call, he said, "Turns out the Coast Guard has a cutter about twenty miles from here. He told them we'll fire a flare when we see their ship."

I smiled at Snake and Justin. "I sure am glad you guys came with us."

"While we're waiting to be rescued, let's discuss how we're going to catch the murderer," Hunter said. "Chances are he's the same guy who blew up the dive boat."

"The boat is a good place to start." I surveyed the surface as waves splashed my face. "Think there's any floating evidence to help us trace the bomb?"

"You and Justin stay with the anchor line while Snake and I look around."

Hunter checked his speargun and gave Justin a protect-her look as he swam away from me. I knew he wasn't being chauvinistic, just a caring uncle, so I didn't object.

Snake swam in the opposite direction. Twenty minutes later, they returned.

"There isn't much left," Hunter reported. "The wind and current carried most of the floating pieces away, and the rest sank."

"I couldn't find anything either." Snake grabbed a float. "The cutter will be here soon. After they drop us off, do we want to nose around Freeport and see if anyone had a vendetta against the boat captain?"

"I can hire people to look into that," Hunter said. "I want my niece back in Florida under guard until we get this solved."

Snake raised his hand. "I volunteer to be Jett's bodyguard."

I laughed. "How nice of you, Snake."

Hunter grinned. "Good idea, Snake. Sophia is going to *love* you."

"Who's Sophia?"

We answered questions about the boat explosion for the Coast Guard and then for the Bahamian police before we could fly back to Florida. After we landed, I called Sophia and told her I'd be home soon with a guest. It was 9 p.m. by the time Snake and I arrived at my house.

Sophia and the dogs greeted us in the foyer. As the puppies wiggled and fussed over Snake, I told the dogs, "Be nice to the alpha male."

He took in the surroundings. "I knew you inherited money, but dang, this place is as big as some hotels."

Sophia eased closer and admired his bulging biceps. "Nice guns."

I smiled. "Snake, I'd like you to meet my dog nanny, Sophia."

He kissed her hand. "It's a pleasure, ma'am."

She cocked her head. "Snake? Didn't your mother like you?"

I laughed. "That's his SEAL nickname. They don't use their real names for security reasons."

"I see." She crossed her arms. "And why did they name you Snake?"

He grinned. "Anaconda is too long for a nickname."

She raised an eyebrow. "I'll be keeping a close eye on you, Mister. No funny business."

"Snake's here to protect me. Someone blew up our dive boat."

"What? Well, if anybody comes here to hurt you, I'll blow him away just like the last guy." She reached under her skirt and pulled out a Glock 26.

Snake's jaw dropped. "You shot somebody here?"

I hooked my arm in his. "Come and sit with us and we'll tell you all about it." I caught Sophia's eye. "We missed lunch and dinner. I'll order a couple of large pizzas."

"Fuhgeddaboudit. I made a juicy pot roast with mashed potatoes and gravy I can have reheated in ten minutes. You kids relax. I'll bring a cold beer for Snake and a merlot for you." She rushed off to the kitchen.

"Let's sit on the terrace. There's a cool breeze, and the puppies can play on the back lawn." I led him outside.

We settled into chairs and watched the dogs romp on the grass in the outdoor lighting.

"Cute pups. What are their names?"

"The male is Pratt, and the female is Whitney, like the aircraft engines," I explained to avoid the inevitable question.

He smiled. "Woman, you never cease to surprise me."

Sophia served our drinks and asked, "Would you like to eat out here?"

"That would be great." I stood. "Can I help you bring everything out?"

"No need. I have it all loaded on a serving cart. I'll be back in a jiffy, and you can tell me all about your trip." She zipped back inside.

I turned to Snake. "Sophia is a treasure. She's far more than a dog nanny. I'm lucky to have found her."

"You don't think she's a tad cavalier about that handgun she totes around?"

"She's the late Don Calabrese's daughter. She grew up around guns and Mafia culture."

His jaw dropped again. "Dang, woman. I thought I'd seen everything in my line of work. Then I spend a day with you, and the surprises keep rolling in."

My backup cell rang. It was programmed to forward calls made to the cell that had gone down with the boat. As a long-time member of Navy Intelligence, I had learned to have backups for communication devices.

It was Gwen. "Who's the hot guy on the terrace with you?"

I laughed. "I guess you're making good use of those high-powered military binoculars I gave you for your birthday. Come over and meet my SEAL friend."

"I'll be right there."

I smiled at Snake. "My best friend is on her way over from next door. Excuse me while I let her in."

When I returned a few minutes later with Gwen, Sophia had the table set and dinner ready to serve.

I introduced Snake and told him, "Gwen's a detective with the Palm Beach Police."

He grinned. "Another armed woman. Maybe you don't need a bodyguard, Jett."

"Uh oh, what happened now?" Gwen asked as Sophia handed her a glass of merlot.

I told her and Sophia everything that happened on the dive trip. "Hunter thinks somebody is keeping tabs on me and doesn't want me to discover the truth about what happened to my parents."

Snake broke in, "That's why I'm sticking around a while to protect her."

Sophia cocked an eyebrow. "I know you bad-boy types. Protecting had better be all you do, Mister. Jett has had a rough breakup and isn't ready for romance."

My backup cell rang again. This time it was Mike.

"I have some news. Are you still in the Bahamas?"

"I'm home, and I have news too. Why don't you stop by? Gwen and my SEAL friend are here."

"I'll be there in five minutes."

# TWENTY-ONE

I explained who had called and why. "I'll let him in."

Sophia put a hand on my shoulder. "Sit and enjoy your meal. I'll get the door." She hustled to the foyer.

A few minutes later, Mike walked out onto the terrace, and Sophia came out carrying beer and wine. She handed a cold beer to Mike and another to Snake. Then she refilled our wine glasses as I made the introductions.

Mike gave Snake a defiant nod and pulled up a chair between Gwen and me. "Manny Delgado was murdered this morning. Cyanide in his coffee. I arrested his wife Dolores for his murder and the mayor's murder."

I paused mid-sip. "How did she expect to get away with that?"

"She claims she's innocent, but that's what killers always say." He focused on Snake. "How did the dive trip go?"

Snake filled him in and explained he was staying to protect me.

Mike gave me a worried look. "Whoever killed your parents must be nearby, watching you to stop you from exposing him. Good thing you're home now with an armed guard patrolling the grounds."

"Hah! The armed guard didn't stop the last intruder, and I'm still waiting for you to return my Glock," Sophia said. "I'm making do with a loaner from Jett."

"Sorry, Sophia, I've been busy with all the murder investigations."

"No worries. I'll protect the ladies," Snake promised with a smirk.

Gwen jumped in, "Back to Dolores. Why did she kill Manny?"

"Rumor was he was threatening to have her killed by one of his Mob connections." Mike swigged his beer. "He was furious about her affair with the mayor."

I chuckled. "What about her affair with Andy Carrigan and his affair with Brenda?"

"Dang, sounds like this little island community is a sexual free-for-all." Snake looked at Sophia. "And you're worried about *me*?"

She smirked. "None of those people are staying in this house with Jett."

Gwen said, "That reminds me, have you seen more intruders, Sophia?"

She glanced back at the house. "I used that big telescope Jett keeps near the terrace doors. Nobody was on the beach or ocean, and the backyard was clear except for the guard on patrol."

"Maybe someone was out front, sneaking around and hiding from the guard." Mike frowned. "That guard can't be everywhere at once."

"If anyone had come near the house, our little darlings would've warned me." Sophia ruffled the pups' fur. "They're always vigilant. Whenever a guard gets near the house, they nudge me, look in his direction, and bare their teeth."

I caressed Whitney, then pulled her up on my lap. "What about you, Gwen? Any luck solving the murders of two rich Palm Beachers?"

"I have a long list of their victims and relatives of their victims to interview." She sipped her wine. "So far, I haven't been able to establish a connection between any of them. I'm working on a theory that some of them got together and hired a hitman."

"That's plausible, but it might be hard to prove." Mike finished his beer.

"I haven't exactly made a good impression on Chief Malone, especially after I knocked over the body in the Rolls." She frowned, then her eyes widened like she'd just remembered something. "Don't forget the charity ball Friday night at The Breakers, Jett. Will Snake be joining us?" She looked at him.

"No, I have to fly back to Virginia Friday morning." He grinned at me as he pulled Pratt up on his lap. "Too bad. I'd love to see Jett in a ballgown."

The doorbell rang, booming "Ride of the Valkyries."

Snake laughed. "*That's* your doorbell? The surprises just keep coming."

Sophia stood. "Relax, Jett, I'll get it." She patted her hidden thigh holster.

A few minutes later, Pierce sauntered out with Sophia and said, "Thanks for putting me on your approved visitors list. The guard opened the gate." He leaned down and kissed my cheek. "Thank God you're all right. I saw a news story on my cell phone about a dive boat near Freeport that blew up. The story said four Americans had chartered it. I tried your cell a few hours ago. No answer. I was worried it might've been you."

"It *was* me." I made the introductions and motioned for him to pull up a chair. "The boat captain was killed, and sharks ate what was left of him. I feel bad for his family."

"Sorry to hear that, but I'm glad you and your dive buddies made it home safely." His gaze moved from me to Snake. "Why did the boat explode?"

Snake seemed to be sizing him up. He said, "We're not certain, but we suspect our boat was bombed by someone in another boat."

"That's terrible. I hope the Coast Guard catches the bomber." He turned his gaze to me. "The news report said you were near Freeport. Did you at least find some good dive spots?"

"No, we found my parents' crash site. Now we're sure the jet was sabotaged, but we have no idea how to prove who did it. I didn't think my parents had any enemies."

"Without a motive, it'll be difficult to find the killer," Mike said. "You'll have to look into all your dad's business dealings as well as your parents' personal lives."

Gwen leaned in. "I just had a thought. What if Atsila was the target? She treated Cherokee patients as a shaman using natural medicine. Maybe one of her patients died, and the family blamed her and took revenge."

"None of Mom's patients died under her care. Some died much later of old age, but that's hardly a motive for revenge."

"I could ask around and make sure it wasn't a Mob hit," Sophia offered. "You know, just to rule that out."

"Good idea," I said, "and while you're asking, find out if they know anything about the boat explosion."

The three men stared at Sophia with their mouths agape.

"What? The daughter of Don Calabrese still has connections. I'll see what I can learn."

"I don't think Jett's parents had any dealings with the Mafia, but you never know," Gwen said. "It's worth checking out."

I elbowed Pierce. "I'll call your dad and ask if anyone ever sued my parents or vice versa. Maybe he knows someone who held a grudge against them."

"He was their lawyer for over twenty years, so he'd know if anyone had a beef with them." Pierce patted my hand. "I'll ask him to review their records and give you a call."

"Thanks, Pierce. Nobody sabotages a jet without a reason. If your dad can help me find someone with a motive, maybe the FBI will nail them." I finished my glass of merlot.

Pierce drained his beer. "Knowing Dad, you can expect his call tomorrow."

Everyone said their goodbyes, and Sophia, Snake, and I carried everything into the kitchen and finished the cleanup while the puppies watched us.

"I bet you two are exhausted after the day you've had." Sophia nudged Snake. "Where's your luggage?"

"It went down with the boat." He held up a small nylon bag. "Hunter loaned me a few essentials."

"Speaking of essentials, I'd better open the gun safe and supply you with a firearm." I led him into the study. "I have plenty of weapons and ammo here. Choose whatever you want." I opened the safe door, hidden behind a bookcase, and switched on the interior light.

He grabbed a Glock 40 and two extra magazines. "Need anything?"

"I keep a Glock 26 and extra mags in my bedroom. Come on, I'll show you to your room." I led him upstairs to a room down the hall from me on the top floor. "Mine's the one at the end, in case you see someone sneaking around up here."

"I can protect you better if I'm in the same room with you."

"Nice try, but I'll have the dogs with me. They're very protective."

"They're little puppies. Better to have a big, strong man close by." He winked.

# TWENTY-TWO

I woke from a sound sleep at midnight when Sophia yelled, "Freeze, dirtbag!" followed by Snake yelling, "Don't shoot!"

I flung open my door, switched on the hall light, and found Sophia wearing night-vision goggles and seated in a chair in front of my room. Her weapon was pointed at Snake.

When the light came on, she dropped the Glock onto her lap, yanked off her goggles, and covered her eyes. "Great, now you blinded me with the light."

"What the heck is going on?" I looked from her to Snake, who wore Navy gym shorts and no shirt. My gaze paused for a moment on his six-pack abs.

"Your crazy dog nanny almost shot me." He snatched up her pistol while her eyes were closed.

"I saw a big man sneaking toward your room and drew on him. It's his own fault for not staying where he belongs." She blinked her eyes and felt her lap. "Give back my gun."

I glared at Snake. "Give her the weapon, and both of you go to bed. I'm too tired for this nonsense." I herded the puppies back to my room and closed the door.

————

Mother invaded my sleep again. She led me into the great hall and ran her hand over the telescope. Then she walked out onto the terrace and returned.

Pratt and Whitney were in my dream, rocketing around the huge room, chasing each other. They misjudged a turn and tumbled into the telescope stand. The long, heavy spyglass toppled toward me. I tried to catch it so it wouldn't smash onto the oak floor. When it hit my chest, I lost my balance and fell backward, knocking over a floor lamp and landing on my back with the telescope on top of me.

My fall and the loud crash caused by the fallen lamp woke me and brought Snake and Sophia rushing into the room. The puppies licked my face.

"Jett, what happened?" Sophia switched on a table lamp and crouched over me while Snake surveyed the room, pistol in hand.

I rubbed the back of my head. "That's going to leave a lump. Help move this heavy thing off me."

Snake leaned down, lifted it up, and returned the tripod stand to its upright position with the telescope secure on top. Then he scooped me up, carried me to a sofa, and sat beside me. "Should I be looking for an intruder?"

"No." My face flushed. "I had another sleepwalking episode. I dreamed my mother led me here and showed me the telescope." I petted the worried-looking puppies. "I thought the dogs were in my dream. They didn't know I was sleepwalking and followed me. I guess they thought it was playtime. They were roughhousing around and knocked the telescope into me."

Sophia scanned the backyard with the telescope. "There has to be a reason she led you here. All the other incidents led to you investigating your parents' deaths."

I stared a moment, remembering. "My parents used to keep the spyglass on the terrace every night until they went to bed, in case they wanted to look at boats, airplanes, or stars. Then they'd bring it inside before they went upstairs."

Snake gave Sophia a sideways glance. "I think Jett's mother is trying to tell her that she and her husband saw something they shouldn't have, and that's why they were killed."

"That has to be it. We just have to find out what happened right before they left on vacation. I'm guessing they saw someone on a boat behind our house."

"All right, children. We'll sort this out in the morning. Go to your own beds and stay there." Sophia holstered her weapon and pointed her fingers at her eyes and then at Snake. "Behave yourself."

"Yes, ma'am." He squeezed my shoulder. "You never said this would be more dangerous than a SEAL mission." He scooped up Pratt and carried him upstairs.

"You'll be safe as long as you stay away from her room." Sophia followed him up the stairs. "I'll be watching. Sleep tight." She slapped his butt.

"Careful what you start, woman. I'm more man than you can handle." He winked at her and continued up.

"If I thought for one second you were serious, I'd be on my back faster than you can say, 'Help, I've fallen on her, and she won't let me up.'"

I carried Whitney past them. "All right, you two, quit fooling around and go to bed. I'm exhausted."

Once Snake and I were on the fourth floor, I led the dogs into my room and closed the door. Moonlight filtered in from tall windows and the glass balcony doors on three sides.

———

The next morning, Snake and I sat at a table on the terrace with my laptop while Sophia fixed breakfast. A warm breeze caressed me as I checked for local news stories that might give us a clue.

"Nothing the week before, but the day they left, there was a story in the evening news about a missing local woman, Lola Brown." I pointed at the item. "She was twenty-two."

He sipped his coffee. "Did you know her?"

"No, she probably moved here while I was away in the Navy."

"She could've gone missing the night before your parents left on vacation, but it wouldn't have made it into the paper until the following night."

"I'll check for follow-up stories." I tapped the keys. "Look. Two fishermen found her body floating in the ocean the next day." I gasped. "And the autopsy showed she was pregnant."

He frowned. "That's a strong motive if the father was a selfish jerk who didn't want to take responsibility. Easier to drown the problem."

I stared out at the ocean. "And maybe my parents saw her on his boat."

"What time did they fly out the next day?" He reached down and accepted the frisbee Pratt offered him. He flung it toward the lawn, the puppies charging after it.

"They left at ten in the morning from the private jet terminal at PBI, which means they didn't know she was murdered, or they would've reported it."

He sat back. "How long were they planning to be away?"

"It was supposed to be a four-day vacation at a casino resort in Freeport." I poured myself another cup of coffee and refilled his cup.

"They wouldn't have learned about the crime until the second or third day of their trip. By then, it would make sense to wait until they

145

returned home to report what they had seen." He stirred cream and sugar into his cup.

"Which is why the killer made sure they never made it home." I bit my lip.

He reached over and gently turned my chin toward him. "None of this is plausible unless the killer was certain they had seen him with the victim. How could he have known they saw him on a boat? He must've been at least a half-mile away."

We were lost in thought, blankly staring into each other's eyes when Sophia rolled out the serving cart with breakfast. The aroma of warm cinnamon rolls, bacon, and eggs scrambled with a sprinkling of cheddar drifted over us.

She punched his muscled arm. "I can't leave you alone with her for five minutes."

He turned. "No need to be jealous. It's not what it looks like."

"That's what they all say. Eat your breakfast and behave yourself." She plopped a plate in front of him.

I chuckled. "He's telling the truth. Our thoughts were occupied with how to explain the conundrum we just discovered."

Pratt and Whitney nudged Sophia and Snake to help them climb onto their laps.

"Don't pick them up." I pointed at the bacon. "They're trying to get closer to this. My uncle gave them some, and now they want it every time they smell it."

Sophia shook her head. "It's lucky Hunter's so good-looking or I'd be mad at him." She settled in for breakfast. "Tell me what's puzzling you."

I explained what we'd learned on the Internet and that it only made sense if the killer knew my parents had seen him with the victim.

She leaned in. "Your parents flew out in a corporate jet, right?"

"Yes, from a private terminal over at Palm Beach International."

"Then the answer is simple." She smiled a smug little smile. "Before they boarded their jet, they ran into someone they knew who also had a jet. One of them probably made an innocent remark about having seen him the previous night on his boat with Lola."

Snake set his cup down. "She's right. Later, when the news stories came out, he realized he'd have to eliminate them before they returned and exposed him."

I leaned forward. "They probably made small talk, like people do, and told him where they were going and when they'd be back."

"If the guy has a jet, he's rich, which means he could afford to hire a pro to make their deaths look like an accident." Sophia pulled out her cell. "If a hitman was used, my family might know about it." She took a stroll on the lawn while she made the call.

I picked up my cell. "I'll ask Mike to stop by. He's been with the Banyan Isle Police several years, and he'll know about the murdered girl." I made the call. "He'll be here in a few minutes."

"What's the deal with him?" Snake asked. "It's obvious he's into you."

"He was my boyfriend until I joined the Navy. Then he stopped speaking to me until the mayor's murder. I don't know where his head's at now."

My cell rang. Pierce's father was calling. "Good morning, Mr. Lockwood, and thank you for getting back to me so fast."

"Please, call me Niles. Your parents were dear friends for many years. I called because a man named Carl Rowan was convicted of embezzling four hundred thousand dollars from Jorgensen Industries five years ago. He was their VP of Finance until he was sentenced to five years in prison. Said he needed the money to pay gambling debts."

"What did that have to do with my parents?"

"He blamed your father for destroying his life because he pushed the D.A. to prosecute the case instead of just firing Rowan. His wife divorced him and took the kids."

"But he was in jail when my parents' jet crashed, wasn't he?"

"I checked with a cop friend. He was released three years early, about six months before they died. Rumor has it he handles the books for a major drug dealer in Miami now, but nothing has been proven."

"Thanks, Niles. I'll ask the police to check him out. Anything else?"

"I suggest you set a meeting with the CEO of Jorgensen Industries and look into whether anyone else had a beef with your father. I knew about the embezzling case because I handled the corporate law account for Jorgensen Industries."

"All right. Thanks for the call and give my best to your wife, Nancy." I hung up feeling shocked and concerned. My parents hadn't told me about any problems within the company.

The dogs cocked their heads, barked once, and stared at me.

"Mike must be here. I'll be right back." I breezed through the terrace door with the puppies on my heels.

I returned with Mike the same time Sophia finished her calls. We all sat together and passed around the coffee pot.

Mike took in our group. "I gather you've learned something new since last night?"

I filled him in. "What can you tell us about the Lola Brown murder?"

"Not much. She was choked and thrown into the ocean. The medical examiner said she'd been in the water approximately two days. We checked the marinas to see if anyone saw her go out on a boat. No luck there."

"Someone must've known who she was dating." Snake bit into a cinnamon bun. "Did you get a name?"

"Her roommate said she was seeing someone but insisted on

keeping it secret. Lola told her she'd reveal his name after they were engaged," Mike said. "Obviously, that never happened."

Sophia pursed her lips. "Sounds like her lover was married, and she was waiting for him to get a divorce. Any chance it could've been the mayor, you know, the guy who was murdered here?"

"Talk about irony." I shook my head. "I guess anything's possible. He was married to a super-rich woman, and a pregnant girlfriend would've ruined the luxurious lifestyle his wife provided."

"That's probably why he switched to middle-aged married women," Mike said. "Less risk."

"Did Mayor Peabody have a boat?" I grabbed a cinnamon roll.

"The Peabodys have a huge yacht with a live-aboard captain and crew, a mid-sized sailboat, and an ocean-going speedboat." Mike took a bite out of a cinnamon bun. "We assumed he took her out on the speedboat, but no one remembered seeing him leave the harbor with Lola the night she disappeared."

I leaned into him. "Was there a record of him taking the boat out that night?"

"His boat was seen in the inlet heading out to sea, but it was too dark to recognize who was at the helm." He glanced at me. "If Mayor Peabody killed Lola, I should be looking at her family to find his killer."

"Wait a minute." Sophia crossed her arms. "You said Dolores Delgado killed him."

"That's changed. A day after we charged her with both murders, her son came forward and admitted he poisoned his stepfather to protect his mother. He handed over the evidence he'd been hiding in a friend's garage."

"What about the mayor's murder?" I asked.

"She's probably innocent, like she says. After you gave me the pictures you took at the restaurant, Dolores admitted she was also having an affair with Andy Carrigan." Mike lifted his hands. "No reason for her to be angry the mayor was playing around when she was doing the same thing. It doesn't look like she was serious about Mayor Peabody."

I turned to Sophia. "Did your people know anything about a hitman hired to kill my parents?"

"They thought the crash was an accident." She frowned. "If a hitter was used, it wasn't anyone they know or they would've heard about it."

I nudged Mike. "What about Carl Rowan? Will you ask the Miami PD to check if he has an alibi for my parents' murders?"

"Yes, and I expect you to stay out of it." Mike checked his watch and stood. "I have to run. I'll call if I find any leads through Lola's family or Rowan. Be careful. Your parents' killer knows you're looking for him."

I called and made a late afternoon appointment with my company's CEO, Frasier Collins.

# TWENTY-THREE

S nake and I decided it wouldn't hurt to double-check the boat traffic from two years ago, assuming anyone could remember that far back. Our first stop was the Banyan Harbor Inn Marina. Seagulls squawked and dived over a fish-cleaning station on the docks. Boats rocked gently in their slips, and lines clinked against the masts of sailboats as a warm east breeze flowed across the Intracoastal Waterway. We stopped at the dockmaster's office.

A man in his fifties with tan, leathery skin, white hair, and hard eyes greeted us. "Jim Jansen, dockmaster. What can I do for you?"

My flirting skills were almost non-existent, but I gave it a shot. I smiled and tossed my hair. "Hi, I'm Jett and this is my friend." I didn't want to put him off by saying Snake's name. "I'm not sure if you can help me. Were you working here two years ago?"

"Yep, been here sixteen years. What do you need?"

"My friend, Lola Brown, went missing two years ago the night of January 15th, and her body was found in the ocean on the 17th. She might have gone out on Phil Peabody's speedboat the night of the

15th. Any chance you saw her that night and remember who she left with?"

"We don't have a lot of crime here." He frowned. "I remember that murder. Like I told the cops back then, I saw Peabody's speedboat leave the harbor, but it was too far away to recognize who was at the helm."

"Did you see a woman on the boat?" Snake leaned against the railing by the water.

"No, but she could have been below. That boat has a huge cabin belowdecks."

"Were you here when the boat returned?" I hoped he'd seen her or Phil.

"No, the man on night duty relieved me at ten, and he quit over a year ago. Sorry."

We thanked him and drove to the island's other marina, which was on the western curve of the crescent about mid-way between the north and south ends of the island.

As we strolled down to the docks, Snake said, "We're probably wasting our time here."

"It's possible the mayor left from the other marina and returned to this one or he picked her up here in his boat." I surveyed the vessels, most over sixty feet.

The dockmaster had recently moved here from Maine and didn't know who we should ask about events two years ago. "We have a lot of turnover with the dock workers. Most of them don't last more than six months before they move on to something better."

We talked to a few dock hands, but they had all been there less than six months. Another dead end.

We hopped into my dad's Bentley sedan, drove over the bridge, and eventually connected with I-95 South to the airport.

The private aircraft terminal at Signature Aviation on the south side of Palm Beach International Airport was the next stop in our fact-finding mission. The curved glass exterior resembled a modern two-story sculpture.

I opened the car's center console. "We'd better leave the handguns here." I put mine in and closed it after Snake deposited his pistol. "Any other weapons on you?"

He grinned. "Jett, darlin', I *am* a weapon."

Focusing on his broad shoulders and hard torso, I momentarily forgot why we were there. I grabbed my handbag. "You certainly are. Let's go."

We approached the reception desk where a tan young woman in her mid-twenties greeted us. "Welcome to Signature. I'm Marni. How may I be of service?"

Snake, looking hunky in snug jeans and a white polo shirt that hugged his muscles, poured on his Texas charm. "Good mornin', Marni. Do y'all keep records of departures and arrivals at this facility?"

She beamed at him. I may as well have been invisible.

"Yes, sir, Homeland Security requires records of all flights, passengers, and crews. Are you expecting someone?"

He thumbed at me. "This here's Jettine Jorgensen. We're lookin' into the last flight her parents took." He turned to me. "What day was it they left in the Gulfstream G650?"

"Victor and Atsila Jorgensen departed here at 10 a.m., January 16th, two years ago in Gulfstream November-One-Juliet-India," I said, reciting the aircraft type and tail number. "We'd appreciate it if you'd give us a printout of all the aircraft arrivals and departures on that day." I gave her my warmest smile, not that she noticed. Her radar was locked on Snake.

A deep voice behind me said, "Jett, is it you?"

I turned and faced Jorgensen Industries' chief pilot, Dan Duquesne. A little taller than me, slim, and fortyish with graying temples and penetrating hazel eyes, he wore a navy-blue uniform with the company logo above his gold wings and four gold stripes on his sleeves.

I hugged him. "Dan, good to see you. It's been ages. This is my SEAL friend, Snake."

He shook Snake's hand and turned to me. "Flying somewhere?"

"No." I explained what we needed but not why. "Will you please assure Marni that I have a legitimate right to the information?"

"Marni, Miss Jorgensen owns Jorgensen Industries, and her company keeps four corporate jets here. She's my boss, so please give her whatever she needs."

"Right away, Miss Jorgensen." Her fingers raced over the keyboard. Seconds later, the printer behind her hummed to life and spit out the page I needed. Apparently, her radar only locked onto handsome men and wealthy customers. She handed me the paper.

I scanned the page and concentrated on maintaining a poker face when a certain name caught my eye. I took Dan's arm and eased him away from the desk. "Got a minute?"

"Anything for you. What's up?" He led us into the pilots' lounge.

I handed the paper to Snake and asked Dan, "Do you know the pilots who fly Gulfstream November-Two-Mike-Whisky-Papa that belongs to Marjorie Wentworth Peabody?"

"Steve Winters is the captain. We've been friends for years."

"How long has he had that job?" I tried to keep my tone casual and friendly.

Dan thought a moment. "About three years. He flew copilot for us before he took the captain seat in the Wentworth jet. We play golf together on our days off. Is there a problem?"

"No, but I might want to talk to him about something he may have seen here two years ago that could help me with a personal matter. Sorry I can't say more right now. I promise I'll fill you in when I have all the facts. It has nothing to do with flight crews. Please ask him if it's okay for you to give me his phone number."

"I'm sure he won't mind. I'll give it to you now." He pulled out his cell and texted me the number.

"Thanks, Dan. We won't keep you. Have a good flight." I waved goodbye.

Snake and I headed back to the car. He stopped me under a shade tree and gently pulled me against him. Looking into my eyes, he said, "Woman, you're wound tighter than the seat springs on my daddy's old farm tractor. Let me help you with that."

He gave me a sensual kiss that curled my toes and melted my nether region. All the tension drained from my body as my heart pumped at the maximum rate, sending blood into every muscle.

He released me and smiled. "Dang, I'm good."

I licked my lower lip. "Can't argue with that. I think I need to sit down now." I pulled out my key fob and clicked open the door locks.

He slid into the front passenger seat and pulled the paper out of his pocket. "This took an unexpected turn. Looks like Sophia was right about your parents running into the mayor before they flew out. What do you want to do about this?"

I started the engine and let the air conditioner run while I recovered from Snake's kiss and the revelation that Mayor Peabody might have been responsible for killing my parents.

"The Russian Mafia is big in South Florida," I said. "I wonder if there's a safe way to find out if Peabody hired a Russian hitman."

"Let's go somewhere for lunch and discuss it. Know a place that serves a good steak?"

"You're in for a treat. Okeechobee Steakhouse is the oldest steakhouse in Florida, and it's not far from here. They have a ribeye that will make you think you're in Heaven, and I owe you a steak anyway." I took Southern Blvd. to I-95 and exited west on Okeechobee Boulevard. We pulled into the parking lot ten minutes after we left the airport.

Once we were settled at a table, Snake with a cold Cobra beer and me with a Pahlmeyer Merlot, we relaxed. We ordered ribeye steaks with the bone in. I planned to give the leftovers and bones to Pratt and Whitney.

Snake took a long pull on his beer. "Too bad your Bentley has center consoles in the front and back seats. We need a place to spend some quality alone time. How about a bedroom at your next-door neighbor's house? Gwen won't tell."

"I told you before, I'm not ready for romance." I took a big sip of wine.

He grinned smugly. "That's not what your body said when I kissed you."

"Fine. I'm human, so shoot me." I crossed my arms.

"I'd rather do something more pleasurable. It'll be our little secret. The government trusts me with bigger things than this, and SEALs never tell."

"Wrong." I arched my left eyebrow. "You tell your teammates everything. Besides, I need to concentrate on solving my parents' murder." I took another nervous sip.

He gently squeezed my hand. "What if we already solved it? If Mayor Peabody had them killed, what can you do? He's already dead."

"I can nail the guy who sabotaged their jet." I drained my glass.

"Baby, if you ask the Russian Mafia about a hitman, you'll end up with a bullet hole in your pretty head." He took another slug of English beer. "Face it, we've reached the end of the road on this quest."

"Oh yeah? What about Carl Rowan? And who blew up our boat and why?" I waved at the waiter for another round.

"Forgot about that." He drained his mug. "I guess we're not done after all."

A server delivered our steaks, plated with baked potatoes and broccoli. The meat was so tender and flavorful it almost melted in my mouth. I gazed across at Snake as he swallowed his first bite.

His eyes closed momentarily. "This is the best steak I've ever tasted. My stomach's about to have a foodgasm."

"I knew you'd love it. Steaks are their specialty, and they only use aged Angus beef."

I waited until we'd finished most of our meal before I steered the conversation back to the murders. "What if the killer isn't a hitman? Might've been Rowan. There has to be a reason our boat was destroyed."

"Call Hunter and see if his investigator in Freeport has uncovered anything about the attack." He took another pull on his beer.

I called my uncle. "Hi, I'm having lunch with Snake, and we're wondering if you have any news about the boat explosion." I put the phone on SPEAKER.

"The captain was also the owner. He was well-liked on the island, and my investigator couldn't find any evidence that the skipper was the target. There were no witnesses to the incident. Bottom line, we were the targets. Any luck on your end?"

I filled him in on everything we'd learned. "But the mayor is dead, so is Rowan targeting us? Or could it be a hitman hired by the mayor or Rowan?"

Hunter took a moment. "What if the hitman killed the mayor to eliminate a loose end, and now he's trying to eliminate any evidence that points to him sabotaging the jet? If he takes us out in what appears to be an accident, our investigation stops. Problem solved."

"Or Rowan could be targeting us to prevent us from finding evidence of him sabotaging the jet. We'd better pay close attention to the condition of our vehicles and your airplanes," I said. "And add extra security measures to your hangar."

"Be careful, sweetheart. I'm glad Snake has your back. Call me later."

I looked at Snake. "Any ideas how we catch a hitman?"

"Anticipate his next move and outmaneuver him."

I checked the time. "We need to get going. Our appointment with my CEO is in twenty minutes."

We valet parked at Jorgensen Industries' waterfront building on Flagler Drive bordering the Intracoastal Waterway. Mauve-colored glass and matching stones covered the structure's exterior. The CEO's office perched twenty-eight stories up on the top floor.

We exited the elevator into an expansive foyer where an executive assistant ushered us into Frasier Collins' office. Floor-to-ceiling windows showcased the waterway and distant ocean. Frasier, a fit man in his late fifties with thick gray hair, stood to greet us.

After friendly introductions, I got right to the point. "We found evidence my parents' jet was sabotaged. I'm looking into who might've had a motive to murder them."

Once Frasier recovered from the shock, he said, "Carl Rowan is a definite possibility."

"We're already looking into him," Snake said. "Anyone else?"

"Werner Dietrich is a ruthless German billionaire who tried to buy Jorgensen Industries, but it's a privately held company, and they refused to sell."

"Why did Dietrich want my family's company?"

"His usual method is to acquire a company, break it up, and sell the assets. He's known for getting his way. Maybe he thought with your parents gone, you'd sell it. Has he contacted you, Jett?"

"No, but I wasn't easy to reach on a military base in Afghanistan the past two years. I haven't been home long. Has he asked you about the company's new owner, namely me?"

"He contacted me a week after the plane crash. I explained the company would be tied up in probate a while and then it would pass to you."

I stood. "Let me know if you hear from Dietrich. Good seeing you, Frasier."

On the way back to Banyan Isle, I nudged Snake. "A billionaire could easily hire a hitman, and Dietrich sounds like the kind of guy who would do that."

# TWENTY-FOUR

We pulled into my garage at 5:10 p.m., no closer to a solution on catching the killer. I closed the big electric door and slid out of the car.

Snake scanned the garage interior. "You could fit ten vehicles in here, easy, and the floor looks clean enough to eat on."

"A century ago, this building housed horses and their carriages."

He stared at a corner. "What's under the blue tarp?"

"Oh, nothing, just my motorcycle." I reached into my handbag for my house keys.

He sauntered over to the bike and lifted the tarp. "Whoa, woman, this is a Harley-Davidson Softail Heritage Classic. I love the teal color." He grinned at me. "I didn't know you were a Harley babe." He held the tarp. "You know, we could be nice and comfy with this cover on the floor. You look tense again." He spread the canvas and beckoned me to join him.

"Sex won't solve my problem." *And I'm too emotionally vulnerable right now.* I didn't want to get hurt again, but he'd be hard to resist if he kissed me like he had at the airport.

"It'll solve *my* problem." He reached for me.

"Slow your roll, cowboy." I pressed my hands against his hard chest.

"Relax, Jett." He slid his arms around me and kissed me nice and slow.

A loud click preceded the side door opening. Sophia and the puppies peeked in. "You two okay in here? I got worried when you didn't come out right away."

The dogs rocketed to us.

"Snake wanted to look at my Harley." My heart pounded as I stumbled over to the tarp and tossed it over my bike.

"Uh huh, that's not all he wanted to look at." Sophia crossed her arms and glared at Snake.

"Give me a break. I can't help it if I'm a hot-blooded Texan." He put his arm around Sophia. "Deep down, I know you understand. How about giving us some quality alone time?"

"Sorry." She leaned into him, enjoying the moment. "My obligation is to Jett. Besides, you're flying home tomorrow. There'll be no loving and leaving in this house. She's been through enough already."

He gave her a gentle hug. "You drive a hard bargain, woman. Got any homemade goodies to ease the pain?"

"Just made a batch of chocolate-chip cannoli. Come with me, sweet cheeks."

I trailed behind on the stone walkway as they strolled to the house. The puppies gave me plenty of kisses, especially after I retrieved the doggie bag from the car. They were mesmerized by the scent of juicy steak and bones.

## GWEN

Gwen started her day interviewing more of Denton Donley's alleged rape victims. First on the list was Josie Perkins. She lived with her parents in a modest home in one of the old West Palm Beach neighborhoods south of the downtown area.

Gwen flashed her shield. "Thank you for seeing me. I'm Detective Gwen Stuart, here investigating Denton Donley."

Josie and her mother welcomed her inside. Both women were blond and petite with delicate bone structure, pale skin, heart-shaped lips, and large blue eyes. They led her into a twelve-foot-square living room and sat on a cloth-covered couch with a cheerful tropical floral pattern.

Gwen sat across from them in a matching armchair. "I'd appreciate anything you can tell me about Denton Donley."

Josie stared at her hands. "He was a player, but he acted all charming and polite so I'd trust him. I met him at an upscale club on Clematis Street. Said he was looking for the right woman so he could settle down and start a family." She paused, collecting herself. "He must've slipped something into my drink. Everything went black, and later, I woke up naked and bleeding."

"And where were you when you woke?" Gwen checked the file on her iPad.

"The backseat of my car, parked at a strip mall near the corner of Forest Hill and Congress. He must've taken the keys from my purse and driven me there or had someone else do it. My clothes were draped over me, the doors were locked, and a window was open an inch."

"What time did you wake?"

"It was about seven the next morning. A cop knocked on my window."

Josie's mother broke in, "The cop was horrible. He arrested my daughter for public nudity and solicitation. Treated her like a prostitute. Didn't even care about her injury."

"By the time I got out on bail and went to the hospital, the doctor said it was too late to collect DNA from my attacker. Bleeding had washed away the DNA on the inside if there was any, and I had wiped the blood off my skin, not realizing I was destroying evidence. My father was so angry about the attack."

Josie's mother wrung her hands. "We hired a lawyer and sued the police and Denton Donley."

"Right, I read the file." Gwen checked her iPad. "You lost the police case, and the Donley suit was dropped for lack of evidence. How did that make you feel?"

"I felt devalued and bitter," Josie admitted. "My doctor warned I might not ever have children because of the damage Donley did to me. For a while, I just wanted to die." She wiped away tears.

"And Frank, her father, wanted to kill him." Josie's mother dabbed at tears with a tissue. "We convinced him it wasn't worth ruining his life to kill that scum. The creep got off without so much as a slap on the wrist."

"Well, he's dead now. Please don't be upset by my next question. I have to ask everyone who had any connection to him where they were last Sunday afternoon so I can rule them out."

"Josie and I work at a shelter for homeless women on Sundays, and my husband plays golf all afternoon with his buddies from work. You can check with the public golf course, and I'll give you the names and numbers of Frank's friends and the number for the shelter."

Gwen took down the information and stood. "Thank you for your help, ladies. I'm sorry to dredge up bad memories. At least you know Donley can't hurt anyone else."

Every interview that day was a replay of the previous ones. All the young women were from modest middle-class families, and every rape account followed a similar pattern. So far, all the affected parties had alibis.

Gwen wrapped up the last interview of the day and headed for Banyan Isle. On her drive home, she called Jett.

"Hi, Jett, I'm headed home. Want to get together for dinner?"

"Yes, I have loads to tell you, and I could use your help running interference between Snake and me. That man is way too good at kissing, but he's leaving tomorrow, and I don't want to get hurt again."

"He made a pass?"

"Twice. He's the kind of guy who can melt away all your inhibitions with one steamy kiss. And I've already had one too many. I need help."

"Want me to lure him over to my house?" She chuckled.

"He's supposed to stay here to protect me. Could you spend the night at my place? If he asks, we could say you're sleeping in my room to stop me from sleepwalking again."

"Okay, I'll stop by home and change clothes, and then I'll show up with a little overnight bag and explain I'm there to help."

"Should I invite Mike to dinner so I can update him at the same time I tell you everything we learned today?"

"Good idea, and Mike can be a buffer between you and Snake." Gwen chuckled. "Think you should invite Pierce too?"

"No, he keeps reminding me he wants to take me out as soon as I'm ready to start dating again. I don't want him to think the dinner invitation is a signal for him to go for it. I've got too much to deal with here."

"All right. I'll see you in an hour." Gwen tapped off and pulled into her driveway.

# TWENTY-FIVE

JETT

We gathered in the spacious dining room. Twenty-foot walls covered in teal silk matched the upholstered mahogany chairs. The hand-carved mahogany table seated forty-four and had leaves that could expand it to accommodate an additional twenty diners. Huge crystal chandeliers sparkled above us, reflecting off the highly-polished golden oak floor.

The seating for dinner worked out to my advantage. Gwen and Sophia sat on either side of Snake, and Mike sat beside me across from them, leaving most of the dining table unoccupied. A delicious aroma of cheese and sausage lasagna and fresh-baked garlic bread filled the air. We chose to dine indoors to eliminate any concern there might be a sniper outside on a boat.

A large decanter of Ménage à Trois Silk blended red wine and an ice bucket filled with cold bottles of Budweiser provided everyone with their drink of choice.

"Gwen, have you made any headway on your murder case?" I asked.

"So far, all the suspects I've interviewed have rock-solid alibis, and we still don't know the cause of death."

"Are you talking about Denton Donley?" Mike set down his beer. "I thought he died of natural causes."

"He and Binky Worthington are considered suspicious deaths, but we aren't sure if they were murdered." Gwen sipped her wine and gave Snake a playful nudge. "What did you and Jett find out today?"

He gave her an admiring glance. "Mayor Peabody's boat left the harbor the night Lola Brown was murdered, and he and his wife flew out of Signature's private terminal the next morning at the same time Jett's parents left. It's reasonable to conclude they ran into each other before departure and had a chat. We think Jett's parents must've let it slip they saw the mayor and Lola on his boat the night before."

Sophia grinned. "My theory was correct. Peabody knew your parents would report what they had seen once the story about the murdered girl hit the news and they returned home, so he hired a hitman to kill them and make it look like an accident."

I frowned. "Or it could've been Carl Rowan, who blamed my parents for his prison sentence and divorce."

Snake added, "Or billionaire Werner Dietrich could've hired a hitman to kill Jett's parents because he wanted their company. He doesn't want us poking around for evidence, so he had the same pro blow up our dive boat."

Mike gave me a gentle nudge. "I hate to burst your bubble, but your theory about a hitman taking care of loose ends makes no sense. If he was worried about the mayor feeling guilty and turning him in, he would've killed him two years ago after he was paid for the hit. And if Dietrich hired the hit on your parents, it still wouldn't fit that the hitter is targeting you now because pros don't leave loose ends."

Gwen added, "The mayor began the heavy drinking and

womanizing two years ago, after Jett's parents died. Maybe the hitman didn't consider him a threat until his risky behavior escalated. Poisoning him made a woman seem guilty."

Snake agreed, "No matter who hired him, the assassin wouldn't want divers finding evidence of sabotage, triggering an investigation. That's why he blew up our boat."

Sophia swallowed a bite of lasagna. "Okay, that makes sense. Jett, do you think whoever it is will try to kill you and Hunter again?"

"Maybe, but only if he can make it look like an accident. With us dead, the investigation would end and my company might be available to buyers." I took a drink of wine.

Snake shook his head. "The hitman needn't worry. Proving who sabotaged the airplane will be almost impossible. There's not enough evidence, and the person who hired him might be dead."

Mike cut in, "Are you saying Jett isn't in danger?"

"Probably not, but she should remain vigilant, just in case." Snake gave me a longing look and then switched back to Mike. "I'm flying home tomorrow. I have to return to my team."

"I hope you're right about Jett no longer being in danger," Sophia said. "Maybe he blew up the dive boat to scare her and Hunter away from the crash site."

"That was a drastic move, and he killed the boat captain." Mike turned to me. "Either the mayor ordered the hit, and he may have died because of it, or it was Rowan or Dietrich. You should stop looking for the hitman. Enough people have died. Let it go."

"That's surprising advice coming from a police detective. Don't you want to catch the murderer, Mike?" I refilled my glass and passed the carafe to Gwen.

"Yes, I do, so leave it to the police and stay out of it. I'd hate to see you get killed."

We locked eyes for a moment, and a warm, familiar feeling from long ago washed over me. Did Mike still love me?

I took a soothing sip of wine. "Everything we have so far is circumstantial. If I were sure the mayor ordered the hit on my parents, then I could let this go. If Rowan or Dietrich did it, I don't want him to get away with it. And the hitman might still be trying to kill my uncle and me. I won't feel safe until I know who's responsible and he's behind bars or dead."

"I understand how Jett feels, wanting justice for her murdered parents. I feel the same way about my parents' killer." Gwen bit her lip. "I'll never have peace until he's caught."

Mike agreed, "And I feel the same way about my brother."

Sophia peered across the table at me. "What's left to do?"

I smiled at my friends. "I still have people to interview. One of them might shed new light on the case."

"Jett, I'd rather you didn't interfere with my investigation. The mayor's murder could be connected to your parents' crash." Mike gave me a stern look. "I don't want you talking to any of my suspects."

"Relax, Mike, I won't mess up your big case. You don't even know one of them."

Gwen interrupted, "Who are you talking about, Jett?"

"Someone who might be able to confirm if the mayor is guilty. If it wasn't him, I'd hate for the real killer to go free. Also, I'd like to know if Rowan and Dietrich have alibis. There has to be somebody who might know a detail that will help me figure this out."

Snake smiled at me. "Now you're talking like a real detective. Just be careful out there."

Gwen leaned into Snake. "Think we should use Jett's telescope and check the backyard and ocean for snipers?"

They momentarily locked eyes.

"Good idea. Excuse us."

Sophia caught me smiling. After they walked away, she said, "I know what you and Gwen are up to, and I think it's a good idea."

"What?" Mike asked.

"Nothing. Gwen's just helping me be a good hostess. Help us clear the table, and if Snake and Gwen give us the all clear, we can enjoy dessert on the terrace." I stood and began stacking plates.

Five minutes later, we checked in with Snake and Gwen.

"No snipers in sight." Snake stepped away from the telescope.

"Good, then we can have Sophia's cannoli out here." I went inside and helped her load the serving cart.

When we arrived with the dessert, Gwen and Snake stood near the back steps.

Gwen announced, "Snake had some cannoli earlier, and I want to show him our lovely beach. We'll be back in a little while."


GWEN

Gwen took Snake's arm, and they strolled across the back lawn toward the ocean. When they opened the beach gate, she used a palm frond to hold it open so they wouldn't need a key to return. She led him on the sand south to her entrance gate next door and pulled a key out of her jeans pocket.

"My backyard has an unusual gazebo I think you'd enjoy seeing." She led him down a path to a raised circular structure made of stone with glass windows and a glass door. "The glass is hurricane-proof up to 200-mph winds." She opened the door, stepped inside, and opened the windows for a cool, cross breeze.

The center was bare, and cushions covered the perimeter seating all the way around. Warm salt air and the soothing sounds of waves breaking on shore filled the gazebo.

Snake sat beside Gwen and took her hands. "This is nice. Now tell me what's really going on. It's obvious Jett put you up to this to get rid of me. Is she tryin' to get back with Mike?"

She gazed into his eyes. "No, she's trying to avoid more

emotional pain. The truth is she finds you very attractive, but you're leaving tomorrow, and she doesn't want to get hurt. She hasn't recovered from the last guy."

"Are you takin' her place or just distracting me?" He ran his hand through her long hair.

"Um, I kind of have the hots for a detective where I work. He hasn't met me yet, but—"

He drew her into his arms and kissed her so passionately she melted into him.

When he came up for air, she was left breathless.

He leaned in for another kiss, and she scooted backward.

"Sorry, Snake. You're really hot, but I don't do one-night stands." She stood. "We should get back."

By the time they returned to Jett's house, Mike had left, and Sophia and Jett had retired to their bedrooms.

Gwen snatched up her little overnight bag. "I'm sleeping in Jett's bed tonight so I can make sure she doesn't sleepwalk again."

He laughed. "If I tried that, Sophia would shoot me."

"She's very protective of Jett."

"You don't have to tell me. She almost shot me my first night here." He took her bag. "Let me carry that, darlin'." He put his arm around her shoulder. "You know, I've got plenty of room in my bed, and it's going to be awfully crowded sharing Jett's bed with her and the puppies."

# TWENTY-SIX

JETT

The next morning, Chef Hugo stopped by to deliver a delicious breakfast of eggs Benedict and cut fruit to the terrace table for Gwen, Snake, Sophia, and me. He was eager to meet Sophia.

When I introduced them, she said, "Ah, it's the French teddy bear I've heard so much about. Give me a hug, big guy." She reached for him and received a warm hug.

It didn't hurt that she referred to the short Frenchman as a "big guy." Of course, everyone seemed big to her at four-foot-ten.

After the hug, he kissed her hand. "My dear, I'm told your cannoli is second to none. You must show me how you make them."

"Tell you what, handsome, I'll share my cannoli secrets if you'll teach me how to make a good Béarnaise sauce."

"It will be my pleasure." He bowed. "Enjoy your breakfasts."

Snake and Gwen smiled as they dived into their meals. The puppies tried to get a good sniff of what was on the table. Sophia gave them a dark look, and they immediately dropped to prone positions on either side of her. Good dog nanny.

Snake gazed across the table at me. "What's your next move in the investigation?"

I checked my watch. "After I drop you off at the company hangar, I'll swing by Signature Aviation and see if Mayor Peabody's pilot is available for a chat. I'd like to confirm if he saw the mayor speaking to my parents the morning they flew to Freeport."

"Why don't you call his cell?" Gwen said. "I know you have a lot to do today. I can drive Snake to the airport." She smiled at him.

"Good idea. I need to swing by Formally Yours on Main Street and pick up my gown for the ball tonight. This will give me extra time in case they need to make alterations." I smiled at them. "Snake, I can't thank you enough for helping me out with the dive and everything. Give my best to your team."

He grinned. "Happy to help. Keep me in the loop. I want to know how this turns out."

Gwen stood. "I'll clear the table while you and Sophia say goodbye to Snake." She stacked the plates and headed for the kitchen.

Sophia reached for him. "Give me some sugar, ya big galoot."

He lifted her off her feet and gave her a soft kiss on the cheek and a warm hug. "You're one unforgettable woman, Sophia. Any chance you might send me a box of your cannoli every once in a while?"

"Anything for you, handsome. Leave your address with Jett." Sophia put the cups on a tray and carried them inside.

He walked around the table and pulled me into his arms in a bear hug. Leaning down, he kissed my neck and said, "Any time you need me, just call."

"Be careful out there, Snake." I gave him one last kiss goodbye. He pulled me in and made it a memorable one. Zowie, that man knew how to kiss.

———

After picking up my gown, which fit perfectly, I drove home and tried calling the mayor's pilot.

No answer. I left a message asking him to call me.

I contacted a friend at the NSA. He gave me the cell number and address for Carl Rowan in Miami and told me Rowan was an accountant for a Columbian drug lord. I had plenty of time before the charity ball to drive to Miami and back. Maybe a face-to-face meeting would reveal his guilt or innocence. I clipped my pistol inside the waistband on my shorts at the small of my back. The shorts and pink T-shirt made me look harmless.

Sophia met me in the great hall. "Going somewhere?"

"Miami. I want to visit Carl Rowan and find out if he killed my parents."

"Good idea, but you need backup." She checked the pistol in the thigh holster under her dress. "I'm going with you."

"What about Pratt and Whitney? Who'll look after them?"

"I have a friend at Silver Lakes, Ruby Glick. She loves dogs, and her condo is only ten minutes away. Want me to call her?"

"Okay, see if she'll babysit the dogs here for four hours."

Ruby agreed, and we picked her up outside her one-story end unit. She was maybe two inches taller than Sophia and much rounder, wearing a purple polyester pantsuit and pink sneakers.

Her eyes widened when we pulled in front of Valhalla. "Ooh, you live in a castle. I've always wanted to live in a castle. Are there knights in armor inside?"

Sophia rolled her eyes. "No, silly, this is a Viking castle. We've got winged Valkyries."

The two statues in the foyer verified Sophia's comment. We had only been gone twenty minutes, and it appeared the puppies had waited for us by the front door. Their tails wagging, they slobbered all over us when we came in.

"Hello, there," Ruby said, bending down and fussing over the dogs.

We spent a few minutes showing her around the main rooms on the first floor and pointing out the water and food dishes for the puppies in the kitchen.

"Help yourself to anything in the refrigerator. We'll be back in about four hours." I double-checked my purse for my cell phone with the info on Rowan.

As we drove away in the Bentley, Sophia said, "I've got two extra magazines in my purse in case we run out of bullets."

"We're not going to a shootout. I just want to talk to him."

"It never hurts to be prepared. Rowan works for a drug dealer. Could be trouble."

"He's just the accountant, but you're right, it can't hurt to be ready for anything."

An hour and a half later, we found his house in an old neighborhood with modest homes built in the 1960s. Canals behind the houses led to the Intracoastal Waterway, which had outlets to the ocean.

I knocked on his front door. A man in his late forties opened the door. He was five-feet-nine with a pot belly, a tanned, half-bald head, and wild hazel eyes. Barefoot, he wore a Miami Dolphins T-shirt and khaki shorts.

His jaw dropped. "Jett? Jett Jorgensen? I recognize you from pictures on your dad's desk at Jorgensen Industries."

"Hello, Carl. This is my friend, Sophia DeLuca. May we come in?"

He stepped back and waved us in. "Have a seat on the couch. Like something to drink?"

"No, thanks, we just want to talk with you for a few minutes." I waited until he sat across from us beside a small table with two drawers and a lamp on top. "I'll get right to the point. I recently discovered someone sabotaged my parents' jet. Did you do it?"

He sat up straighter, his eyes wide. "Their plane crash wasn't just a happy accident?"

"There was nothing happy about their deaths." Sophia glared at him.

"I hated them for sending me to prison. My wife divorced me and took everything. Truth is I was disappointed they were killed in the crash. It ruined my plan for revenge."

"What did you have in mind?" I asked, struggling to maintain my composure.

"A buddy in the joint arranged my accounting job with the Colombians. Once I earned their trust, I asked for help arranging a hit on your family." He frowned. "Everything was working out great. The Columbians aren't very smart. I've skimmed almost a half mil, and they have no clue." He chuckled. "They agreed to let me use their hitman, but then your parents' plane crashed, and I felt cheated."

I could barely contain my contempt for this loser. "It wasn't my parents' fault you ran up a huge gambling debt and stole money from the company. That's on you."

"If they hadn't pressed charges, I wouldn't have lost everything and spent two years in prison." He reached inside the top drawer, pulled out a SIG pistol, and pointed it at us. "But now I have their daughter, and I can get my revenge on a Jorgensen. Get up. You and granny. Take your purses. We're going for a boat ride." He waved toward the back door, his eyes glinting with a hint of crazy.

As he walked behind us, I hoped he wouldn't notice the slight bulge mid-waist on my shorts.

He did.

"Stop. Don't move or I'll shoot you right here." He reached under the back of my shirt and pulled out my Glock. "You won't need this where you're going." He shoved it in the front of his pants beneath his beer gut.

"And exactly where are we going?" Sophia asked over her shoulder.

"The ocean, in the middle of the Gulf Stream. I'll make you real bloody for the sharks." He shoved me through the sliding-glass door behind Sophia.

She must've spotted a neighbor across the canal. She waved her arms and yelled, "Help! We're being kidnapped! Call the cops!" Then she dropped and rolled onto the grass.

Carl held his weapon close to his side and yelled, "Never mind! She's joking!" He grabbed me and held me against him. "Be quiet and get in the boat."

I elbowed him, stomped his foot, dropped, and rolled onto the dock.

He raised his weapon and pointed it at me.

Sophia yelled, "Freeze, dirtbag! Hands in the air!"

He turned and fired at her.

He missed.

She didn't.

Carl jerked, dropped his gun, and fell backward. He landed beside me with a hole in his forehead.

The gory image churned my stomach. "You okay, Sophia?"

"I'm good. Better call the cops."

"Sorry I got you into this mess." I pulled out my cell and called 9-1-1. After explaining what happened and that they should send police, two thugs stepped out onto the patio. They appeared to be South American.

One said, "Why you shoot Carl?"

"He tried to kidnap us in his boat." I stood and brushed myself off.

He smirked at Sophia. "*You* too?"

"He planned to kill us and dump us in the ocean, so I blew him away. You got a problem with that?"

"He stole money. Boss wanted him dead. You did our job."

"You'd better go." I held up my cell. "Cops will be here any minute. I called."

They gave us each a nod, turned, and left as sirens blared in the distance.

I called to Sophia. "Thanks for saving me. Again. Better sit where you are with your gun on the ground and your hands on your head." I did the same.

"Don't worry, I know the drill." She smoothed her dress and put her hands on her head.

Moments later, Miami police officers charged onto the scene, shouted orders, and collected the weapons.

I explained Carl tried to kill us, that we were licensed to carry weapons, and I was an officer in the U.S. Navy. "This is Detective Mike Miller's cell number. He'll vouch for us."

The detective stood, hands hooked on his belt, looking us over. "Who made the kill shot?"

Sophia waved her hand. "I did."

He scrutinized her and then me. "Let me get this straight. You're an officer in the Navy, but Rowan disarmed you, and the senior citizen over there shot him?"

My face reddened. "He got the jump on me, and he didn't know she was armed."

After giving me a hard time, Mike vouched for us. We gave the cops detailed statements, leaving out the part about the Colombian thugs. The detective allowed us to go home, but he kept our weapons for the formal investigation.

I glanced over at Sophia as we drove out of the neighborhood. "This was a bad idea. I never expected to get you into a gun battle with Carl. I'm so sorry."

"No worries. What time do you need to be ready for the ball?"

I checked my watch. "I'll barely make it. Will you drive Ruby home?"

"Of course. I can't wait to tell my friends at Silver Lakes about the shootout."

When we arrived, Ruby handed me a business card. "A nice man from Germany stopped by to see you. He'd like you to call him right away."

I read the card. Werner Dietrich of Dietrich Enterprises based in Hamburg, Germany. The billionaire who wanted Jorgensen Industries. I tapped his number on my cell.

"Hello, Mr. Dietrich, this is Jett Jorgensen. I understand you'd like to speak with me."

A male voice with a German accent said, "Ah, Jett, you have an impressive home. Sorry I missed you. I'd like to meet and discuss my purchase of Jorgensen Industries. Are you free tonight?"

"I'm attending a charity ball this evening, but there's no point in us meeting. I have no interest in selling my company and wouldn't want to waste your time."

"No hurry. Think it over. By the way, your puppies are beautiful dogs. You should watch them closely. Animals will eat anything, and there are so many poisonous things everywhere. It would be a shame if they died, especially so young." He chuckled. "I'll be in touch."

I sucked in my breath and tried not to panic. "Ruby, was that German guy ever out of your sight while he was here?"

"No, he never left the foyer. He handed me his card, asked that you call him, petted the dogs, and left. Why?"

"He made a vague threat about poisoning the puppies. I just wanted to make sure he didn't have an opportunity to poison their food or water." I reached down and ruffled their fur.

"No, but maybe you should check the front yard," Ruby said. "He could've tossed some poisoned food on the grass before he drove away."

We left the dogs inside and searched the front yard. I paid close attention to grassy areas near the driveway where he could've tossed something from his car.

No poison.

# TWENTY-SEVEN

GWEN

G wen watched Snake saunter into the private terminal before she drove away. He lived in Virginia Beach, and she had no illusions about a romance with him. And that was fine, because she had her sights set on Palm Beach Detective Clint Reynolds. A few high-ranking police officers always attended Palm Beach events. She hoped she'd see him at the charity ball. *He'd look fabulous in a tux.*

The day sped by, and soon it was time to dress for the ball. She pulled on a floor-length silk gown that clung to her curves. Sleeveless with a plunging neckline, it was more daring than what she would normally wear, but Snake had given her the confidence to take a chance and maybe snare Clint. Matching stilettos and her mother's diamond teardrop earrings and tennis bracelet completed the ensemble. She checked her reflection in the three-way dressing-room mirror.

Hugo and Leo greeted her downstairs in the foyer. They wore

matching black tuxedoes in a traditional style that made Hugo appear taller and slimmer. Leo looked good in anything.

"Gentlemen, you're quite dashing this evening. Would you like to ride with Jett and me to the ball?"

"Gwen, darling, you look divine in that emerald gown." Leo gave her a light kiss on the cheek. "We'll take our own vehicle in case you get lucky or have to dash off on police business."

Hugo tugged at his bowtie. "That gown matches your eyes." He cocked his head. "There's no room for your Glock in the tiny purse."

She patted her leg. "Thigh holster, inner thigh, left leg."

Hugo crossed his arms. "But how will you reach it?"

She turned sideways and moved her right leg to demonstrate the slit that rose almost to her hip. "I'll reach in through here and pull out my weapon. No problem." She drew her pistol and then holstered it and straightened her gown.

Leo grinned. "That's our girl, ready for anything. We'll see you at the ball."

They opened the door just as Jett pulled up.

Hugo held the door. "Madam, your chariot awaits."

Gwen waved and slid into the front passenger seat. "Hi, Jett, ready for a fun night?"

"Oh yes, especially after the day I've had." She filled her in on the encounter with Carl Rowan and then gazed down at her ruby gown. "What do you think? Is the red too much?"

"Good thing Sophia was with you today. And that red is more like a claret. The color looks perfect with your black hair and golden skin."

"Thanks, Gwen. I'll check into Dietrich tomorrow, but tonight we'll be the belles of the ball, especially with you in that sleek silk gown."

Fifteen minutes later, Gwen smoothed her dress and waited while Jett gave her keys to the valet. They headed for the grand ballroom at

The Breakers. Inside, an ornate coffered ceiling held enormous crystal chandeliers, and tall windows with red velvet curtains lined the long, ocean-side wall.

It was the season's most popular charity ball. They entered the vast ballroom, and an usher seated them next to Liz and Clive at the guests-of-honor table beside the dance floor, facing the thirty-piece orchestra.

"Thanks for inviting us. We love seeing all the beautiful gowns." Gwen kissed Liz's cheek.

Liz squeezed her hand. "Gwen, darling, we wouldn't dream of coming without you. You look lovely in green silk, and Jett looks fetching in that wine-colored satin."

Clive raised a glass of Ruinart Blanc de Blancs Champagne. "To Liz, Gwen, and Jett, the three most beautiful women in the room." He turned to his niece. "How is your case progressing?"

"It isn't. Not a good way to launch my detective career." She scanned the room. "Have you seen my designer friend, Cam Altman?"

Liz smiled. "Yes, dear, he's floating around the room, fussing over all his clients."

"Isn't that Marjorie Wentworth Peabody, the mayor's widow, seated at the next table?" Jett stood. "Please excuse us. Gwen and I need to have a word with her."

Gwen stood. "Right. We have questions she might be able to answer." She led Jett to the grand dame of Banyan Isle and made the introductions.

Marjorie stood and offered her hand. "Jett, dear, I owe you an apology for my late husband's appalling behavior in your home."

"What happened has been far worse for you. How are you holding up?"

She adjusted her full-skirted royal-blue renaissance gown. "The worst thing is the police suspect me for the murder. Can you imagine?

A far worse punishment would have been to divorce him and cut off his lavish lifestyle. Our prenup was airtight."

"We were hoping you could help us with something that happened two years ago on the night before you flew to New York to see *Cats* on Broadway," Gwen said.

"Oh, my, that was a long time ago." Marjorie smoothed her perfectly coiffed, golden-blond hair. "What do you wish to know?"

"Did Phil take your speedboat out that night?" Gwen asked.

Marjorie's face paled. "You think he killed that pregnant girl, Lola Brown? I worried he might have done that, but he assured me he was alone on the boat, destressing from a trying day."

"One more thing," Jett interjected. "Did you or Phil happen to speak to my parents at the airport the next morning?"

"I didn't because I stopped in the ladies' room, but I saw Phil talking to them when I came out. They left before I had a chance to say hello."

"Thank you, Marjorie, you've been a big help." Gwen led Jett back to her relatives' table.

Jett leaned close to her. "It sure seems like the mayor killed Lola and maybe my parents, but what if I'm missing something?"

"You'll figure it out. Oh, look, here comes Pierce looking debonair in his tuxedo." Gwen nodded in his direction. "You should dance with him."

Moments later, Pierce said, "Good evening, ladies. You look smashing in those gowns."

"And you look hot in a tux." Gwen kissed his cheek. "Where are you sitting?"

"My parents roped me into sharing a table with them and the Berendsens, who just happen to have their unmarried daughter with them." He shook his head. "I wish they would stop playing matchmaker."

"Maybe you should deter them by dancing with Jett." Gwen nudged her forward.

Pierce offered his hand. "May I have this dance?"

Jett smiled and followed him onto the dance floor. Meanwhile, Gwen peered around, hoping to spot Clint. She knew he usually attended the Palm Beach charity functions, but it was difficult to find him among three hundred people. Weaving through the crowd, she greeted many of her parents' friends.

An hour later, Gwen refreshed her lipstick in the ladies-room mirror before returning to the table. Her relatives had disappeared, no doubt circulating among the many guests. They were quite the social butterflies. She scanned the room and spotted Cam Altman gliding toward her, dressed like eighteenth-century royalty.

"OMG, Gwen, your aunt and uncle are divine! I'd love to get my hands on that extraordinary antique brooch and matching ring the duchess is wearing. I've never seen anything like them—gold and crystal with rubies and sapphires."

"Aunt Liz wears them everywhere." She hugged him. "You look striking in that period ensemble, Cam. What's new in the fashion world?"

"Oh, you know, the other designers kiss my face and stab my back—business as usual. My antique-style jewelry and renaissance gowns are all the rage." He pointed at a woman in a satin-and-lace cream gown. "That's one of my creations. Isn't it fab?"

"It's lovely. Did you design the matching pearl-and-diamond necklace and earrings?"

"I design all the jewelry for my unique gowns. My clients love dressing like Old-World royalty." He touched his finger to his lips as he gave her the onceover. "I could make you look like a princess in a rose gown with a tiara made of diamonds-and-rubies with matching earrings. The corset bodice would accentuate your robust cleavage and help you snare a rich husband." He nudged her. "We should do something soon, girlfriend. At twenty-eight, you're rapidly approaching old-maid territory."

"Thanks, Cam, but I don't want to blow my trust fund on diamonds and rubies. My new job is my top priority. I'll focus on catching a husband after I collar some major criminals."

"Oh, Gwennie, I know who you're hunting. He's long gone, dear. Forget him and enjoy life. Your parents would want you to move on."

"And let him destroy more families? I'll get him. You'll see. But first I have to catch the person who killed Denton Donley and Binky Worthington. I don't want to fail on my first case."

Cam shook his head and scanned the room. "Here comes the duchess. I'll have another chance to gush over her jewelry."

Liz beamed and clasped his left arm. "Cam, darling, you simply must design a gown for Gwen. Your creations are superb."

"We were just discussing that very thing. Unfortunately, your niece is more interested in catching criminals than a husband." He focused on her brooch. "Your jewelry fascinates me. May I remove your brooch for a closer look?"

Liz placed her hand over the large antique pin. "Sorry, darling, Lloyds of London has strict rules. It must remain on my person or locked in my safe if I wish to keep my insurance. This piece is a centuries-old heirloom."

Cam peered over Gwen's shoulder. "Hottie alert. Check out Mr. Tall, Dark, and Dashing behind you."

"That's Clint Reynolds," Liz said as Gwen turned. "He's a detective with the Palm Beach Police. I met him earlier this evening. Would you like an introduction?"

"Yes, indeed." Cam grabbed Gwen's hand. "Come along, Queen Guinevere, and meet your Sir Lancelot."

"Geez, Cam, dial it down a few clicks. You're salivating." She pulled her hand free. "He's probably here with a date."

Liz turned to her. "I checked. He's solo."

Cam grinned at Liz. "Well done. I love a woman with an eye for details." He shifted his glance to Gwen. "FYI, I can have your dress ready in time for a June wedding."

She rolled her eyes, but inside, her heart was pounding. "Let's get this farce over."

Just then, the object of Gwen's desire smiled at Liz.

She stepped forward. "Clint, darling, I want to introduce my niece and her friend." She half-turned to Gwen. "Detective Gwen Stuart, meet Detective Clint Reynolds."

Gwen extended her hand and gazed into his intense eyes. "Pleased to meet you. I've been meaning to catch you at the police station."

He lifted her hand to his lips, his eyes piercing her like twin laser beams. "The pleasure is mine. I heard you were promoted recently. Sorry I haven't had a chance to connect with you at work."

Cam cleared his throat and looked expectantly at Liz.

"Clint, I'd like you to meet Cam Altman. He's with the fashion police."

The men shook hands as Cam said, "I'd arrest you for stealing James Bond's fabulous tux, but you look better in it than he did."

"Thank you, I—" Clint pulled out his vibrating cell phone and read the text. "Excuse me, duty calls. It was a pleasure to meet you both." He smiled and strode to the exit.

Cam smirked at Gwen. "That smile was for you, girlfriend. I'm thinking satin and antique lace with lots of pearls for your wedding gown."

Her gut told her his call was connected to her case. "I'm going after him."

"You go, girl."

She rushed outside and spotted him heading for the oceanfront walkway that ran along the seawall behind the hotel. He followed the brick path north sixty feet and stopped at a bench where a man sat slumped against the seatback, a whisky and a cigar beside him. Two uniformed officers were taping off the area.

She caught up with Clint. "Check his neck for a tiny puncture wound."

He spun around, clutching his electronic tablet. "Excuse me? You've been a detective for maybe five minutes, and you're telling *me* what to do? This is my case. Go back to the ball." He turned away.

"Is he a wealthy man who escaped prosecution and appears to have died of natural causes?"

He hesitated before facing her again. "What if he is?"

"I'm working the Denton Donley/Binky Worthington cases— wealthy alleged criminals with no obvious causes of death. Both men had pinpricks over their right carotid arteries."

The medical examiner arrived, and Clint said, "Check his neck for a needle puncture near a carotid artery."

The M.E. examined the man's neck with a bright light and a magnifying glass for about a minute. "Yep, found a puncture over his right carotid. Are you thinking poison?"

Clint gazed at Gwen.

She shook her head. "No poison. His condition mirrors two recent murder victims. They both had non-lethal doses of sleep sedatives in their bodies."

The M.E. arched an eyebrow. "Who are you?"

"Detective Gwen Stuart, Palm Beach P.D."

"All right then." The M.E. checked the body. "No injuries or signs of a struggle. Liver temp indicates he died about an hour ago." He bagged the man's cocktail glass and cigar. "I'll check these for toxins. Is this a high-profile case?"

"He's Barrett Branson, a wealthy Palm Beacher and alleged pedophile. He escaped prosecution several times by buying off the parents. Somebody did the community a big favor here." He turned to her. "Eh, Gwen? Sorry about earlier. Looks like our cases are connected. Let's meet after the autopsy and compare notes."

She stared into his handsome face for a long moment, giving him time to regret his earlier snap judgment of her, then pulled her personal card from her purse. "Apology accepted. Call my cell when you're ready."

Gwen walked back to the ball feeling superior for the first time since she'd made detective. She told Jett all about it on the way home. Maybe she'd solve the case and impress Clint.

# TWENTY-EIGHT

Sophia and I enjoyed breakfast on the terrace. A gentle ocean breeze carried the scent of the sea as we basked in the early-morning sun. The January temperatures were perfect. Cool nights and mid-to-upper 70s during the days.

"Find out anything new last night?" Sophia poured coffee into my cup.

"The mayor's wife confirmed he took the boat out the night before my parents left and that he talked to them at the airport. She was concerned he might've murdered Lola Brown."

"What's your problem then? He was our prime suspect, and it looks like we were right about him." Sophia poured herself another cup of green tea and stirred in a dollop of honey.

"If someone hadn't blown up the dive boat, I'd consider this case closed." I stared out at the ocean. "I have this nagging feeling there's another killer lurking in the shadows."

"Right, the hitman the mayor hired." Sophia patted my hand.

"He's probably long gone by now."

"What if there never was a hitman?" Without thinking about it, I handed each dog a piece of bacon. "What if it wasn't the mayor on the boat with Lola, and someone else killed her and my parents?"

Sophia set down her teacup. "Everything points to the mayor, but if it was someone else, then he'd want you to die in an accident, and if that didn't put a stop to the investigation, he'd arrange for Hunter to die too. Or… maybe the mayor killed Lola, but Werner Dietrich hired the hitman who killed your parents."

The dogs' ears perked up. One quick bark from them preceded the doorbell booming.

Sophia laughed. "No wonder all your friends knock instead."

"Dad bought that doorbell as a tribute to his great-grandfather." I jumped up. "I'll get the door." The puppies followed me.

The dogs started wagging their tails before I peeked out and spotted my uncle. I opened the door and hugged him. "Hey, I'm glad you're here. We have a lot to discuss."

He leaned down and ruffled the fur on Pratt and Whitney. "Sorry about the doorbell. You didn't hear me knock. I have the gate code and a door key, but I'll never just let myself in. Wouldn't want Sophia mistaking me for an intruder. I decided to swing by and check on you now that Snake's gone." He whispered, "Did you two hook up?"

"No, I didn't want to get involved with someone I'd hardly ever see. Snake understood."

"Got any coffee brewed?"

I took his arm and walked with him through the foyer and great hall. "We have some on the terrace. Have you had breakfast?"

"Much earlier." He opened the door for me. "Coffee will be fine."

Sophia grinned. "Oh, joy, my favorite man has arrived." She reached for him. "Give an old lady some sugar."

Hunter scooped her up and planted a soft kiss on her lips. "Now I won't need sugar in my coffee." He set her down.

She grinned at me. "Any chance he could move in with us?"

"I wish, but we'd put a crimp in his bachelor lifestyle." I poured him a cup of coffee and filled him in on everything I knew.

"Sounds like you might've solved the case." He took a sip. "Better make sure the hitman is gone."

I expressed my suspicion about Dietrich hiring the hitman.

He took my hand. "Maybe it's time to let go. If there is a hitman, it would be almost impossible to catch him anyway."

"That's why I think maybe there wasn't one." I gazed from him to Sophia. "Think about it. Why draw attention to his existence by blowing up our dive boat? If he's a pro, there wouldn't be any evidence pointing to him personally. Hence, no reason to come after us, unless Dietrich wants me dead so he can buy my company."

Sophia agreed, "She has a point."

"But then Dietrich would have to deal with me as your heir, and I won't sell either." He turned to me. "And the mayor's wife told you Peabody took the boat out the night Lola disappeared and that he talked to your parents the next morning." He poured another cup. "What am I missing?"

"Yes, he told her that, but she didn't see him do it, and he's lied before. And maybe the real killer also talked to my parents the next morning. I should've asked Marjorie if anyone was with the mayor when he spoke to them. Peabody could be innocent of all the murders, or he might've had an accomplice. Or Dietrich had my parents killed. Ugh!"

"Forget about Dietrich for a minute. Are you speculating that a close friend of the mayor's killed him and your parents?" Sophia asked.

"It's possible, especially if the mayor knew his friend borrowed his boat to take Lola on a date." I tried to imagine the scenario.

Hunter shook his head. "If you're right, why did his friend wait two years to kill him?"

"I don't know, but the first step is to find out if someone borrowed the boat and also talked to my parents at the airport. Once I have his name, I can figure out the rest."

"How do you intend to get his name?" he asked.

"I'll talk to Marjorie again and also check with her pilot to see if he saw anyone else talking to my parents that morning."

"Is there anything I can do to help?" He patted my hand.

"Come with me to the pet shop. I'd like to get two or three huge bags of dog food and fill the dry-food hamper without throwing out my back. The puppies are eating like bears who just came out of hibernation."

"As I recall, your dad bought the Bentley a month before the plane crash. Is that right?"

"Yes, why do you ask?"

"Mind if I drive it to the pet shop? A friend asked me about the newer sedans. He's thinking of buying a used one and wanted my opinion."

"No problem. The trunk is huge. Plenty of room for forty-pound bags of dog food. Want to go now?" I stood.

"Right after we help Sophia clear the table." He stacked plates and grabbed the coffee pot.

Sophia smiled. "Could he be any more perfect?"

We deposited the dishes in the kitchen and headed for the garage. I handed him the keys.

After a quick drive to The Pampered Pet, we headed home with a trunk full of dry dog food. We had just turned onto Ocean Drive when a white toy poodle ran into the street. Hunter hit the brakes and stopped short of her. He switched on the emergency flashers.

"Help me catch her." I jumped out and eased around the passenger side while he came around his side.

There wasn't any traffic as the chubby little dog turned and trotted down the middle of the street. We ran after her. A hundred feet from the car, an explosion slammed us forward onto the pavement. We landed on our forearms and knees inches from the stunned dog.

Hunter grabbed the poodle, turned, and sat on the road. "Someone blew up your Bentley. Still think there isn't a hitman?"

Flaming car parts and thousands of singed kibble pellets covered the street in every direction. Flames engulfed the remainder of the vehicle, and searing heat radiated outward as sirens approached.

He tapped my shoulder. "You okay? We'd better get off the street."

My body trembled every bit as much as the poodle he held in his arms.

He guided me to a bench on the sidewalk under a giant banyan tree. Branches over the car were burning. My hands and forearms were scraped and bleeding. So were my knees. Hunter had worn jeans, but blood seeped through over the knee areas. His hands and arms were scraped like mine.

The little poodle buried its face in Hunter's arms. He petted it, trying to soothe her. "This dog saved our lives."

I stared at the burning car. "Someone must've planted a bomb while we shopped."

"He probably had a remote detonator with a long range and waited until we drove out of sight to activate it." He turned when an unmarked police car with grill lights flashing screeched to a halt in front of us.

Mike jumped out as a firetruck roared past and stopped in front of the Bentley. "What happened? How bad are you hurt?"

Before we could answer, an EMT truck pulled up and two paramedics ran to us.

"We're bleeding from road rash where our skin scraped the pavement, and my ears are ringing." I held up my arms.

"We jumped out to rescue this dog, and she saved our lives."

Hunter cuddled her.

"That's Mimsy Farnsworth's dog, Muffin," Mike said, checking the collar. "Ever since Mimsy put her on a diet, she's been sneaking away to beg food from tourists. Poor thing is old and forgets how to find her way home."

"We're lucky she picked today to sneak out again, or we'd be dead." I reached over and scratched her ears.

The paramedics checked us over, cleaned and bandaged our wounds, and took our blood pressure, which, of course, was sky-high.

One said, "You should stop by the E.R. and get a thorough checkup."

I nudged Mike. "We've got bigger problems. Somebody tried to blow us up."

The fire chief walked over to us, holding something in his gloved hand. He held it out to show Mike. "I found this on the grass over there." He pointed. "It's the filler tube from the gas tank with what's left of a detonator with a remote-control antenna wedged inside the tube. The blast shot it well past the fire, preserving it."

"Any chance we can get prints off this?" Mike took pictures of it with his cell.

"It's small, but forensics can try. I'll give it to the CSU." The fire chief turned as a white CSU van pulled up. "That was fast. They must've been in the area." He walked to the van.

"Mike, I need to talk to you about this." I glanced at the paramedics. "In private."

The EMTs packed up their gear. "We're done here. Better get tetanus shots and also antibiotics to prevent infections. The hospital E.R. will take care of you." He and his partner headed back to their truck.

Hunter and I told Mike everything we knew and also my new theory that there might not have been a hitman or Dietrich might've hired one.

Mike beckoned us to follow him. "Come on. I'll take you to the hospital."

"But—"

"You're going. Both of you. Get in the car." Mike opened the back door.

Hunter tapped his shoulder. "Better drop Muffin at home first."

"Right. Her owner lives a few doors north." Mike climbed in and started the car.

I turned to Hunter. "That's my second cell phone blown up this week. I should get a quantity discount at the Apple store."

"Not me. This time, mine was in my back pocket." He kissed Muffin's little head. "She's a sweet dog."

"We'd better call Sophia and let her know we're okay."

He handed me his phone.

After I made the call, I tapped Mike's shoulder. "Please let us know if you spot someone on Pampered Pet's security tape planting the bomb. It might've been Werner Dietrich. I think he's staying here in a condo on the beach."

"It had to have happened at the pet shop." Mike peeked at me in his rearview mirror. "You said the Bentley was locked in your garage before you went out."

"That's right." I nudged Hunter as we pulled into Mimsy Farnsworth's driveway. "I'm glad we weren't in your McLaren. I'd hate to see such a beautiful work of art destroyed."

Mike opened the door and took Muffin from Hunter's arms. "Be right back."

———

Before he was halfway to the door, Mimsy rushed out and teetered toward him in stiletto sandals better suited for someone forty years younger. She wore floral yoga pants and a loose, hot-pink silk top with matching lipstick. A rich widow, she worked at looking young and hip.

"Ooh, Muffin, you naughty girl! Mommy was worried sick." She snatched the dog out of Mike's arms. "What am I to do with you?" The little dog licked her nose and wagged its tail.

"Don't be too angry with her." Mike caressed Muffin's fur. "She saved the lives of two people. That loud noise you heard was their car exploding while they were chasing your dog."

"Oh, my goodness, that explains all the sirens." She nuzzled her dog's nose. "Would my little heroine like some ice cream?" The poodle wiggled with delight as Mimsy said, "Mike, thank you for returning my precious princess." She turned and took her dog inside.

———

Mike hopped back in and drove us to the hospital against our wishes. "You could have been concussed by the explosion. Better to be cleared by a doctor now than pass out later and die. And remain vigilant in case the killer shows up at the hospital."

"That reminds me." I reached behind me and checked the holster hidden under my shirt in the small of my back, attached to the waistband of my shorts. A Glock 26 from my gun vault was still there. "Uh, Mike, I've got a handgun hidden in my shorts. Can I keep it with me?"

Before he answered, Hunter said, "I've got mine too."

Mike gazed back at us. "You're both licensed, right?"

"Yes, but firearms aren't allowed in hospitals unless they're carried by police." I peered at his face reflected in the rearview.

"I'll tell the doctors you're working undercover and to ignore your weapons." He gave us a hard look. "You might need them, but try not to shoot up the hospital."

# TWENTY-NINE

GWEN

Gwen went to her cubicle at the Palm Beach Police early on the morning after the charity ball to get a jump on the triple murders and maybe find something to impress Clint. She switched on her computer and read the files on Barrett Branson's numerous pedophile arrests. Each case was dropped shortly after the parents of the alleged victims became millionaires. The payoffs were obvious, but the district attorney couldn't prosecute Branson without the victims' cooperation.

The injustice churned her stomach.

She reread the files for the three murdered men and compiled a list of their victims, relatives of their victims, their occupations and contact info. Every now and then, she'd check Clint's office. Where was he? She hadn't seen him all morning.

Right after she returned from lunch, her cell phone rang.

"Gwen, it's Jett. Someone blew up Dad's Bentley." She told her everything. "Mike gave us a ride home from the hospital."

"How badly are you injured?"

"Just scrapes and bruises from surfing the pavement. The main thing is we still don't know who did it. Mike said the security cameras at the pet store weren't working."

"Sounds like things are escalating. Want me to come to your house?"

"I'm safe here with Hunter, Sophia, and the armed guard. Besides, you have three murders to solve. Any progress on that?"

"No, but I'm supposed to meet with Clint and compare notes after the autopsy comes in. I haven't heard from him yet."

"Good luck with that, personally and professionally. He sure is a hottie. I'll call you if anything major happens here."

"Be careful." Seconds after Jett hung up, Clint called.

"Hello, Gwen. The autopsy results are in. Can you meet me at The Colony for dinner tonight at seven?"

"Hang on a sec while I check my schedule." She silently counted to ten. "Ah, yes, seven o'clock will work."

"Good. See you then."

A hint about the autopsy report would've been nice. He must be the strong, silent type. She flashed back to his handsome face, then reminded herself this was for police business, not romance. That didn't stop her from agonizing over what to wear. She wanted to see approval in his mesmerizing eyes.

Gwen spent the rest of the day organizing her notes. A clever theory to impress Clint with her detective skills eluded her. She'd have to depend on her electric-blue cocktail dress. She convinced herself her usual detective attire wouldn't be right for The Colony on a Saturday night.

It was exactly seven o'clock when she strolled into the restaurant where Clint waited for her at a secluded table in a dark corner. His navy suit fit perfectly on his tall, muscular physique as he rose to pull out her chair. She sucked in her breath and attempted to control her heart rate.

"Good to see you again, Gwen. You look amazing in that dress." He gave her a dazzling smile.

"Clint, you look dashing in that suit. I guess we don't look like detectives. Then again, this is hardly a restaurant for cops."

"I'm trying to make amends for being a jerk at The Breakers. I shouldn't have pre-judged your detective skills. Care for a glass of Bordeaux?" He signaled the waiter.

The waiter poured from a vintage bottle of Pavillon Rouge du Chateau Margaux and presented them with menus.

"Wow, dinner at The Colony and a legendary wine. This is too much. I already accepted your apology. Let me split the check with you." She took a sip of the divine wine.

"No way. You're my guest tonight. Relax and order whatever you like."

"You're too nice. Thank you." She smiled at the jazz trio across the room. "I love the mellow music here."

"It helps me unwind. That triple murder case has been vexing me. Palm Beachers aren't known for their patience." He breathed in the wine's bouquet.

She gazed into his eyes. "Dare I ask what Branson's autopsy turned up?"

"Same as the others, but this time the M.E. figured out what killed him—a massive stroke triggered by an air embolism from air injected into the carotid artery." He sat back and waited for her response.

"Brilliant—almost instant death with no obvious cause. The killer must be a clever pro."

"The M.E. suggested we look for someone with medical expertise. Too bad we didn't find a hypodermic syringe at the scene."

She pulled out her case notes. "This is a list of Donley's, Worthington's, and Branson's victims and their family members, including their occupations." She scanned the list for medical personnel. "The father of one of Donley's victims is a brain surgeon. I see a veterinarian and two nurses among Branson's victims' parents. The mother of one of Worthington's late wives is a phlebotomist." She handed him the list.

"Looks like we hit the motherlode." He stared into space, then smiled. "I wonder if they got together and agreed to something similar to a *Strangers on a Train* scenario."

"Like Hitchcock's movie based on Patricia Highsmith's novel. Two strangers meet on a train, discover they each want someone dead, and agree to commit murder for each other. No one would suspect them of killing someone they didn't know." She pondered the idea. "A simple yet brilliant plan, just like the murder method."

Clint focused on her. "Well, now that we know who to investigate, we can dispense with the cop talk. Would you like some decadent red meat with our wine?"

"Sounds good. What do you suggest?" She scanned the steak section on the menu.

"How about the aged prime rib?" He signaled the waiter.

"That's my favorite beef entrée, and this Bordeaux will complement it perfectly. I'm in gourmet heaven. How did you know the food and wine I like?"

"A lucky coincidence. They happen to be my favorites too. I guess we have a lot in common." He gave their order to the waiter.

They enjoyed a scrumptious meal, fine wine, and lively conversation. Turned out they did have a lot in common. The climax was when they walked to her car, and he gave her hand a gentle kiss before opening the door for her. She was amazed his simple gesture ignited such a blazing inferno inside her.

Maybe she could catch criminals and a husband simultaneously.

# THIRTY

JETT

Hunter took me to buy a new cell phone. Then he arranged for an extra guard on my property and also tightened security at his home and business in Aerodrome Estates. Satisfied I was safe, he drove home to check on his house, airplanes, flight school, and maintenance hangar. He had a lot more exposure than I did.

Gwen stopped by after her fancy dinner with Clint. Her face glowed as she described their time together. "And he kissed my hand before he helped me into my car."

Sophia grinned. "Somebody's smitten."

"What did Branson's autopsy reveal?" I asked.

"Definitely murder. Sorry, but the method is too sensitive to discuss with civilians. We don't have any solid suspects. Could be the victims' families got together and agreed to kill for each other. We're hoping if we squeeze them hard enough, somebody will purge their guilty conscience."

"You're assuming three killers used identical methods and killed someone they have no connection to?" I sipped a glass of merlot, my nerves still a bit jangled from the explosion.

"Kinda like that old Hitchcock movie? Clever." Sophia cuddled Pratt while he slept in her lap.

"Wouldn't that be wild?" Gwen shook her head. "At first, I thought the families got together and hired a pro, but I couldn't find any evidence of that. If they swapped murders, I have to find a way to prove they planned it. This is a tough one."

"It's no more puzzling than figuring out who killed the mayor, my parents, and is trying to kill Hunter and me." I emptied my glass and poured another.

"Did you make any headway with Marjorie or her pilot?" Gwen reached over and stroked Whitney, who was sound asleep on my lap.

"Marjorie's housekeeper said she's down with a migraine and isn't taking calls. I tried her pilot, but it goes straight to voicemail."

Sophia's face lit up. "I have an idea. What if the mayor said he was taking the boat out so he could get out of the house for a tryst? And then he met up with one of his married women while a friend took Lola out on the ocean. His boat would be seen leaving the dock in case his wife got suspicious. Meanwhile, he's somewhere else playing hide the sausage." She sat back.

"That's a great idea," I said. "No reason for any of the women to deny it. Everyone already knows they were having affairs with the mayor. I'll talk to them and see if one met him away from the boat that night."

"At least then we'll know somebody else was on the boat with Lola. It's a good start." Gwen smiled at Sophia. "You're good at this detective stuff. Any ideas how to catch the killer or killers in my triple-murder case?"

"If it's not a hitman, it has to be somebody who thought the men deserved to die for their alleged crimes." She tilted her head, thinking.

"What if the killer has no connection to the victims and simply sees himself as an avenger of evil?"

Gwen groaned. "If that's the case, I'll never catch him unless he makes a mistake."

Jett's new cell phone rang.

"Hello, Jett. It's Werner Dietrich. I heard your car exploded today. Good thing you were not in it."

"Thank you for your concern. If there's nothing else, I have to go."

"Wait. Let me take you to dinner tomorrow night at The Islander Grill on Singer Island. It's a fun place with delicious food and musical entertainment. If you will give me a chance, I am certain we can arrive at a mutually beneficial agreement."

"Thank you, but I don't want to waste your time or mine. I have no intention of selling my company, especially not to someone who wants to break it apart and sell off the assets."

"Why do you care? You're in the Navy. Someone else is running the company."

"My great-great-grandfather founded that company, and thousands of employees depend on it for their living. You'd put them all out of work without a second thought."

"Darling, you're taking this too seriously. It's just business. Your employees will find work elsewhere, and you will have one less responsibility to worry about. Take a look at my proposal. It's a fair offer."

"I said no, and I meant it. Don't call me again." I hung up, and an instant later, my cell rang. I checked caller ID and answered.

"Jett, are you okay?" Pierce asked. "I drove down to Miami this morning and was out on the ocean all day deep-sea fishing with clients. On the drive home, I heard the news on the radio."

"Hunter and I are fine, thanks to Mimsy Farnsworth's poodle, but my Bentley's toast, and the local birds feasted all day on roasted kibble." I explained what happened.

"Sounds terrifying. What are you going to do?"

"Hunker down here with two armed guards while the bomb squad, fire department, and police investigate. They're trying to get prints off the detonator part they recovered."

"Good, I hope they catch who did this and put the matter to rest. You don't want to live in fear, wondering when he'll strike again."

"I'm worried my uncle is in danger too. He's all I have left, except for some distant relatives. We're not sure if he's being targeted or if it was a coincidence that he was with me when the car blew up."

"Well, if nothing happens to him while he's away from you, you'll have your answer. The thing is, I'm probably not on the killer's radar. You're welcome to stay at my place until he's caught."

"Thanks, but I'm safe here. Ask your parents to think again if there's anyone who might have held a grudge against my family, especially my parents. Maybe someone from their distant past when I was a child."

"I'll look into it and get back to you. In the meantime, stay safe."

As soon as I clicked off with Pierce, Mike called. "Jett, are you up?"

"Sophia and I are in the great hall with Gwen. Would you like to stop by?"

"I'm pulling into your driveway now. Good thing I have the new gate code."

Gwen stood when we heard a knock. "You two have the dogs on your laps. I'll get the door."

When she returned with Mike, I patted the seat beside me on the sofa. "Have a seat and tell us what's up."

He settled next to me.

Still standing, Gwen peeked at her watch. "I'd better go. I've got a long day tomorrow. Goodnight, everyone."

After she left, I asked Mike, "Did you catch the bomber?"

"Not yet." He pulled a paper out of his pocket. "We couldn't find anyone at the pet store who saw someone messing with your car, but I have a list of customers who made credit card purchases that morning." He handed me the paper. "Recognize any of the names?"

I studied the list. "No, sorry." I handed it back. "Did forensics get any fingerprints from the detonator?"

"Nothing, and they weren't able to trace where it was purchased because it was from a batch made over ten years ago." He consulted his notes. "Whoever is doing this is a pro. No mistakes. I tried talking to Dietrich. He said to call his lawyer and slammed the door in my face. I don't have any evidence to arrest him or get a warrant to search his condo. Sorry."

"Are we back to thinking it's a hitman?" Sophia asked. "Maybe the mayor hired a pro from the Russian Mafia here in South Florida like we thought." She turned to Mike. "Can you find out if he had dealings with them?"

"I can try. I'll put the word out to all law enforcement agencies between here and Miami and see if there's any word on the street about a Russian hitter blowing up a Bentley on Banyan Isle or poisoning the mayor. Somebody's informant might know something."

"My gut tells me it wasn't a hitman." I stared at the family telescope. "Maybe my parents' murders aren't connected to the mayor's murder, and this has been a string of strange coincidences."

"Stay out of it, Jett. Nosing around almost got you killed in the Bahamas, Miami, and here in the street. I expect you to remain home and leave the investigating to law enforcement officers." Mike strode to the front door.

# THIRTY-ONE

GWEN

O ver the next few days, Gwen and Clint pursued the *Strangers-on-a-Train* suspects, but they couldn't find any evidence the medical professionals had ever met or communicated with each other. They all had alibis, leaving her and Clint with no leads.

The major events Liz and Clive had come for during the Palm Beach social season were over, and they returned to their castle in England.

Gwen sat at her desk in the cop shop and stared at the files, searching for something she'd missed, when her cell phone played "If I Could Turn Back Time" by Cher. Cam was calling.

"Hey, girlfriend, how's it going with Detective Hottie? Should I get started on your wedding gown?"

"It's going great personally, slow and steady, but we aren't making any headway professionally. What's new with you?"

"I was researching antique jewelry, and I found drawings of your aunt's fabulous brooch and matching ring. Turns out they may date back to the reign of King Arthur."

"I guess you didn't know Aunt Liz is my mother's older sister. They were born in England, and their noble bloodline traces back to Queen Guinevere. My mother married a wealthy commoner from America, and Aunt Liz married Clive Pendragon, the Duke of Colchester, whose bloodline connects to King Arthur. Wild, huh?"

"That explains a lot. Legend claims Merlin himself created the brooch and ring with magical properties. King Arthur asked Merlin to forge the enchanted jewelry for his queen's protection after Queen Guinevere was kidnapped by Mordred and rescued by Sir Lancelot."

"I had no idea. How do they work?" Gwen tried to visualize Liz's ring and brooch doing something magical.

"Unfortunately, I couldn't find anything on that, and I'm dying to know. Would you be a dear and ask your aunt?"

"I'll ask her, but chances are the secret was lost centuries ago."

"Well, you know what they say, 'Nothing ventured ...' Anyway, call me after you talk to her. TTFN."

She checked the time. Almost 11 p.m. in England. Too late to call her aunt.

The next day, she was assigned a robbery investigation and forgot to call her.

## JETT

After breakfast, I called Brenda Carrigan. "Hi, Brenda, it's Jett Jorgensen. I'm thinking of selling some of my family's antiques. Can you stop by around ten this morning and take a look?"

"I'd love to." After a brief pause, she said, "I guess you changed the gate code."

"Yes, just press the call button, and I'll open the gate. See you at ten." I hung up before she had a chance to ask questions.

Sophia grinned. "She's coming?"

"Yep, she took the bait." I checked my watch. "We have plenty of time to deal with the breakfast dishes before she arrives."

"Let's hope she doesn't cancel on us." Sophia stacked the plates. "We should meet with her in the great hall. All the swords, spears, and battle axes hanging on the walls will intimidate her."

Thirty minutes later, the buzzer indicated someone was at the front gate. I checked the security camera and recognized Brenda. Memories of the incident in a guest bedroom with her and the mayor flooded my mind as I hit the button to open the gate.

Sophia said, "We'd better get our roles straight. You play good cop, and I'll play bad cop."

"Something tells me you've played that role before." I smiled and headed for the front door when the bell rang.

Brenda entered the foyer and ignored the puppies, her eyes eagerly scanning the room, searching for potential treasures. Her eyes paused on a life-sized oil painting of a Viking chieftain, mounted on the wall beside the south staircase.

I took her arm. "Let's go into the great hall first." The dogs followed.

As we passed the statues guarding the twin staircases, she pointed. "Are the winged Valkyries for sale?"

"They fit so well with the doorbell's theme they should probably remain in the foyer." I indicated one of the sofas. "Have a seat and I'll tell you what I have in mind." The dogs reclined at my feet.

She sat, her head on a swivel, taking in all the paintings, antiques, statues, and weapons in the room. Her gaze landed on a Viking broadsword gleaming on the oak-paneled east wall between tall windows.

"Brenda, this is my dear friend, Sophia Calabrese of the New York Calabreses."

Sophia indicated a tray on the coffee table filled with cups, saucers, cream and sugar, and a large pot. "Nice to meet you, Brenda. Care for a cup of coffee?"

Brenda sat up straighter. "Uh, you're not related to Don Francesco Calabrese, right?"

Sophia kept a deadpan expression. "I'm his daughter. You got a problem with that?"

"No, no, of course not." Brenda wrung her hands. "It's a pleasure to meet you, and I'd love a cup of coffee."

I waited until Brenda had stirred cream and sugar into her cup. "The real reason I invited you is I'm looking into my parents' murders, and I need to know one thing from you."

"Your parents were murdered?" She set her cup down. "I thought they died in a plane crash."

"They did, but the airplane was sabotaged." I held up a hand. "Relax, I know you had nothing to do with it. The thing is, I've traced the clues back to the night before my parents left for Freeport. It was the same night Lola Brown went missing two years ago. Do you remember that story?"

"Yes, it was a mild Friday night in mid-January. I remember because Andy and I attended an outdoor charity event that night on the waterfront terrace of the Banyan Harbor Inn. The mayor was supposed to M.C. the event, but he claimed he had the flu and couldn't make it." She frowned, like she was recalling something that made her angry. "I heard the low rumble of a big inboard engine and spotted his speedboat leaving the harbor. That lying snot!"

"Did you recognize Peabody at the helm?" I asked, excited.

"No, it was too dark to see his face, but *Lusty Lady* was illuminated by the stern light. It was definitely his boat." She shook her head. "That should have been my first clue I couldn't trust him."

Sophia smirked. "Your first clue should have been that he was cheating on his wife with you."

"Hey, we all make mistakes, and I'm paying for mine big time.

My divorce will be final next month, and the cops still consider me a suspect in the mayor's murder." She huffed. "I'd bet anything his wife offed him."

"Maybe she did." I stood. "Sorry to bring you here under false pretenses, but thanks for coming."

Brenda stood. "Happy to help. I owe you after that fiasco upstairs." She turned to Sophia. "Good to meet you, Mrs. Calabrese." She hurried to the door.

Sophia picked up the coffee tray. "One down and two to go. Who's coming next?"

"Dolores Delgado will be here at eleven-thirty. She thinks I want to hire one of her personal trainers to do in-home training." I opened the terrace door and led the puppies outside.

Armed guards moved to either side of the backyard so the dogs could do their business. I waved to the men. Everything seemed peaceful. I doubted the killer would try anything with so much security at my house.

At 11:30, Dolores made a fuss over the puppies when she entered the foyer. "What adorable little doggies. Are they German shepherds?"

"Almost." I explained their parentage and led her into the great hall, where Sophia had placed a tray of iced glasses with a pitcher of iced tea on a coffee table.

"Dolores Delgado, meet my dear friend, Sophia Calabrese of the New York Calabreses." I motioned for her to sit beside Sophia on the sofa by the coffee table.

"Nice to meet you, Dolores. Iced tea?" Sophia handed her a full glass.

"Thank you, Sophia." She set her glass on the table. "You're not related to the late Don Francesco Calabrese, are you?

"He was my father, may he rest in peace," she said, crossing herself. "You got a problem with that?"

"Oh, no, no, it's just that my late husband probably knew him. He had ties with the New York Mafia. I didn't know any of them personally." She took a big gulp of iced tea.

"I'm glad you understand how the family works." Sophia paused for effect. "Let's get down to business. Jett, tell her the real reason she's here."

I explained what I needed to know and why. "Any chance you were with Mayor Peabody that night?"

"Later that weekend, Lola's body was found by fishermen, right?" Dolores asked.

"Yes. Do you remember what you did that Friday night?" I reached down and stroked my puppies' little heads.

Her face lit up. "Yes, that was the weekend Manny took me to New York. I went shopping on Fifth Avenue while he met with suppliers." She glanced at Sophia. "He was probably meeting with your relatives."

"Did you fly commercial or private?" Sophia refilled her glass.

"American Airlines, first class. We always flew with them. Very safe." She took another big sip and drained the glass.

I stood. "Sorry to waste your time, but I needed to know if you were with Peabody that night."

She smiled. "No problem. Let me know if you decide to work out with a trainer. My guys are pros, and they're easy on the eyes, if you know what I mean." She winked.

"I'll keep that in mind. Thanks for coming, Dolores." I escorted her to the door.

Sophia peeked at her watch. "What time is Victoria Master coming?"

"After lunch at two o'clock. I'm hungry. Let's make grilled ham, tomato, and cheese sandwiches." I headed for the kitchen and plugged in the George Foreman grill.

Our lunch was ready in minutes. We sat on the terrace under a big sun umbrella and enjoyed our sandwiches.

"What if Victoria wasn't with the mayor that night? Any other ideas?" Sophia took another bite of her grilled sandwich.

"Let's cross that bridge when we come to it. We deserve a break in this case. I'm feeling optimistic that Victoria will be the missing piece of the puzzle."

Our last hope arrived promptly at two o'clock. She wore a cream sheath and a navy linen jacket. When she spotted the dogs, she said, "They're cute, but I can't get dog hair on my clothes. I have meetings with clients all day. You understand."

When we settled in the great hall, I introduced her to Sophia the same way I had earlier with the other women.

Victoria stiffened, and her eyes widened. "Jett, I heard your great-great-grandfather came here from Denmark by way of New York, but I didn't know your family was *connected*."

Sophia, in her most serious tone, said, "Some things are better left unsaid, capiche?"

"Yes, of course, forget I mentioned it." Victoria took a long drink of iced tea.

"Let's get down to business." Sophia gazed at me and back to her. "Jett has something she needs to ask, and it's important you answer truthfully."

I explained my quest to find my parents' killer and that I knew it wasn't her. "I just need to know if you were with Phil Peabody that night. If you were, I promise no one need know. I'm just trying to narrow down some leads."

She stared at her hands and swallowed. "Phil met me at my real estate office that night. My husband was in Vegas for a real estate lawyers convention." Her face flushed. "I have a sleeper sofa in a back office. We were … you know."

"Victoria, I can't thank you enough for telling me this. Any chance you know who took out his speedboat that night?" I tried not to look excited.

"Sorry, he didn't mention his boat." She frowned. "He knew I never went out on the water. Motion sickness."

"Thanks for coming today. You've been a big help." I walked her out.

When I returned, Sophia said, "That's a major piece of the puzzle. If Peabody's wife can tell us who borrowed the boat, we might have our killer."

I rubbed my temples. "She already said she thought her husband took it out."

"Then ask if he ever loaned it to anyone and hope it's a short list."

"If her pilot would return my calls, maybe he could tell me if anyone was with the mayor when he talked to my parents at the airport." I licked my lips. "We're so close I can taste it."

I called Hunter and filled him in.

"Sounds like maybe the killer was Peabody's friend, like you thought, and something made him think he couldn't trust him anymore, even though it had been two years since Lola's murder. Better look into news stories, like you did when you figured out the motive for your parents' murders."

"First, I'll try to get the name of the man who borrowed the boat the night Lola was killed. It'll be easier to know what to look for in news reports if I know who to connect with the story." Worried about him, I asked, "How's everything at your place? Anything suspicious happen?"

"Everything's good here. Keep your head down until we nail that guy, and don't tell anyone other than Gwen and Sophia that you suspect it wasn't Peabody or a hitman."

"Okay, and you be careful too. I don't want to lose my favorite relative, and Sophia lives for a glimpse of you."

He laughed. "I wouldn't dream of disappointing Sophia or you. Take care, sweetheart."

I called Gwen and brought her up to speed on everything we'd learned.

"You're way ahead of me, Jett. My investigation is going nowhere, but the good news is Clint asked me out to dinner again tonight. I really like him."

"Good, have fun and tell me all about it later."

# THIRTY-TWO

GWEN

She sat in front of her police computer and slowly scrolled through the case files, desperate to find something that would help her solve the murders. Close to noon, her cell played "God Save the Queen." It was Uncle Clive.

"Gwen dear, Liz has become quite ill. Her heart is failing. She may not last long, and she's asking for you. Can you come right away?"

"Yes, of course. I'll catch the Miami-to-London flight tonight. I'll call you when I know my arrival time." She booked the British Airways flight to London online and waited for the printer to spit out her boarding pass.

How had Aunt Liz changed from vibrant to terminal so quickly? She was only seventy. Surely the doctors were mistaken.

Chief Rod Malone was very understanding and told her to take as much leave as she needed. What a relief. Her next call was to Clint.

"I have to cancel our date. Aunt Liz is seriously ill, and I'm flying out tonight."

"Sorry about your aunt, Gwen. I'll drive you to the airport. What time should I pick you up?"

"Four o'clock this afternoon. Thank you for taking me." She hung up and called Jett, explained the situation, and promised, "I'll call you when I know more."

———

Her flight left on time. The next morning, Gwen awoke to the scent of warm croissants and coffee in the first-class section. The jet landed in Heathrow on schedule, and Clive's chauffeur was waiting for her in the arrivals area outside U.K. Customs. He ushered her into the back seat of the Rolls and deposited her luggage in the trunk. She fell asleep on the long drive to the castle.

Her uncle awakened her with a kiss on the cheek. "Thanks for coming, Gwen. I fear I'm losing my dear Elizabeth. She suffered a massive heart attack yesterday. The doctor said there's nothing he can do." He sounded sad and exhausted. "She's been asking for you."

"I'd better see her right away." She hugged Clive and followed him into the centuries-old castle perched on a hill overlooking Colchester.

In a large bedroom on the second floor, a massive antique four-poster bed seemed to swallow her frail aunt. She had an oxygen mask strapped to her face and an IV line connected to her left arm.

Gwen sat on the edge of the bed and took her hand. "Aunt Liz, how are you?"

She pulled the mask off and spoke in a weak voice. "My dear Gwen, we need to talk." She implored her husband, "Leave us, darling. We won't be long." She gave him a reassuring smile.

Clive squeezed Gwen's shoulder. "Look after her. I'll wait outside." He walked to the heavy oak door and gently closed it.

Liz pointed at her nightstand. "Open that drawer and hand me the small red leather box with King Arthur's royal seal."

When Gwen handed her the box, Liz said, "I'll teach you the steps to unlock the sacred box." She performed an intricate sequence of pushes, twists, and pulls to unlock the puzzle box before lifting out her ring and brooch.

"I haven't much time, so listen carefully. You're next in line for the secret weapon passed down from Queen Guinevere." She pulled a leather pouch filled with white powder from the box. "This is a powerful sedative." She pressed the center ruby on her ring and the jeweled top popped open. "Fill the ring with this powder and snap it shut. The sedative is tasteless and dissolves instantly in a beverage. Use it to immobilize your target."

"Aunt Liz, what are you talking about?"

"Patience, my dear." She held the antique brooch, pressed the ruby center, and withdrew a large-volume crystal tube that ran through it horizontally. A short gold needle was connected to one end of the crystal syringe, and a ruby was embedded in the handle. "This is Guinevere's Lance. Use it to inject air into your target's carotid artery, causing a massive stroke. Death is almost instantaneous. Choose only criminals of great evil who have escaped justice."

Gwen sucked in her breath as if she'd been gut-punched. "Aunt Liz, did you murder those three Palm Beach men?"

"No, dear, I fulfilled my sacred duty and executed them." She answered the shocked look on Gwen's face. "My private detectives had mountains of evidence against them, but it was illegally obtained and wouldn't hold up in court. Not only did Denton Donley rape twenty-eight young women, he used his money and influence to destroy their reputations and ruin their lives. They were sweet, decent girls who thought they had met their Prince Charming, only to be drugged and brutalized. He injured some women so badly they'll never be able to bear children."

Flooded with outrage and confusion, Gwen paced beside the bed. "What about Binky Worthington? Did four marriages earn him an execution?"

"Binky was a serial killer who killed for money. He murdered his four wives so he could inherit their fortunes, and he devastated their families. My investigators know how he killed each one, making the deaths appear accidental, but they can't prove it in court. Too many evidence rules." She paused. "Parents lost their beloved daughters."

"And Barret Branson? What about him?" Her mind raced, not able to comprehend her beloved aunt had killed those men.

"He was a serial pedophile. At least twenty children between the ages of six and twelve were molested, and those were just the ones my investigators were certain about. There were probably many more. That sort of thing does permanent damage to a child mentally and sometimes physically too. Some even grow up to become molesters themselves. Branson's wealth allowed him to behave like a monster without suffering consequences. Think of all the children who are safe now that he's gone."

"Are you saying you sent your detectives to various places seeking out heinous criminals, and then you chose your targets?" A wave of nausea swept over Gwen.

"It was never that simple, and recently at my advanced age, I could only execute men who would welcome an elderly woman of high social status. I had to sit beside them and pretend to be fascinated by their conversation while I drugged their drinks and executed them."

"This is a lot to take in, Aunt Liz. I don't know what to think." She studied the pale face of the woman who had stepped into the role of mother when her parents were murdered. How could such a warm, loving person be a killer?

"This secret calling has been passed down to noble women in Queen Guinevere's bloodline throughout the centuries. It's time to pass that sacred duty to you, my dear. Will you accept your inheritance?" Liz slid the crystal syringe into the brooch, placed it in the box with the ring and pouch, and offered it to her.

Gwen's mind reeled. "Did my mother know about this?"

"The woman who wields Guinevere's Lance must bear the burden alone. I couldn't share the secret with my younger sister or with my husband. I told you because you're the heir. I realize this must come as a shock, but surely you know this is your destiny. You've always been keen for justice. My dear Gwen, you're the perfect woman to wield the ancient weapon designed by Merlin himself."

Gwen bit her lower lip. "Aunt Liz, I swore an oath to uphold the law, not go around executing criminals."

Liz hesitated. "There's something else. I know who murdered your parents. My private detectives have been following his trail of crimes. They're sure it's him, but they don't have enough hard evidence that would be admissible in court. If you accept Guinevere's Lance and agree to continue the noble commission, I'll give you his name, address, and photo."

"And if I don't accept? Will you allow the man who killed your sister, who killed my parents, to remain free?" Gwen replayed the gunshots in her mind.

"If you refuse, I'll pass the box to your second cousin, Juliet, and send her after him. The authorities will never prosecute him. He tossed the gun and shipped your parents' car to a foreign country years ago. You told the police he wore a ski mask, so you can't pick him out of a lineup."

"I'd recognize his evil eyes. They're burned into my soul."

"You're a police officer. You know that's not enough for a conviction. Meanwhile, he continues to destroy families. Guinevere's

Lance must put an end to him. Shall I give the sacred weapon to Juliet?"

Gwen couldn't imagine meek little Juliet becoming an executioner, especially using a weapon as intimate as the crystal syringe. She flashed on the horrific carjacking scene and felt the searing pain of the bullet ripping through her midsection. She stared once again into the murderer's evil eyes and heard his sick laughter. How many people had he killed? How many more families would he destroy if she refused her inheritance?

Justice demanded action.

Her stomach churned.

What should she do?

# THIRTY-THREE

JETT

Mayor Phil Peabody's widow, Marjorie, was still indisposed with a migraine, which I found frustrating in the extreme. I was desperate to know who had borrowed Phil's speedboat the night Lola was murdered. And Marjorie's pilot hadn't returned my calls either.

I paced on the tiled terrace, a brisk breeze swirling my hair as the puppies played on the grass. What could I do?

I pulled out my cell phone and called Dan Duquesne, Chief Pilot for Jorgensen Industries.

"Hi, Jett, what's up?" Dan's deep voice was somehow comforting.

"Maybe you can tell me why your pilot friend, Steve Winters, isn't answering his cell phone and why he won't return my calls? I'm desperate to reach him."

"Oh, sorry, he had a few days off and went fly fishing in Montana. He's somewhere out in the boonies where there's no cell reception. I'm sure he'll call you just as soon as he returns to civilization."

"When is he due back?" I continued pacing as I peered at the ocean.

"I think he said he'd be back tonight, which means he'll be at an airport with cell reception any time now."

"Good, but if you hear from him, please ask him to call me. It's urgent. Thanks, Dan."

Two minutes after I ended the call, my cell rang. It was Steve Winters.

"Miss Jorgensen, I apologize for not returning your calls sooner. I was in the wilderness in Montana. What can I do for you?"

"For starters, please call me Jett. I need you to dig way back in your memory to Saturday, January 16th, two years ago, when you flew the Peabodys to New York to see the Broadway show, *Cats*. It was the same morning my parents flew out to Freeport in the G650."

"That was a long time ago. What were you hoping I'd remember?"

"Did you see Mayor Peabody talking to my parents before he boarded your flight?" I held my breath, praying he'd remember.

"He had a few minutes because Mrs. Peabody had stopped in the ladies' room. I saw him talking to your parents."

"Good. Now for the crucial question: was anyone else talking to my parents?"

He paused a few seconds. "Yeah, a friend had given the Peabodys a ride to the airport, and he stayed a few minutes to chat with your parents. It was that lawyer, Pierce Lockwood. I remember him well because he let me fly his L-39 fighter jet."

"Pierce Lockwood? You're certain?" My stomach churned.

"Yeah, Pierce is a nice guy, and his fighter is a real thrill to fly. Hey, I didn't get him in trouble, did I?"

"No, no, nothing like that. I'm just trying to piece together my parents' last few days before they died. Please don't mention this to him. It's not important to anyone but me."

"No problem, Jett. It will stay between us. If there's nothing else, I have to board now."

"Have a nice flight home, Steve, and thanks for the help." I hung up feeling nauseous.

Pierce Lockwood murdered Lola Brown, my parents, and the mayor. Or did he? I had to be sure. A few discreet inquiries would convince me one way or the other. Where to start? Marjorie Wentworth Peabody, the mayor's widow. I went upstairs and changed from jean shorts into something elegant but casual—white linen pedal pushers, a pastel-pink floral Lily Pulitzer shirt, and matching pink wedge sandals. I still had scabs on my palms, my knees, and the undersides of my forearms from the car bomb, but at least the bandages were off. Good thing the pants covered my knees.

I found Sophia in the kitchen, having just fed the dogs.

She whistled. "Don't you look sporty! Are we expecting company?"

"No, I have a plan. I'll use the puppies to cure Marjorie's migraine while I ply her for information."

She raised an eyebrow. "Are you sure that'll work?"

"Maybe. Mother taught me wolves have magical healing powers, especially if the patient pets them. It's worth a shot." I searched around. "Do you remember where you put their harnesses and leashes?"

She pointed. "They're in that chest in the pantry with some of the other puppy stuff."

I opened the chest and pulled out a blue harness with a matching leash for Pratt and pink ones for Whitney.

"Better let them do their business out back before we get them suited up. Food goes through them fast." Sophia led the dogs out through the terrace door.

While I waited, I called Marjorie. Her housekeeper answered. "Miss Wentworth is unavailable."

I noted Marjorie was back to using her maiden name, probably distancing herself from her late husband's scandalous behavior. "This is her neighbor, Jett Jorgensen. I have a guaranteed cure for her migraine. Tell her I'm bringing it now. I'll be there in a few minutes." I hung up before she could say "no."

Sophia returned with the dogs and helped me wrestle them into their harnesses. I clipped on the leashes and grabbed my handbag. Looking down at them, I said, "We're going for a ride in the car, and then we'll visit a nice lady who isn't well. Your jobs are to make her feel better."

They wagged their little tails and gave one bark each. Such good dogs.

I loaded them in the back of the SUV and drove over to the Wentworth estate. It was a five-minute drive counting the time it took to leave my driveway and enter hers. I pulled into her porte cochère and lifted out the dogs.

The moment the housekeeper opened the door, I smiled, eased around her with the puppies, and asked her to lead us to Marjorie. It worked. Moments later, we were upstairs in her dark bedroom.

I leaned down and whispered to the dogs, "Don't make any noise. Just give the nice lady kisses." I lifted them onto her bed.

Pratt and Whitney snuggled against either side of her and licked her hands. She ran her fingers over their warm fur and opened her eyes.

"What have we here?" Marjorie glanced at me. "Are they yours?"

"Yes," I said softly. "They're half-wolf, and they have special healing qualities. Your migraine will be gone any minute."

She smiled at my cute little darlings, and they kissed her cheeks. She couldn't help caressing their fur and cuddling them close to her.

"I can't believe it, Jett. My headache is gone. Your puppies cured me." She sat up. "Just to be sure, open my curtains a crack, and see if the light sets me off again."

I pulled back one of the heavy curtains a few inches to let the bright sunshine in. "Shall I open them wider?"

"Yes, draw them fully open."

Sunlight flooded her bed with bright light. She squinted. "No pain. I'm cured until next time." She pointed. "Hand me my robe, please."

We accompanied Marjorie to a table and chairs under a wide sun umbrella on her oceanfront terrace.

"Would you like a lemonade?" She rang for the housekeeper.

"Yes, thank you." I waited until her helper left to get the drinks. "Are you still feeling well?"

"Thanks to you and your doggies, I'm pain-free. I really appreciate this. Is there anything I can do for you?"

"If you can answer a few questions, you might help me more than you know." I accepted a glass of lemonade and took a sip.

"Of course, ask away." She tasted her drink and set her glass on the table.

"Was Pierce Lockwood a close friend of Phil's?" I watched her face.

"They were best friends for years, ever since they attended prep school together in New England." She reached down and petted the dogs sitting on either side of her.

"Do you remember which school it was?" I hoped she would remember and save me a lot of searching.

"Ashcroft Academy in Vermont. They were roommates all four years. I have pictures if you'd like to see them." She rang for the housekeeper again.

"Yes, I'd love to." I took another sip, trying to appear casual. "Did Pierce ever borrow Phil's speedboat?"

"Oh, yes, he loves to go fast. He used it many times until he bought one recently at a government auction for vehicles seized in drug raids."

"Did Pierce give you and Phil a ride to the airport two years ago when you flew to New York to see *Cats*?" I almost crossed my fingers as I awaited her answer.

She took a moment. "Yes, our Rolls was on the fritz, and Pierce had court in downtown West Palm Beach later that morning. He drove us in his father's Bentley and even spent a few minutes chatting with your parents before they flew out. I remember because I saw them when I came out of the ladies' room. They left before I crossed the lobby."

The housekeeper returned with a photo album.

"This album has pictures from Phil's four years at Ashcroft." Marjorie handed it to me. "Good thing you visited before I tossed his things in the trash."

I flipped through the pages, looking for pictures with Phil and Pierce together. The photos were divided into four sections, each section labeled with the year and his age. A photo in the third section caught my eye. A lovely young girl stood between Phil and Pierce. "Was Ashcroft co-ed?"

"No, it was strictly for boys, but there was a small town nearby."

I pulled out the photo and checked the back. It was inscribed: *My 16th birthday with Cindy and Pierce*. "May I keep this?"

"Keep the whole album if you like."

"Thanks so much, Marjorie. You've been a huge help." I finished my lemonade.

"Why all the questions about Pierce? Do you think he killed your parents?"

I lied to protect Marjorie as well as myself. "I wasn't going to mention this, but you have a right to know. When Phil took the speedboat out the night before you flew to New York, it was as you had feared. He'd been having an affair with Lola Brown, and she became pregnant. She probably threatened to tell you if Phil didn't get a divorce and marry her. He didn't want to spoil his cushy lifestyle with you, so he killed her and tossed her overboard."

"But what does that have to do with your parents?" She seemed dismayed and confused.

I explained the scenario with the telescope, the conversation the next day, and Phil's assumption they'd figure out he killed Lola if her death was reported later. "So, he hired a hitman to sabotage their jet and make the crash appear to be an accident."

"That creep! How could I have married a man like him?" She shook her head. "But what about Pierce? Why did you ask about him?"

"We started dating recently. I wanted to know if he's the kind of guy I can trust, so I've been comparing what he told me about various things to what other people said about the same things. If he lied about the little stuff, he'd lie about big stuff. It turned out he was honest with me, so please don't tell him I've been checking up on him. I don't want to lose him."

"My lips are sealed." She gave me a sad look. "Jett, I'm so sorry about your parents."

"Please don't give it another thought. You had nothing to do with their deaths." I stood and picked up the album. "We'll leave you to enjoy your day. If you ever get another migraine, give me a call."

I returned home feeling proud of my puppies and concerned Pierce was probably the killer I'd been hunting. He didn't seem like that kind of person.

When we walked into the house, Sophia said, "Well? How did it go?"

"Pierce and the mayor were best friends since prep school, where they were roommates all four years. I need to check something on the computer."

Sophia helped me unharness the puppies. "A rain shower is

headed this way. I'll take the dogs to the ballroom and play with them while you fire up your computer."

I carried the album into the study and powered up Dad's desktop. Soon I was deep into an Internet search for news stories posted right before the mayor's murder. There was nothing relevant in the local news. On a hunch, I typed in the town in Vermont near Ashcroft Academy.

I found big news there that had made the national papers. A body had been unearthed by a bulldozer preparing the ground for a new resort in the forest. The rushed DNA results verified it was a girl who had disappeared eighteen years earlier at age sixteen. A smiling photo of Cindy Thompson almost leaped off the page at me. I compared it to the one I had pulled from the album. It was the same girl. Goosebumps erupted on my arms.

I printed the news article and took it and the photo from the album with me to look for Sophia. She was in the ballroom, throwing frisbees for the dogs.

She smiled at me. "Ready for some iced tea?"

I waved the page. "I'm going to need something stronger. But first, I want to show you this."

We settled on chairs along the interior wall, and the dogs bounded up and stuck their little heads in the water bowls she had placed there for them. The rain shower ended, and sunlight streamed into fifteen-foot-tall windows that lined the three outer walls enclosing the ballroom at the north end of the castle. Red velvet draperies framed each window, and massive crystal chandeliers hung above the polished oak floor.

Sophia studied the article and compared the photos. "This is what convinced Pierce to kill the mayor. Peabody had to know about Lola. Maybe he even knew that's why your parents died, and unearthing the teenage girl he and Pierce had killed was too much for him. With all his drinking and womanizing, he was primed to break down and confess their crimes." She thought a moment. "Poisoning his Scotch was a stroke of genius because women tend to use poison for murder, and one of Peabody's many playmates would be blamed."

"There's more. After Pierce took Lola out on the boat, he and the mayor talked to my parents the next morning. I verified it with the pilot and Marjorie."

She clenched her fist. "Call Mike and have him arrest Pierce."

"I wish it were that simple. All the evidence is circumstantial. Pierce's lawyer would argue that Peabody killed both girls, and Pierce knew nothing about any of it. He'd say the mayor hired a hitman to kill my parents."

"What are you going to do?"

"I want to know how Pierce managed to kill my parents and blow up the dive boat and my car. If I can figure that out, maybe I can devise a way to prove he did it all. For example, where did he acquire expertise with explosives?"

"Call Hunter. Don't tell him anything on the phone, just in case. Ask him to come here."

"Good idea." I called him on my cell and asked him to come right away. When I hung up, I said to Sophia, "He'll be here in thirty minutes."

# THIRTY-FOUR

Hunter arrived mid-afternoon. A worried look clouded his face. He hugged me and then Sophia. "Are my two favorite girls safe?"

"Safe is a relative term. Come and sit with us. There's beer in a cooler on the terrace, and I have a lot to tell you." I walked with him through the great hall.

Between my sips of cold chardonnay, I covered everything and ended with, "We're pretty sure Pierce is the killer, but we can't prove it in court."

"What can I do?" He drained his beer.

"We're missing four pieces of crucial information." I organized my thoughts. "We need to learn where Pierce acquired expertise with explosives, not to mention where he got all the components for the bombs."

"There are plenty of how-to manuals on the Internet, but that wouldn't explain where he bought the bomb materials." Hunter frowned. "What did Mike say about the detonator?"

"He said it was more than ten years old and impossible to trace, so

I'll look for a job Pierce could've had more than ten years ago. Something between college semesters—a job that could involve the use of explosives, like construction projects where they have to blast into the bedrock."

Sophia perked up. "Maybe one of his relatives owns a construction company."

"That would be too easy." I stood. "Hang on a minute while I grab my laptop."

I returned with my computer. After several tries, I said, "Nothing for Lockwood Construction Company or derivatives of that name."

"What was his mother's maiden name?" Sophia asked.

It only took a few moments. "Nancy Lockwood's maiden name was Caldwell." I tried the Caldwell name in a search for construction companies. "Here it is: Caldwell and Sons Construction. They build high-rise condo buildings on the beach."

Hunter smiled. "I have a friend who does that. They use explosives to blast through the coral bed so they can insert the foundation pilings thirty feet into the base."

I did an Internet search on Pierce. "Pierce is thirty-four. He graduated Yale at age twenty-two and started Harvard Law that fall. Assuming he worked for his uncle in his early twenties during summer breaks, that would be over ten years ago."

Sophia added, "The sick creep probably stole everything necessary for bomb-making and squirreled it away in a storage unit just in case he might need it someday."

"He told me he has big political ambitions. His ultimate goal is to be elected U.S. President. That's a scary thought."

Hunter pulled another Coors out of the cooler. "All right. We've probably solved the mystery of his expertise with explosives. What's next?"

"Find out how he gained access to the Jorgensen jet." I poured another glass of chardonnay. "We already know he's a pilot who has worked on enough airplanes with you to know how to sabotage one."

"I can fly to Freeport tomorrow and look into whether he was there the same time the Jorgensen jet was parked on the ramp." He peered out to sea. "If he flew an airplane over there, maybe he managed to park it right next to their jet."

"Also check whether he flew there the day we went diving or if he sneaked over in his speedboat and blew up our dive boat. But first, I'll make a call and find out what time his deep-sea fishing charter left the dock the day my car exploded."

I searched the Internet for deep-sea charter companies in Miami. One advertised itself as a luxury experience, so I called them first. "Hello, this is the accounting department at the Lockwood Law Firm. I just need a few minor details for Pierce Lockwood's expense report pertaining to the charter he took Saturday."

"What do you need?" a woman asked.

"Nothing much. Just the time the boat left the dock, the time they returned, and how many clients he took with him."

"Let's see, Mr. Lockwood took four clients on a private charter departing at 1 p.m. Saturday and returning at 5 p.m. Captain Bowman was the skipper."

"Thanks for the help. Now I can wrap up this expense report. Have a nice day." I turned to Hunter and Sophia. "Pierce lied. The boat didn't leave the dock until one o'clock. Plenty of time to plant the explosive in my car and remotely detonate it before he drove to Miami."

"I bet he had a false alibi for the day your dive boat exploded." Sophia cuddled the puppies. "Can you check if he was actually in court when you were diving in the Bahamas?"

"Court cases are usually public records. Let me see if I can pull up the cases for that day." My fingers raced over the keyboard. "His law firm had four cases, but he wasn't on record as being there for any of them."

"Which means he could have gone to Freeport and bombed our dive boat." Hunter clenched his fist. "All this time, I thought he was a good guy. I took him under my wing and taught him how to work on airplanes as well as fly them."

I leaned forward. "None of this is your fault."

He squeezed my arm. "If he's responsible for killing that girl in Vermont, Lola Brown, your parents, Mayor Peabody, and the captain on our dive boat, that's six people, not counting his attempts to blow us up. I think that qualifies him as a serial killer."

I took a deep drink. "And, like most serial killers, he doesn't show any signs of remorse. He must be one of those rare people with no conscience."

Sophia leaned forward. "Sounds like the definition of a psychopath—no conscience and anti-social behavior, the extreme being murder."

My cell phone rang. It was Gwen.

"Hi, Jett, I'm still in England." She sniffled. "Aunt Liz died the day before yesterday. I waited to call until I could talk without crying."

"I'm so sorry, Gwen. Liz was a wonderful person."

"I've been consumed with helping my uncle deal with all the necessary arrangements. Her funeral is tomorrow afternoon, and I don't have time to shop. Any chance you could come and bring my black sheath with the three-quarter-length sleeves and the black netted hat I keep for funerals?" She sounded sad and exhausted.

I checked my watch and mentally added five hours. "Of course, I'll come. I'll fly out tonight in one of the company jets. Want me to bring Hugo and Leo with me?"

Her voice cracked. "Yes, please, I need my house family."

"Consider it done, and you should plan to fly home with us."

"Thanks, Jett. I knew I could count on you. Uncle Clive will send a car to Heathrow. I booked a hotel suite near Westminster Abbey so I can dress for the funeral. After the service, we'll drive to Colchester Castle for the interment and the reception afterward. Text me with your arrival time."

I hung up. "Gwen's Aunt Elizabeth died. She needs me with her at the funeral, so I'll be gone a couple days."

Hunter hugged me. "I'll see what I can find out tomorrow in Freeport, and if I have time, I'll look into whether he took his speedboat there the day our dive boat exploded. After that, I have to work a three-day trip with the airline. We'll compare notes when you return from England." He held us in his gaze. "Be careful. If Pierce knows we're onto him, there's no telling what he'll do."

Sophia tried to play the helpless female card. "Maybe you should stay here tonight and protect me and the puppies."

He didn't buy it. He leaned over and gave her a little kiss. "You and the puppies will be fine. Pierce is the one who should worry if he messes with you."

"I need to call the company's flight department and book a jet. Then I'll run next door and pack a few things Gwen needs for the funeral, return, and pack my stuff." I hugged him. "Thanks for coming. I'll see you when I get back."

He left, and I booked the jet. "Is Captain Duquesne available? Good. I'll be there at seven tonight. Thank you."

I touched Sophia's arm. "I'm going next door to pack Gwen's clothes."

"Would you like me to cook a nice dinner for you, say around five?"

"Only if you were planning on cooking anyway. Otherwise, we can order out."

"Let me feed you. It satisfies my mothering instincts. How about chicken parmigiana?"

I hugged her. "Sounds wonderful. I'll be back in less than an hour." I petted the puppies and left.

Next door, Leo opened the door for me. "Jett, darling, thanks for inviting us to fly with you. Gwen just called and explained you would bring her funeral clothes." He led me upstairs to her top-floor bedroom, where everything she had requested was laid out and ready to put into her bag.

"This should be everything." He scrutinized my arms and legs. "You had better wear a long-sleeved ankle-length dress and gloves to cover your scabs from the explosion. Gwen's aunt was a duchess, which is high up on the nobility scale, and she was a close friend of the queen. The funeral will be held in Westminster Abbey, and the queen will attend with other royals—a high society event with media coverage."

"Oh. Didn't think about that. Poor Gwen. This will put a lot of pressure on her at a time when she's already burdened with grief." I hugged him. "Thanks for the heads-up."

He hung her dress in the bag.

"Did you pack black heels for her?" I was lucky Leo was such a fashion expert. Looking good mattered to me, but I had never been a slave to fashion. And I was out of touch with the latest trends after wearing a Navy uniform for six years.

"I packed her black Manolo stilettos." He smirked. "One can never be too tall at events like these."

"Gwen will tower over the queen in those five-inch heels."

"Jett, darling, everyone towers over the queen." He zipped up the clothes bag.

# THIRTY-FIVE

A few hours before our scheduled departure, I called Mike and asked him to arrange for a bomb-sniffing dog to inspect our aircraft at 7 p.m., right before departure. "I'll happily pay for it. I'd rather be safe than sorry, especially with so many lives at risk."

"I think that's a smart move," Mike said. "And give my condolences to Gwen."

My next call was to our pilot. "Hi, Dan, I don't want to alarm you, but there have been two attempts on my life, both involving explosives. I've arranged for a bomb-sniffing dog and his handler to inspect the jet before departure. In the meantime, I'd like you to go over every inch of the airplane, removing inspection plates and checking inside."

"All right, and I'll arrange for extra security. Any idea where a bomb might be placed?"

"My parents' jet was sabotaged with small explosives placed where bolts attach the tail section to the fuselage."

"Thanks for the warning, Jett. I'll take care of it."

I pocketed my phone, and Sophia served us a delicious dinner.

I patted my lips with a napkin. "Thanks for a wonderful meal. You're such a good cook."

"I enjoy cooking, especially in your kitchen. It has everything a chef could want." She walked around to my side of the table and hugged me. "Be careful out there."

"You too." I petted the dogs. "Be good and protect Sophia while I'm gone."

An airport limo picked me up and drove next door to collect Leo and Hugo. I rang the bell because I wanted to ask Leo something about Gwen's funeral outfit.

Leo opened the door. He wore an elegant navy silk suit. "I'm waiting for Hugo. He'll be right down."

"I forgot to ask if I should bring some jewelry for Gwen's funeral outfit. Did she mention anything to you about that?"

"Oh, right, she said something about honoring her aunt by wearing some of Liz's jewelry." He turned when Hugo trotted down the stairs. "Really? You're wearing *that*?"

Hugo looked down at his khaki cargo shorts and black T-shirt with *French Men Do It Better* printed on the front. "It's an all-night flight. I want to be comfortable."

Leo rolled his eyes. "Fine, but you'll change into a nice suit before arrival. We can't have you showing up at the funeral wearing casual clothes." He waved to the limo driver. "Put these in the trunk, please." He indicated their matching set of Louis Vuitton luggage. Turning back to me, he said, "Hugo's gay card should be revoked. The man has no fashion sense."

"Don't be silly." I hugged him, and then I hugged Hugo. "I'm glad I have two strong men coming with me. Gwen and I will need you to lean on, especially at the funeral."

They smiled, and Hugo said, "Anything for our girls."

After a twenty-minute limo ride, Captain Dan Duquesne greeted us in the lobby at Signature. He had porters standing by to load the luggage after the K-9 sniffed everything.

A gorgeous blond flight attendant in her mid-twenties greeted us with glasses of Dom Perignon. "Welcome aboard. After takeoff, I'll hand out silk robes if you'd like me to hang up your clothes. All the club seats fully recline." She closed and secured the entry door.

"Thank you." I led the way into the spacious cabin with its wide overstuffed leather recliners and individual entertainment centers. "Make yourselves comfortable, guys. We'll have some drinks and a gourmet snack. Then I suggest we get as much sleep as possible before our inflight breakfast is served in the morning."

"Sounds good to me." Leo sat beside a window, and Hugo sat next to him and pulled his seatbelt snug.

The pilots started the engines, and soon we were taxiing to the runway.

Dan announced via the public address system, "We'll be taking off momentarily. The weather en route is good, and eleven hours of flight time will put us on the ground at Heathrow at eleven in the morning local time. If you'd like to reset your watches, London is five hours ahead of Eastern Standard Time. Enjoy your flight, and I'll make an announcement about the weather at our destination an hour before arrival."

––––––

We pulled onto the private jet ramp at Heathrow right on schedule, 6 a.m. Florida time and 11 a.m. London time. The weather was a cold forty-two degrees with a light rain. After breezing through U.K. Customs, we found Clive's driver waiting for us with a huge umbrella beside a Rolls Royce limo. Hugo had changed on the airplane into a dark-blue gabardine suit with a crisp white shirt and a red silk tie, all chosen by Leo. There would be no wardrobe faux pas.

Gwen greeted us in the hotel suite. She hugged me, then Leo and Hugo. "Thank you for coming. How was your flight? Did you sleep?"

"Oh, yes, we zonked out right after a small snack and champagne." I hugged Clive. "I'm so sorry for your loss. Elizabeth was such an extraordinary woman."

He forced a brave smile. "I shall miss her terribly. Come and meet my niece, Juliet." He led us to a seating area and made the introductions.

Gwen's second cousin stood only five feet in heels and was as pale as a freshly embalmed cadaver, her delicate skin a bluish white. Dark blond hair and large, doe-like eyes complemented her timid personality.

Juliet offered a limp hand and said in a high, squeaky voice, "Thank you for coming."

"Would you like tea?" Clive gestured to his butler, who called down to the restaurant.

Gwen checked the time. "We have to leave for the funeral at Westminster Abbey in an hour. Just so you know, Queen Elizabeth will be there, but she won't be attending the burial and reception in Colchester afterward. It's a long drive from London. I'm sorry to put you through such an exhausting day."

"We're well-rested and ready to assist you, right gentlemen?" I nudged Leo and Hugo.

"Yes, we're here for you and the family. Don't worry about a thing." Leo hugged Gwen.

Tea, cucumber sandwiches, and biscuits were served. We spent a half-hour making small talk, and then we freshened up for the funeral.

––––––––

Westminster Abbey was filled with two thousand dignitaries, friends, and villagers from Colchester.

I marveled that every inch of the structure was a work of art. I sat in the front row on the left side with Clive, Gwen, Leo, Hugo, and Juliet. The queen and several royals sat in the right front row. The traditional funeral lasted an hour.

Colchester was an hour and a half drive from London. As the Rolls climbed the hill to the castle, the winding driveway was impressive even in winter. A moat full of water fed by a nearby river encircled the base of the hill, and a gated drawbridge allowed access to the other side. Eight hundred years old, Colchester Castle loomed above us, dominating the landscape with its towering turrets and imposing ramparts and parapets.

A brief interment ceremony was held at the burial site in the family cemetery. Then we greeted one hundred invited guests at the reception in the castle.

Two hours later, I finally had a moment alone with Gwen after all the guests had departed. "I see you're wearing your aunt's favorite jewelry. The brooch and ring go well with your plain black sheath."

Gwen put her hand over the brooch. "She gave these to me before she passed. They're family heirlooms that go back centuries. According to legend, they were forged by Merlin for King Arthur's beloved Queen Guinevere."

"What an awesome history. I'm sure you'll treasure them always." I admired the unique brooch and ring.

She lowered her voice. "There's something else. Uncle Clive made a drastic, unorthodox maneuver yesterday, but it was totally legal."

"What did he do?" I braced myself for shocking news.

"He adopted me so that all his holdings, including Colchester Castle, will pass to me when he dies. It's tricky in England for titled families. Clive has no male heirs in his family line and no children.

I've always been more like a daughter than a niece to him and Aunt Liz, especially after my parents died. My new legal name is Lady Guinevere Stuart Pendragon, and someday I'll be Duchess of Colchester. Wild, huh?"

"I didn't see that coming. Does this mean you'll have to live here when you inherit?"

"Only for brief periods of time throughout the years. It'll be fun attending royal balls and such. And I expect you to be my wingman. Two girls from Florida playing princess." She smiled.

"I guess we'd better have Cam add to our meager ballgown wardrobe." I grinned. "I do like dressing up. Any chance we'll meet handsome princes?"

"Clint fills that role for me, and I thought maybe you and Pierce might get there when you're ready to date again."

"OMG, you don't know! Is there a place we can sit and talk privately?" My tone and facial expression conveyed the gravity of my words.

"Come with me." Gwen led me into a quiet sitting room and closed the door. "Is this about Pierce?"

We sat beside each other on a velvet-covered loveseat.

I took a breath. "Brace yourself. The short answer is Pierce might be a serial killer." I let that sink in a moment and then told her everything I'd learned about all the murders.

"Are you saying we can't nail him in court because the mountain of evidence is all circumstantial?"

"Yes, but Hunter may have a few more pieces of the puzzle by the time we get home."

Gwen pursed her lips. "Then we have to figure out a way to trap him and make him confess."

"He's very clever, and if he suspects we know, I'm not sure what he'll do. Murder isn't a problem for him. He would kill all of us if he could figure out a way to do it without getting caught."

She bit her lip. "We'll have to pretend we still think a hitman killed your parents and the mayor. Don't even mention Lola Brown or Cindy Thompson."

"Right. He's a dangerous man. We need to tread lightly and come up with a plan."

# THIRTY-SIX

Our flight home departed Heathrow at noon and landed at Palm Beach International Airport at 4:30 p.m. local time. Leo, Hugo, and I hadn't been in England as long as Gwen, so we hadn't adjusted to the five-hour time difference. We were bleary-eyed when we climbed into the limo.

The driver dropped Gwen and the men off first, then drove next door to my house.

Sophia and the puppies greeted me like I'd been gone for months. It felt good to be missed.

"Tell me everything." Sophia sat beside me on a comfortable leather sofa in the great hall.

After filling her in on the highbrow funeral, I asked, "Any news from Hunter?"

She held up a fancy box. "Hunter sent us these Sweet Dreams chocolates today. The label says they're infused with relaxing herbs that aid sleeping. I can't wait to try them."

"What about the investigation? Did he learn anything new?"

"He called yesterday. Turns out Pierce got a waiver to fly his fighter jet to Freeport two years ago to give the Chief Councilor of Grand Bahama a ride at a small airshow. He parked next to your parents' jet the night before they were scheduled to return home. We think he faked working on his airplane late at night and sabotaged their jet when no one was looking."

"I can't believe he fooled me. How could he murder Mom and Dad and the pilots without the slightest bit of remorse?" I balled my fists, wishing I could punch something to release my anger, but I didn't want to upset the puppies.

Sophia shook her head. "The guy is a genuine psychopath."

I blew out a sigh. "What about blowing up our dive boat? Any news on that?"

"Pierce bought an offshore speedboat that had been confiscated in a drug bust. It has extra-long-range fuel tanks and can easily make the short round trip between here and Freeport nonstop. He probably sped to your dive site, blew up the boat, and cruised home without ever docking in the Bahamas. There's no proof of him having been there."

I strode to the terrace doors and back while I brought my anger under control. Pausing, I gazed down at Sophia. "I told Gwen about Pierce, and she thinks we should tell him we're sure a hitman hired by the mayor committed the murders. We need Pierce to think he's safe so we can trap him."

Sophia cocked her head. "How do you intend to do that?"

I spread my hands. "Not a clue. Any ideas?"

"A few, but they all end with me shooting him in the head."

"You never know. It might come to that. In the meantime, we'd better play it cool around him." I rubbed Pratt and Whitney's ears.

Sophia smirked. "Right, play it cool and keep our guns cocked."

The gate signal buzzed, and I checked the security monitor. "Uh oh, it's Pierce." I turned to Sophia. "What should I do?"

She patted the pistol hidden in a thigh holster under her dress. "Let him in."

I pressed the button to open the gate and ran upstairs to grab my handgun. I racked the slide, shoved the weapon into the inner band of my stocking, and trotted back down the stairs.

The doorbell blasted "Ride of the Valkyries" just as my breath recovered from the sprint. In my state of heightened nerves, the forceful tune hit me like an air-raid siren and made me feel like diving for cover.

I took a moment to compose myself and paste a big smile on my face before I opened the door. "Hello, Pierce. Good to see you. Come in." I hugged him.

"I heard you were due home late this afternoon, so I took a chance and stopped by." He followed me into the great hall. "Hello, Sophia."

She forced a smile and stood. "Hi, Pierce. Can I get you a drink?"

"Actually, I'd like to save you the trouble and take you lovely ladies out to an early dinner at the Bistro. We won't stay long. I'm sure Jett's tired after her trip to England." He admired my blue dress. "Looks like you're ready to go out."

"Dinner sounds nice, but we haven't left the puppies home alone yet. They're only three months old."

"If you keep them leashed, they're allowed on the restaurant's outdoor deck. It might be a good experience for them." He leaned over to pet the dogs, and they backed away. "Huh, they're acting shy now."

"I'll get their harnesses and leashes." Sophia walked into the kitchen.

"Well?" Pierce looked at me, his eyebrows raised.

"Okay, let's go." I slung my purse over my shoulder and helped Sophia wrestle the dogs into their harnesses.

My cell rang. It was Gwen. I excused myself and stepped away.

"Jett? Are you okay? Is that Pierce's dad's Bentley in your driveway?"

"Pierce is taking Sophia and me to dinner on the waterfront terrace at the Bistro, and we're bringing the dogs. Should be interesting."

Pierce walked up. "If that's Gwen, ask her if she'd like to join us."

She heard what he said. "Yes, swing by and pick me up. I'll bring my gun."

I slipped the phone into my purse. "She would love to come."

"Good. Let's go. I'm dying to hear all about your trip and the royal funeral."

———

We followed the hostess along an outside path to the waterfront terrace and settled at a round table bordering the Intracoastal Waterway. The puppies snuggled on the deck between my chair and Sophia's, and Pierce sat between Gwen and me.

After the server delivered our drinks, Pierce lifted his wine glass. "A welcome back toast for Gwen and Jett."

"It's good to be home." Gwen took a sip of chardonnay. "It's been a draining experience." She smiled at Pierce. "Thank you for the flowers you sent to the castle. They were lovely."

"Are you up to talking about the funeral?" he asked gently.

She nodded. "There were over two thousand people at Westminster Abbey, including the queen and several members of the royal family." She explained, "The royals didn't attend the reception at the castle, so that relieved some of the pressure. But we still had to contend with a hundred guests for the dinner."

"Sounds like it was a memorable but stressful event." Pierce patted Gwen's hand.

Sophia joined in. "What have you been up to, Pierce?"

"I saw Marjorie Wentworth yesterday. My firm is handling her late husband's will. She mentioned she had a visit from Jett and her dogs." He studied my face for a reaction.

I smiled. "Yes, my puppies cured Marjorie's migraine. Mom taught me animals have healing powers, especially wolves."

If Pierce was expecting a panicked look from me, I disappointed him. I played poker with Navy SEALs and usually won. I'd make sure his fishing expedition was a bust, but I'd have to be careful to hide my anger.

He took a sip of merlot and grinned at us. "I stopped by the marina to check on *Juris Prudence* yesterday. One of the dockhands said he saw Hunter looking at her."

Sophia crossed her arms. "Who the heck is *Juris Prudence*?"

"She's my Cigarette speedboat. The name fits, don't you agree?" He grinned smugly.

I gazed into his innocuous blue eyes, unnerved that someone so evil could appear so normal. Goosebumps prickled my skin, and I rubbed my arms. "My uncle is looking to buy an ocean-going speedboat. Is yours pretty?"

"She's navy blue with a light blue interior. Nothing flashy, but she's scary-fast on a calm day."

"Sounds fun." Gwen bit her lower lip. "Do you take it out often?"

"Not lately. Too busy with court cases." He searched our faces. "Any new leads on the murders?"

Sophia shook her head. "I told Jett to drop it. Mayor Peabody hired a hitman to kill her parents, and then the hitman probably killed Peabody for reasons we'll never know. He must be long gone now, and she'd never be able to prove he did it anyway. Better to fuhgeddaboudit."

"She's right. I wanted to know what happened to my parents. Now

I know, and it's time to move on." I took a long drink of merlot and leaned back as our meals were served.

We ate in silence for a few minutes, then made small talk. When the waiter came to take dessert orders, Gwen said, "No, thanks. Hunter sent me a box of Sweet Dreams chocolates, and I'm having one or two of those tonight."

"Hunter sent us a box too." I smiled at the waiter. "Sorry, no dessert for us."

Pierce leaned back. "My mother loves those chocolates. She claims they have just enough CBD oil and valerian root to help her sleep without ruining the taste of the chocolate."

I stifled a yawn. "I hate to eat and run, Pierce, but the jetlag is catching up with me. Thanks for a delicious meal."

He signaled for the check, and soon we were back at Valhalla.

He walked us to the door. "Are you sure I can't drop you next door, Gwen?"

"Don't bother. A walk on the beach will do me good, especially after the cold, wet weather in England. Thanks for the nice dinner. Goodnight, Pierce."

He retreated to his dad's Bentley. We watched him drive away and then went inside.

Sophia helped me unharness the dogs, and we took them out back for a run. As they romped on the grass, I settled beside Sophia and Gwen on terrace chairs.

Sophia nudged us. "Well, girls, I think he knows we know."

Gwen tensed. "What do you mean? I'm sure we didn't give anything away when he questioned us."

I answered, "No, but he knows you're a detective, and I work in Navy Intelligence. Maybe he assumed we'd figure it out."

"The thing is, clever lawyers never ask a question if they don't already know the answer," Sophia said. "He probably nosed around while you were gone, found out about the questions you and Hunter have been asking, and put two and two together. The dinner was an attempt to confirm his suspicions."

"What do you think he'll do now?" I asked.

Sophia leaned forward. "The way I see it, he has two options. He can steal as much of his parents' money as possible and flee to a country with no extradition, or he can find a way to eliminate you and Hunter and make it look like an accident."

"What about you and me?" Gwen asked Sophia.

"I don't think he sees me as a threat, and if Jett were dead, I'd be out of a job and have to move away." Sophia patted Gwen's hand. "Don't take this the wrong way. He'd use your parents' deaths and the loss of your aunt against you and claim your judgment is clouded. A good lawyer would blame everything on the mayor and his nonexistent hitman. Pierce might even try to ruin your career as a police detective, painting you as unstable."

"But, I'm—"

Sophia held up a hand. "None of it's true, but that doesn't mean a scumbag lawyer couldn't paint a picture with a bunch of lies coupled with your recent loss."

I bit my lip. "This is bad, and Hunter is out of town until tomorrow afternoon."

Gwen yawned. "We know Pierce is a careful planner, so he's not going to do anything tonight. We'll get a good night's sleep and then come up with a plan."

I grabbed my keys. "Forget the walk on the beach. I'm driving you home."

When we pulled up in front of Gwen's house, I walked her inside. Hugo and Leo had left the box of Sweet Dreams chocolates out with a note. "Hope you don't mind. We tried a few. They're very tasty."

Gwen laughed. "We're all chocoholics."

"Hunter knows us well." I waved goodbye.

Thirty minutes later, Sophia was tucked into bed and sound

asleep. I chose a chocolate from the box as I headed to my bedroom with the dogs.

By the time I'd changed into my nightgown, I could barely keep my eyes open. The last thing I remembered was hiding my pistol under a pillow and petting the puppies.

# THIRTY-SEVEN

Pierce

Pierce's parents were deep asleep after consuming drugged chocolates like the ones he had sent to Jett, Sophia, and Gwen in Hunter's name. He went downstairs and loaded a continuous-loop recording into the security system. It showed an empty backyard and no activity outside the rear of the mansion. His parents didn't have interior cameras for privacy, and their staff were daily with no live-ins.

Once again, he read the backup fake suicide note he'd written:

*I'm still devastated by my parents' murders and too despondent to carry on knowing the killer will never be caught. I drugged Sophia and Gwen so they can't interfere. It's time to join my parents at Odin's endless banquet in Valhalla. I leave my entire estate to my uncle, Hunter Vann, and ask him to end my parents' murder investigation and allow me to rest in peace.*
*Forgive me,*

*Jettine Jorgensen*

Pierce intended to write the note on Jett's desktop computer and use her printer for authenticity, but if that wasn't possible, he had this copy ready. He peeked at his watch. Almost three in the morning. He checked his dart-gun, loaded with tranquilizer darts intended for Jett's guards, and two extras for Sophia and Jett, but only if the drugged chocolates failed to knock them out. A pint of cheap whisky rested in a vest pocket. He had everything he needed.

Dressed in black, he felt like James Bond as he spread his black paraglider on the beach, donned the engine backpack, and secured the chute to his harness. He checked his untraceable SIG P226 pistol and silencer, secure in a hip holster, and the night-vision gear strapped to his head. A moonless, cloudy sky and a fifteen-mph wind from the northeast made his task simple. He gave the risers a firm yank, and the chute rose above him. He turned into the wind and gunned the engine to full power as he ran across the beach.

A few steps and he was airborne. He climbed over the ocean and circled back to the beach as he rose to a thousand feet. It was unlikely the engine's snowmobile-like roar would penetrate air-conditioned houses, and he would shut it off long before nearing Gwen's and Jett's homes.

He headed north along the waterfront. When he reached the southern border of Gwen's estate a mile up the beach, he cut the engine and glided in silence to Jett's house. His meticulous planning, as always, would ensure success.

Exhilarated by the cool sea breeze, he circled over the guards who stood together for a cigarette break. Like most people, they didn't look up. He shot tranquilizer darts into their backs as he glided over them from behind. In seconds, they collapsed onto the ground, unconscious.

Pierce landed on the beach and spread his parasail on the sand for a quick getaway. He slipped out of the engine backpack and harness, climbed over the beach gate, and rushed to the fallen guards.

He pulled the darts from their backs and sealed them in a hard case. Pocketing it, he pulled out the pint of whisky and poured it into the guards' mouths and over the fronts of their uniforms to make them appear passed out drunk for the investigation that would follow Jett's suicide. His gloved hands left no prints, but he curled a guard's fingers around the bottle, then did the same with the other guard so it would appear they had shared it.

He took Jett's house key from a guard. The security code was written on the tag, and he used it to enter through the front door. He keyed in the code to disable the system, then went to the master box in the study and erased the video from the past three hours. The drugged guards would be blamed for the blank video as a ploy to hide their drinking.

The desktop computer was asleep, but not locked. He brought the screen to life and opened a new Word document where he typed the suicide note from memory, double-checking it with the backup copy. Satisfied, he stuffed the backup in his pocket and hit PRINT. The printer had also been in sleep mode. It came alive and spit out a copy of the fake suicide note.

He saved the Word doc and left it open, slipped the note into a pocket, and ascended the stairs, eagerly anticipating the kill. *Might take a while. Don't know which bedroom is Jett's.* His parents had told him there were fourteen rooms on the second floor. He wasn't sure how many were on the third and fourth floors.

When he reached the second-floor landing, he turned left and entered the north wing. He spotted a closed door on the ocean side of the house, eased it open, and peeked inside.

Empty.

Moving to the next door on that side, he found Sophia snoring softly in a big, antique bed.

He crept close and nudged her, ready to shoot her with a tranquilizer dart if she woke. Deep in drug-induced slumber, she didn't react. He checked his watch. *Might be fun to smother her after I kill Jett. Make it look like she died in her sleep. Or maybe Jett will be blamed.*

Pierce continued his search, confident in his plan. He'd wrap Jett's hand around his gun while she slept, press it against her temple, and pull the trigger. He knew even if her death didn't go exactly as planned, he'd shoot her and get away clean with no evidence linking him to the crime. Then he'd be free and clear to continue his political career all the way to the White House.

Slowly and steadily, he worked his way to the top floor.

## MIKE

Mike's cell woke him from a sound sleep. He fumbled for the phone. "Hello."

"Detective Miller, this is Elite Security. You said to call day or night if there's a security issue at the Jorgensen property."

Mike snapped fully awake. "Right, what's the problem?"

"The guards failed to check in with their hourly texts, and I can't reach them. Both their cells ring until they go to voicemail. Miss Jorgensen isn't answering either."

Mike shot out of bed. "Thanks for calling. I'll check it out."

He pulled on his clothes, slipped his feet into sneakers, and called Jett's cell.

No answer.

He tried Gwen's cell.

No answer.

A sick sensation twisted his gut as he grabbed his badge and weapon and rushed out the door. Mike lived in the carriage house on his parents' property down the road from Jett's home. He raced out the gate in his unmarked police car and turned north on Ocean Drive. The road was deserted at that hour, and he decided a stealth approach without a siren or flashers might give him an edge.

As he punched in Jett's gate code, he prayed she was safe and it was all a big misunderstanding. He raced to her house and gently closed his car door to avoid making noise.

His heart sank when he spotted the castle's entrance door ajar.

Mike rushed in, gun drawn, and waited to let his eyes adjust to the dark house. He listened for movement but heard nothing.

He raced up the south staircase as quietly as possible.

He had to save Jett.

Would he reach her in time?

## PIERCE

He found the last bedroom on the top floor in the north wing empty. *She must be in the south wing, probably in the end suite. That would have a view on three sides like the north suite.*

He rushed down the long hallway, eager to find his prey. If she wasn't in the far end, he would work his way back, checking each room in the south wing on the top floor.

Pierce reached the south end and listened at the closed door. Were those soft growls? *Jett keeps the puppies with her.*

He drew his weapon and eased open the door, careful in case she hadn't eaten the chocolates.

## JETT

I dreamed my mother was dabbing my face with wet washcloths and saying, "Wake up, Jett!" The wet cloths felt real. I reached for my mother's hands and felt warm fur.

My dogs licked my face and nudged me with their cold little noses. Groggy, I struggled to open my eyes.

Sniffing something outside, Pratt and Whitney jumped off the bed and ran to the open balcony door on the beach side.

Stumbling to the dogs, I grabbed the Navy night-vision binoculars I kept on a table beside the French doors. After fumbling with the controls, I finally managed to focus on my back lawn. As I scanned the yard, I spotted both guards lying on the grass. It was impossible to tell if they were dead or unconscious. Everything moved in slow motion.

*Did Pierce do this? Has he come to kill me?*

I stumbled back to my bed, climbed onto it, and reached for my pistol under the pillow on the far side. The puppies leaped onto the bed, following me. They turned and growled softly in the direction of my bedroom door.

A tall, dark figure opened the door. Wearing night-vision goggles that glowed an eerie green, he crept into the room.

Sensing danger, the puppies rocketed off the end of the bed and leaped onto the intruder's chest, knocking him back a step. They slid downward and sank their razor teeth into his pant legs at his ankles, acting like furry anchors.

My heart raced as he lifted his right hand, aiming at me.

I rolled off the bed a fraction of a second before a bullet tore into the covers where I had been.

From somewhere down the hall, Mike yelled, "Jett!"

I stayed low, my heart pounding as I crawled along the side of my four-poster bed. As I rounded the corner post, the shooter turned toward Mike and fired. Concentrating on holding the gun steady, I aimed for the back of his head from my low position so I wouldn't hit Mike.

I squeezed the trigger, the gunshot echoing down the hall.

Mike fired at the same instant and put a round through the

intruder's heart, exiting his back.

Our bullets made the intruder jerk like a marionette whose strings had been cut. The weapon slipped from his hand as he collapsed onto the floor. In the greenish glow of his NVG, a dark pool formed.

The coppery scent of fresh blood mixed with the caustic smoke from spent gunpowder invaded my nostrils.

I scrambled up, kicked his gun away, and switched on the bedroom light. "It's okay, Mike. We got him. He's down."

Mike rushed through my bedroom door. "Jett? Are you hurt?"

"No, just a bit wobbly, like I've been drugged." I noticed his left shoulder, soaked in blood.

"You're wounded. I'll call an ambulance."

"I'm okay. It's just a flesh wound." He stepped over the body and pulled me into his arms. "I was afraid I was too late." Looking into my eyes, he ignored his shoulder and poured six years of pent-up emotions into one searing kiss that could melt steel.

Even though my muscles were slow to react, I responded with six years of repressed passion, matching his intensity.

My puppies broke the spell. They were still snarling and tearing at the intruder's pants.

My heart raced as Mike released me and leaned over, turning the body onto its back. I recovered my breath and looked down at Pierce's bloody face.

*Hard to believe someone who seemed so normal could be a cold-blooded killer. His trail of bodies ends here.*

The dogs let go and rushed to me, checking me over, sniffing and licking.

Good dogs.

I plucked a paper sticking out of his pocket and read my suicide note. My stomach churned as I handed it to Mike. Then it dawned on me that the gunshots hadn't brought Sophia running.

I clutched Mike's arm. "Where's Sophia?"

Adrenaline drove us as we turned and rushed downstairs to the second floor with the dogs on our heels.

The puppies leaped onto Sophia's bed and licked her face.

No reaction.

I checked her pulse. "She's alive. The chocolates we had must've been drugged. I only had half a piece because I didn't like the coconut filling. That must be how I was able to wake up." I slapped my forehead. "Hunter didn't send us those sleep chocolates. Pierce did."

"He must've planned this well before you returned from England." He looked at Sophia. "I'm calling an ambulance, just in case."

"Good, I couldn't bear it if anything happened to her."

Mike made the call. Then he called in the troops.

I nudged him. "Better call paramedics for Gwen, Leo, and Hugo. They ate the same chocolates, and the night guards might need ambulances too. They're lying on the back lawn."

Mike swore under his breath and made the calls. Soon, my home was swarming with police officers, CSU techs, a medical examiner, and paramedics. The EMTs took Mike to the hospital over his objections.

I dressed quickly and leashed my brave puppies. Before I loaded them into the SUV, I told the nearest cop, "I'm going to the hospital to check on everyone."

That late at night, it was cool enough to leave the dogs in the locked car parked in the hospital lot with the windows cracked.

I paced in the waiting room, worried but relieved my dear friends were safe and under medical supervision.

My thoughts drifted back to Mike's hot kiss. Did it mean something, or had it been just an adrenaline-filled, heat-of-the-moment reaction? It sure felt like more than that.

Thirty minutes later, the doctor emerged and assured me everyone would recover.

I smiled. "My friends who were drugged are going to be surprised when they wake up in the hospital, especially when I tell them what they missed."

# THIRTY-EIGHT

"I can't believe I missed all the action." Sophia punched the air. "Darn those chocolates!"

"I'm grateful you're home now. How do you feel?"

"Well-rested like you can't believe. How long did I sleep?"

"All last night and most of today." I squeezed her shoulder. "The doctor said if you had eaten one more candy, you would have died."

"It would take more than some drugged chocolates to take out a Calabrese." She petted the dogs. "I hope they bit the crap out of Pierce."

"They were fierce. I'm so proud of them." I scratched their ears.

"Think the attacks on us are over now that he's dead?"

"Mike said they couldn't find evidence Pierce was working with anyone."

The gate buzzer interrupted us, and I checked the video monitor. "It's Werner Dietrich. Should we deal with him?"

Sophia checked her gun in the thigh holster under her dress. "Let him in."

Still jittery from last night, I felt for the pistol at the small of my back under my shirt. "We may as well see him now and put an end to this." I pressed the button that opened the gate. "Keep the puppies away from him. We don't want to give him an opportunity to poison them."

She grabbed their collars and held tight.

I steeled myself as the doorbell heralded his arrival. Wearing my most serious poker face, I opened the door. "Why are you here, Dietrich?"

"I would like a brief word with you and your pet nanny. I promise this will not take long."

"Very well. Come this way." I led him through to the terrace. "Sophia, Werner Dietrich is here for a chat."

She nodded and continued holding the dogs.

His eyes darted from her to me. "I have done some checking. I know Sophia is the daughter of the late Mafia kingpin, Don Calabrese. Earlier, she killed an intruder here, and she also killed Carl Rowan. Then, you and a detective killed that lawyer, Pierce Lockwood, last night."

I crossed my arms. "You left out the part about my dogs attacking him first. Why do you think Sophia's holding them back?"

He swallowed and peeked at Pratt and Whitney. They were snarling in his direction. "My point is now that I understand who I am dealing with, I have decided to abandon my pursuit of Jorgensen Industries. It's not worth contending with such dangerous women. You will not hear from me again."

"Good. I'll walk you out." I escorted him to the door and watched him drive away.

When I returned to the terrace, Sophia said, "That went well. We can probably stop worrying about him now."

"You may be right, but I intend to search the front yard anyway, just in case he tossed poisoned food onto the lawn."

"Good idea. By the way, does Hunter know what happened last night?"

"I called him. His flight landed an hour ago, and he's on his way here."

The doorbell sounded. "Be right back." I trotted to the front door and found my uncle waiting outside.

He pulled me into his arms in a bear hug. "Thank God you're all right." He searched my eyes. "Who made the kill shot? You or Mike?"

"We fired simultaneously. I put one through Pierce's head, and Mike got him in the heart. He died instantly."

"Too bad he didn't suffer first and then die." He released me.

"The puppies bit him several times. That should count for something."

"How's Sophia?" he asked, as we strolled onto the terrace.

Hearing him, she said, "Upset I didn't get to shoot the bad guy, but I'll be fine as soon as my favorite man gives me a big hug and kiss." She reached for him, and he fulfilled her wish.

Gwen called my cell. "Is Hunter there?"

"He just arrived. Come and join us on the terrace."

"I'll be right there." She clicked off.

The doorbell boomed again.

Hunter chuckled. "Your dad sure loved that doorbell."

I opened the door to Mike as Gwen pulled up behind his car. "Mike, I'm glad you're here." I hugged him, careful of his wound. "How's your shoulder?"

"Not bad, just a little sore." He turned and smiled at Gwen. "How are you feeling?"

"Well-rested and ready to celebrate." She kissed his cheek.

We joined Sophia and Hunter on the terrace. The men popped open cold beers, and Gwen, Sophia, and I sipped wine.

I smiled at the group. "Now that Mom and Dad's murderer got

what he deserved, they can rest in peace, and I can have closure and move on with my life."

Sophia smiled. "Right, and no more sleepwalking."

I reached down and ran my hands over soft puppy fur. "I'm done with the military. It's time for a change."

"Any idea what you'll do?" Gwen asked.

"Besides expanding the shelter for battered women and providing college scholarships, I have a new career in mind." I nudged Sophia. "And I hope you'll continue as my dog nanny. I can't imagine living without you now."

"Sign me up." Sophia grinned.

"Have you decided to join the police force?" Gwen sounded pleased.

"Too many rules. I'd rather be a licensed private investigator and help people that way."

Gwen clapped. "Perfect. And I can assist you with the police database."

Mike frowned. "I didn't hear that about the database."

I glanced at Mike. He hadn't said a word about the hot kiss he gave me last night, but maybe that was because he didn't know until now that I had decided to stay on Banyan Isle. Time would tell.

I reached out and squeezed Gwen's shoulder. "Sorry you didn't get closure for your parents' murders."

She shrugged. "Hey, what doesn't kill me makes me stronger. And I have a feeling that case will be wrapped up sooner than you think."

# EPILOGUE

## GWEN

It had been a week since her Aunt Liz's funeral, and Gwen was on bereavement leave. She hunched down in her roadster's front seat and checked her watch—9:15 a.m. *There he is, walking out the front door.* She focused her binoculars on a white, middle-aged man with thin, gray-streaked brown hair and then studied the photo Liz's private investigator had given her.

*Definitely Gary Barnes. Hard to believe he's responsible for fifteen murders.*

Barnes had just left his North Miami townhouse, driving a white, late-model Cadillac SUV. Gwen had run the license plate through the stolen vehicles database on her police laptop. Although the car wasn't registered to him, it hadn't been reported stolen.

She ducked as he drove past her, then pulled out and began tracking the man who'd killed her parents ten years ago. No one knew she was surveilling Barnes, not even her police captain or Jett.

Gwen wasn't planning an execution. She would catch the killer in the act of carjacking, arrest him, and prevent another murder. This time, she knew where to cast her line. Honoring her aunt, she wore Guinevere's Lance, pinned to a sash around her waist. Emboldened by the ancient weapon disguised as a fancy brooch, Gwen thought of all the noble women in her family line who had fought for justice.

Barnes was clever, having escaped prosecution for almost two decades. Catching and convicting him through legitimate law enforcement tactics wouldn't be easy, but she would find a way. Her moral compass didn't include murder, even if she knew the target deserved it.

Gwen followed Barnes onto I-95N, a busy twelve-lane divided expressway. He darted from one lane to another, and she lost sight of him behind a big FEDEX truck. By the time she passed the truck, the white Cadillac had vanished.

"Darn it, where is he?" She sped ahead, trying to spot him.

Gwen never noticed that Gary Barnes had maneuvered behind her.

———

Fifteen minutes earlier, Barnes had spotted a white Mercedes roadster following him near his house. *The same car one of my clients wants, but why am I being followed?*

Always careful, he led his tail onto the expressway where he weaved in and out of traffic. He timed it just right to get behind his quarry and take a picture of the license plate. Then he dropped back and took the first exit her Mercedes had passed.

Barnes pulled behind a building and called his paid informant in the Miami Police Department. "Hey, Bennie, it's Gary. I need you to run a plate for me." He recited the info and waited. In seconds, he had the name, address, and occupation of the car's owner. "Huh, a detective with the Palm Beach Police. Thanks."

He called his crew and arranged for them to keep tabs on her.

From then on, whenever she followed him, they followed her. Barnes noticed she always used her own vehicle. *Is she doing this for personal reasons?*

He called his inside man at the Miami P.D. "Bennie, I need a background check on Palm Beach Police Detective Gwen Stuart. Go way back. I'm looking for a personal connection to me."

Thirty minutes later, Barnes got the report. "Ten years ago? Oh, right, the white Mercedes on Banyan Isle with three people." He listened a moment. "*She's* the daughter? Thanks." *Perfect, I can take care of her and get the car I need.*

———

Gwen discovered Barnes drove a different car every day, exchanging them at a large maintenance garage in Miami. His daytime activities varied, so she had to spot him leaving home first thing in the morning, or she'd lose him for the day. She had a better idea: meet him at a sleazy bar in Hialeah where he spent most of his evenings. She would wear a wire. *I'll go there near closing time. Maybe he'll be plastered by then and let something slip I can use against him.*

Later that night, her heart hammered her chest as she parked behind the bar in a dark corner of the lot and switched on her two-hour recording device. Wearing a long, black, human-hair wig, she strutted toward the rear entrance tarted up in a low-cut top, miniskirt, and red spike heels.

She never made it inside. Two brutes rushed up and grabbed her arms.

Gwen screamed, "Let go!" and tried to kick them.

A third guy plunged a needle into the side of her neck, and in seconds her muscles became sluggish.

"Noooo!" She made a feeble attempt to jerk free.

As she collapsed onto the pavement, a man took her purse, fished out her car keys, and popped open the trunk. The other two guys picked her up and dropped her inside.

As they were closing the lid, one said, "Here's her purse and keys, boss. I gave her just enough ketamine to leave her awake and weak."

Gwen lay in darkness, trembling and terrified, her muscles sluggish and unresponsive. Who had taken her, and where were they going? She was unarmed and helpless. They had her purse with her Glock and cell phone. Would she end up like her parents?

After twenty minutes, the car stopped. Struggling to move, she managed to turn her wrist and check her watch—12:25 a.m. When the trunk lid popped open, the only light came from the bulb in the trunk and moonlight filtering in through the high windows inside an empty warehouse. She gasped, her eyes widening at the man who had opened the trunk.

Gary Barnes grabbed Gwen and yanked her out onto the cement floor. He dragged her ten feet from the car.

*He's smiling the same way he did the night he killed my parents.*

"We meet again, Detective Gwen Stuart. This time, I'll have a little fun with you before I finish what I started ten years ago."

Her eyes filled with tears as she realized her fatal mistake.

He stroked her wig hair. "Good choice. I like brunettes. And thanks for the car. I needed a new Mercedes roadster for a buyer in South America."

His cell rang. "I hope you don't mind waiting while I take this." He turned and walked past her car.

Gwen managed to move her head slightly, side to side, and spotted an old clawfoot bathtub nearby. A five-gallon can of gasoline sat beside it.

*Oh God, he's going to burn me alive!*

Gwen struggled to clear her mind, clenched her jaw, and

concentrated on moving. Her right hand slowly crawled over her sash. Fumbling, she withdrew the syringe from Guinevere's Lance, pulled back the plunger, and filled it with air. She hid it under her hand, close beside her body as she lay on the hard concrete. *Hope I can inject him if the opportunity comes. He won't be sedated like the others were, and he might not die fast.*

Barnes returned and flipped open a switchblade, holding it in his left hand. "Did you notice the tub and gas can?" He sneered. "It'll save your relatives the cost of cremation. But first, I'll cut off your clothes and enjoy making you regret going after me." His evil eyes danced with anticipation.

"Please," Gwen whispered, fighting for control, her heart racing. "Answer one question." Each minute she delayed him increased her strength.

He kneeled between her legs and leaned forward close enough for her to smell his whisky breath. "What?"

She cringed. "Why did you shoot me and my parents? You already had the car."

He laughed, licked his lips, and leaned inches from her face, his hands braced on the floor. "I *enjoy* killing people."

Summoning all her strength, Gwen seized the moment and stabbed the short needle into his left carotid artery. His evil eyes were inches from hers as she pushed the plunger to the stop, injecting him with a lethal dose of air.

His knife clattered to the floor as he grabbed at her hand, but it was too late.

Crippling pain shot through his chest as his face contorted. Barnes stiffened, eyes bulging as he clutched his chest and keeled over onto his right side, gasping and writhing in agony.

Gwen's body shook as she pulled out the crystal syringe and breathed in quick gasps. She slid the syringe inside the brooch and felt around for his knife. Mustering her strength one more time, she grasped the hilt, reached across herself, and plunged the knife into the exact spot where the needle had entered his neck, masking the needle mark. She pushed it in as far as it would go, soaking his shirt with blood seconds before his heart stopped.

As she watched him die, she thought about her parents. Ten years of repressed anger and hatred turned to numbness in an instant. Her fierce passion for justice, inherited from noble women across the centuries, had been satisfied without violating her moral code. She shuddered and burst into tears.

Gwen lay trapped beside his body, unable to move anything but her arms. Praying the ketamine would wear off fast, she gazed down at the ancient weapon that bore her name and considered the ironic turn of events. Guinevere's Lance had saved her life, despite her refusal to act as an executioner.

As she lay on her back beside the dead serial killer, a terrifying reality hit her. *What if his buddies come before the drug wears off?*

She strained, listening to every sound and constantly testing her legs. *I have to get out of here!*

It was thirty minutes before she gained enough control to stagger to her feet. She sucked in a deep breath and looked at the man who had orphaned her ten years ago. His murderous rampage was over.

Not wanting to explain any of this to the police, Gwen ensured she'd left no trace of herself on the knife, the body, or the floor. Better to just put it behind her. She slid her hand under her shirt and turned off the recorder. *Insurance I hope I'll never need.*

She stumbled back to her roadster. Her purse with its contents intact lay on the passenger seat. During the drive home, Gwen relived the horrific scene in the warehouse.

*Never killed anyone before. I feel sick.*

Her gut twisted. She pulled off the road, opened the door, and stumbled around to the passenger side. Dropping to her hands and knees on the grass, she put her head down and vomited.

Wiping her mouth, she realized her nightmare was finally over. She had slain the dragon in self-defense.

No matter what the future held, she'd never be the same.

# AFTERWORD

Banyan Isle is a fictitious residential barrier island on the east coast of South Florida, north of Singer Island and south of Juno Beach.

The Breakers Hotel in Palm Beach and its famous Seafood Bar are real places, and so are the many beautiful ballrooms in the hotel. The ceilings are spectacular works of art, and the entire property is a delightful blend of Old-World elegance and modern luxury with several fabulous restaurants, a beach, four swimming pools, tennis courts, and a golf course.

All the restaurants in the story, except for those on fictional Banyan Isle, are real and are as described. The Kravis Center for the Performing Arts in downtown West Palm Beach is real, and I've enjoyed concerts, operas, ballets, and plays there.

There are many pilot communities in Florida, but Aerodrome Estates is a fictitious place. The nearby international speedway with the two-mile, ten-turn road course is real.

Pura Vida Divers on Singer Island is a real dive shop with top-notch personnel, dive equipment, and instruction. I've never dived below 100 feet, so PADI Tec Deep Instructor Justin Newton from

Pura Vida Divers advised me on the deep-water dive scenes and agreed to be a character in the book.

There are several Aero L-39 Albatros fighter-trainer jets owned and operated by pilots in South Florida. When the Soviet Union broke apart, Russia sold many of their Czech-manufactured jets to private U.S. citizens for reasonable prices. The sleek, tandem-seat fighter jets are often seen at airshows.

Jett's Timber-shepherd puppies are based on Timber-shepherds I had for fourteen years. Their names were Pratt and Whitney, named after my favorite aircraft engine manufacturer. They never had an accident in my house, and they took a protective stance when a stranger approached me their first day at our home.

# ACKNOWLEDGMENTS

First and foremost, I thank my Lord and Savior, Jesus Christ, for my many blessings.

Because of the pandemic, I was unable to enjoy my favorite restaurants and writing spots. But that didn't stop Niko Bujaj, the kind and generous owner of The Islander Grill and Tiki Bar on Singer Island, from bringing care baskets to my home to ensure I never ran out of essentials, like toilet paper, hand sanitizer, masks, and gloves. He did the same for many others, gratis. And I can honestly say his restaurant is my absolute favorite. The food is always delicious, and the live music provides a fun atmosphere for dining and dancing. Thank you, Niko.

Many thanks to authors Jeffrey Philips, Nancy Cohen, Ray Flynt, Dallas Gorham, Laura Burke, Richard Brumer, and D.M. Littlefield for their helpful advice.

My sincere thanks to the good people at Pura Vida Divers on Singer Island, Florida. The owners previewed and approved the dive chapters, and PADI Tec Deep Instructor Justin Newton advised me on correct procedures and equipment for deep dives. He also helped me include the varied sea life my divers would encounter at depth and was a good sport about being a character in the novel. I highly recommend their dive shop to anyone for a safe and rewarding dive experience.

A big thank you to marine biologist and long-time scuba diver Kip Peterson for his sage advice. Author Jeffrey Philips is also a long-time scuba diver who retired from Pura Vida Divers. His critiques of my dive scenes were very helpful. Thank you, Jeffrey.

I especially want to thank my brilliant critique partners, mystery authors Fred Lichtenberg and George A. Bernstein, for their hard work and helpful insights that always improve my writing.

I am grateful to my beta readers, Robert Metz, Suzanne Berglind, and Tina Chippas for their valuable insights and helpful observations. Thank you.

# DROPPED DEAD

## A JETTINE JORGENSEN MYSTERY, BOOK 2

Just when I thought my life had returned to normal, the strangest thing happened.

My dog nanny, Sophia, who had become a trusted friend, strolled beside me as we followed my four-month-old Timber-shepherd puppies across the broad back lawn. A cool breeze blew in from the Atlantic Ocean on my six-acre estate on Banyan Isle, a residential barrier island off the eastern coast of South Florida.

She pointed at the dogs and laughed. "I love to watch them wrestle and play."

"They're smart too. I think it's the timber wolf in them." I watched as they stopped under a tree and stared up at something.

"That's odd. Look how still they're sitting with their noses in the air."

I glanced up. "Buzzards are circling."

"Something stinks, but it doesn't smell like a dead fish." She wrinkled her nose. "Maybe a hawk left his kill up there."

I called, "Here, Pratt! Here, Whitney!"

The puppies, named after my favorite aircraft engine manufacturer, looked back at us, hesitated, and ran to me.

Pratt, a honey-colored male, and Whitney, a black and tan female, were agitated about something. Each dog gave a sharp bark then bounded back to the tree.

Sophia frowned. "Might be an intruder hiding. Where's the armed guard?"

"I think he just started his check of the front yard, and I didn't bring a weapon. I thought the danger ended last month." I pulled out my cell phone in case I had to call for help. "I wasn't expecting trouble, especially this early in the morning." The ground was still moist with dew.

"No worries." She pulled a Glock from under her shirt at the small of her back. "I've got us covered."

At five-nine, I towered over her four-ten, slender frame. Sixty, she seemed too tiny for the weapon in her hand, but she wasn't afraid to use it. The feisty daughter of a late New York Mafia kingpin feared nothing.

The massive banyan tree, its canopy spreading over multiple trunks, was like a small forest. We eased under it to where the puppies sat, their noses skyward.

I looked up and gasped. "Holy cow, I wasn't expecting this!"

Glassy blue eyes, wide open in a macabre look of terror, stared down at me. His clothes ragged and torn, a man in his late twenties, tangled in stout branches, had his arms bent at odd angles. A thin line of dried blood ringed his neck. But it wasn't until my gaze traveled to his lower legs that murder was evident. His feet formed the most bizarre pieces of the puzzle, mired in cement-filled buckets wedged between branches.

Sophia, accustomed to encountering corpses during her Mafia days in New York, commented, "Looks like somebody meant to fly over and drop him in the ocean but hit fifty yards short." She shook her head. "Reminds me of my family. I don't approve of what they do, but they're pros. They wouldn't have missed the water."

My stomach churned. "This is terrible. His family will be devastated, and what will the police think when I call in another dead body?"

"Who cares what the cops think? You don't know the guy in the tree, right?"

I studied his face. "Oh geez, I didn't recognize him at first." Memories of awkward teenage kisses and fun dates to the movies flooded my brain. We had been classmates at Banyan Isle Prep School all four years and briefly dated in our junior year.

"Who is he?"

"Chad Townsend. His parents live five houses down." My voice caught. "Haven't seen him since about four years before I joined the Navy."

"A sad waste of a handsome man, and his parents will be crushed." Sophia put an arm around me. "I'd be devastated if anything bad happened to one of my sons."

I bit my lip and hit the number for Mike Miller, my old boyfriend from college days, now a detective with the Banyan Isle Police. Six years ago, he stopped speaking to me because I joined the Navy. Recent events had forced him to talk to me again, and his cold attitude toward me had thawed now that my stint in the Navy had ended.

I put my phone on SPEAKER for Sophia. "Mike, it's Jett."

His deep voice answered, "You sound upset. What's wrong?"

I hesitated, not sure how he would react, considering the murders here last month. "Sorry about this, but I found a dead guy in one of my trees."

Silence for a few beats. "Are you sure he's dead?"

"Positive."

"I hope he isn't hanging from a noose."

"No, I think he fell from the sky."

"His parachute caught in the tree?"

"No parachute."

He groaned. "How high up is he?"

"About fifteen feet, but you'll probably need Fire Rescue and a CSU."

"What makes you think he was murdered?"

"His cement overshoes were my first clue, and the bloody ring around his neck looks like a garotte injury."

A sharp intake of breath on his end was followed by, "Do you recognize him?"

I choked out the words, "It's Chad Townsend. We were friends in prep school."

Another groan. "Did you touch anything?"

"No way. He's fifteen feet above me."

"Okay. Which tree?"

"The one with the buzzards circling it."

———

**Available in Paperback and eBook from Your Favorite Bookstore or Online Retailer**

# ABOUT THE AUTHOR

S.L. Menear is a retired airline pilot. US Airways hired Sharon in 1980 as their first woman pilot, bypassing the flight engineer position. The men in her new-hire class gave her the nickname, Bombshell. She flew Boeing 727s and 737s, DC-9s, and BAC 1-11 airliners and was promoted to captain in her seventh year.

Before her pilot career, Sharon worked as a water-sports model and then traveled the world as a flight attendant with Pan American World Airways.

Sharon also enjoyed flying antique airplanes, experimental aircraft, and Third-World fighter airplanes. She has flown many of the airplanes in her Samantha Starr Series featuring a woman pilot: *Flight to Redemption*, *Flight to Destiny*, *Triple Threat*, *Stranded*, and *Vanished*, Books 1 - 5. Samantha Starr will return soon in Book 6.

Jettine Jorgensen Mysteries will continue with Book 2 – *Dropped Dead*.

Sharon also co-wrote *Life, Love, & Laughter: 50 Short Stories*, with her mother, D.M. (Dorothy) Littlefield. They also co-wrote a standalone cozy mystery, *Sniffers Agency-The Nose Knows* and two children's novels, *Journey into the Land of the Wingless Giants* and *Enchanted*.

Sharon's leisure activities included scuba diving, powered paragliding, snow skiing, surfing, horseback riding, aerobatic flying, sailing, and driving sports cars and motorcycles.

Her beloved Timber-shepherds, Pratt and Whitney, were her faithful companions for fourteen years, and they produced eight darling puppies. When she lived in Texas, Sharon enjoyed riding her beautiful black and white paint stallion, Chief, who kept her mother's mares happy, fathering several adorable foals.

Retired now, Sharon lives and writes on an island in South Florida. She is an active member of Mystery Writers of America, International Thriller Writers, Sisters in Crime, and Florida Writers Association.

Sharon can be contacted at…

**www.slmenear.com**

 facebook.com/slmenear

CPSIA information can be obtained
at www.ICGtesting.com
Printed in the USA
BVHW031147010921
615786BV00008BA/187